The Victoria Lie

SARAH MARIE GRAYE

To Julie
Hope you enjoy
The Victoria Lie

The Butterfly Effect

Book 1: The Second Cup
Book 2: The Victoria Lie

Acknowledgements

The Pict Publishing team; editor Karl Drinkwater; the Whitstable Biennale team for their inspiration; the Book Connectors who answered my plot questions; my blog tour operator Rachel Gilbey (Rachel's Random Resources); all the book bloggers who support my work; and Phlebas the Phoenician.

And a special thank you to indie author Em Taylor for her accidental inspiration.

To Kate Spade & Anthony Bourdain,
People choose suicide for complicated reasons.

Believing your own lies

Tell yourself a lie enough times, it feels like the truth. It seeps into the cracks and your sponge brain becomes swollen with it. It becomes part of who you are.

If anyone questions it, you're horrified, indignant – of course it's true. It's only later you remember, sheepishly, it's not.

How many of the certainties in your brain started as lies?

There are many times we are adamant something is absolutely the case only to find other witnesses of the same conversation or event remember it differently. Maybe you're reading the situation differently? Or maybe you've been lying to yourself?

And how *much* of a lie does a lie have to be before it stops being a white lie? If you tell a lie to comfort someone or to connect with them, at what point is it manipulation? At what point does it stop being the right thing to do?

Is it when you end up lying about who you are?

And how do you know who you are if your brain has been bathed in lies – lies that have now become truths?

1 lifebuoy

ZOE

The entrance to Brixton tube station looks like a modern glass cinema, all shiny and lustrous, except there's a massive roundel in place of where the blockbusters should be. It's ludicrously large and almost ecclesiastical. Do we enter the church of Transport for London each morning? Urghh.

The iconic symbol for the Underground reminds me of a lifebuoy. Which is fitting as all of us need rescuing from our commutes as we drown in the stench of body odour, our skin attempting to breathe through clothes heavy with sweat.

Today the symbol pleases me; today I will need rescuing.

Tube stations are an irritating mix of escalators and steps. Why it can't just be escalators is anathema to me. Changing from one to the other breaks the stride of the snaking commuters and leads to blockages, slowing down the serpents of people.

But maybe that's the point, to slow us down, an attempt to slow the flow of bodies into the station, the trains already too overcrowded to cope.

It's not these stops-and-starts that are the real issue, but the likelihood of strangers bashing into you – of unwanted physical contact, of your clothes becoming moist with someone else's excretions. And I'm pretty sure some creeps use the excuse of accidental contact to grope you.

Don't let this physical contact fool you though: the tube is the best place in the world if you want to be surrounded by people and yet totally alone. For my plan to work, I need the former; for my sanity, I need the latter. It's the reason I've chosen the tube.

A whole day on the train and I won't have to speak to another soul.

There are two platforms and both are for trains to Walthamstow: Brixton is the end of the line. During peak times, the trains alternate between platforms – and any seasoned commuter who is able to wait three minutes goes for the second train, rather than fighting for space on the first.

Occasionally this tactic will result in getting a seat, but to guarantee it you have to wait for the first train to leave and get on the one replacing it, standing by a set of doors on the first train so you're perfectly positioned for the next one.

This second technique is one I only resort to when I have a hangover as it means sacrificing six minutes. Urghh. Anyone who knows London commuters will know this is an *unacceptable* amount of time to waste.

Today I'm at the station much later than usual, so I'm able to find a seat simply walking down the platform to a carriage near the front. I manage to get an end-of-row seat. They're officially "priority seats" but fully abled people sit in them all the time.

And there'll come a point on this journey when I'll have earned it.

The adverts above the seats opposite me are for holidays, dating and vitamins.

We cram ourselves into packed trains and the adverts laugh down at us from their lofty vantage point, mocking us for not being out there enjoying ourselves, out having a fuller life, for not looking after ourselves better.

I settle down in my seat trying not to think about just how many germs must be festering in the fabric beneath me. Urghh. I lean the side of my head against the Perspex, fully aware that it too will be teeming with life.

I wonder if the metabolites poisoning my liver are like creatures too.

As we pass in and out of each station, a harsh-edged female voice updates us on our journey. I usually find her irritating. Today she is soothing: her dulcet-but-dull tones lull me into a trance.

When my automated friend announces "Green Park" I'm jolted from my daze. I shift in my seat, ready to get up. Except I'm not changing onto the Jubilee line today. I try to resettle myself in my seat.

Two stops later, she informs me Warren Street is the station for University College Hospital. I've planned this better than I thought. When the waiting is over, I won't even need an ambulance. And the waiting is important. It's the most tedious part of the process, but also one of the most crucial.

When we reach Walthamstow – the end of the line – the bodiless voice says "all change please" and I find myself annoyed with her: the phrase is nonsense. The unlistening masses accept it. For some reason, I can't. Every time I hear it, it grates.

Everyone else deserts the train and heads to the exit. I don't – I go only as far as the platform to stretch my legs.

Down here with the artificial strip lighting, it could be any time of day. I check my watch – 11.22am. It's the kind of mid-morning that's too late for commuters but too early for all but the most enthusiastic tourists (not that you'd expect to find many of them in Walthamstow).

Only a handful of people board before the train departs again – and I'm one of them.

For the return journey, I take the seat opposite my original one. It means I travel right shoulder first – which just *feels* the right way round. It also ensures most of the platforms are behind me, which reduces the risk of making accidental eye contact with a stranger. I don't have the energy to do the half-smile-then-look-away manoeuvre.

In my new seat, the left-to-right Walthamstow-to-Brixton map is now in the right direction, which pleases me. I don't understand why they haven't printed two versions (one for each side of the carriage) and why *other people* don't care enough about the details.

I can now view the adverts that were originally above my own head.

The first advert is for what claims to be a mattress but which looks like something out of a horror film. I make a mental note never to try a Simba. And then I remember that I'm *never* going to try anything new. Ever again.

The second ad space is empty: the bare metal rectangle instead showing off cream paint in all its splendour – although Alison would disagree that cream could ever be splendid. The patch is usually covered with cardboard, protected from the dirty air of the tube system, so its clean shininess is otherworldly.

It's nice to have a spot to stare at that's not laughing back at me.

The grooves in the flooring reflect in the curved glass of

the doors, creating a mirage of industrial air condition piping – the type that was often exposed in pubs in the 90s. It mocks me in the saturating heat.

All my fastidious planning and I didn't get further than choosing a comfy outfit that could double as pyjamas. It never occurred to me to wear a bikini!

The nicest part of the journey is each time the train pulls out of a station, as it sends a warm, dirty breeze through the train. The only point where the air seems to cool on the journey is Victoria station itself. Each time we pull in, an awkward shiver ripples through me.

We're soon back in Brixton, ready to head back out the way we came in. I'm the only passenger not to disembark and the few people who get on throw me strange looks, but I'm quickly forgotten and just as quickly ignored.

For the journey back out of Brixton, I don't swap seats again. It means I spend the journey out with my left cheek leading the way, which makes me feel out of sorts. But soon I'm not going to be up to switching seats, so it makes sense to adjust to that now.

It means my next journey is peppered with views of the platforms. The tiled walls are welded with grime from years of dirty marks and greasy handprints. The London Underground must be one of the dirtiest places in the UK. I've been breathing the filthy air for over and hour now – I wonder how many cigarettes I've effectively smoked?

The thought dries my throat and I take a few sips from my water bottle. Just enough to keep my thirst at bay: if I'm going to use the heat of the tube to act as a catalyst, now is not the time to be hydrating.

At Blackhorse Road the picture in the tiles is a black horse, which makes sense. At Seven Sisters there are seven trees in an unpleasantly asymmetrical pattern. I wonder which sisters they represent. Finsbury Park has pistols, which is a tad disconcerting.

I crave Google — to find out what the pictures mean. Should I fight the urge? Or should I carry on questioning everything until the very end?

I get my phone out ready to do the painstaking "tube search". We won't stop in any station long enough for a complete search so you have to type in the search you want and wait until you're just pulling into a station to click go. If you're lucky, the page will have loaded before you pull out again and lose signal. It's then a wait until you're arriving at the next platform before you can click on the first option in your results to see if it's any good.

We don't need Wi-Fi at tube stations; we need it on the trains. But I won't see that in my lifetime. Not with a time bomb ticking inside my chest.

I could get off at any of the stations and do the full search there, but I'm lightheaded and a little queasy, so I want to stay put. I'm not sure if my current symptoms are psychosomatic, so I'm waiting for the pain to kick in before I leave this seat again.

My Google search is fruitful, but uninteresting: the elm trees are the sisters themselves; the guns represent the men who used to meet at Finsbury Park to defend their honour. How disappointing. Why do I always want more from everything?

My favourite is at Brixton where the tiles design is a ton of Bricks. Bricks-ton. What a shame that most people who use the station will never know: its brilliance will be ignored by ignoramus locals.

When it gets to lunchtime, the train fills up, particularly between Victoria station and Green Park and again between Kings Cross St Pancras and Euston.

During those parts of the journey, everybody sitting down has to take up the "tiptoe position" because there's not enough floor space for you to all put your feet flat and for people to be able to stand along the aisle.

Everyone gets on the tube with some urgency, but people leave at a different pace, from last-minute nonchalance to last-minute panic. Those who get up as soon as the train pulls out of a station are met with a chorus of tuts, as they will be in the way until they get off. Everyone is expected to know the commuter dance.

I eat my shop-bought sandwich, ignoring the few disdainful looks I get from other passengers. It's the only time someone else will look at you on the tube: when they want to impart their dissatisfaction. Although there are *no* rules against eating on the train, some people still take issue with it. But if you work long hours, can't afford to eat out all the time and want *any* kind of social life, grabbing a sandwich or sushi and eating it on public transport while on the way to somewhere is a way of life.

I only manage to eat one triangle of sandwich before I start feeling queasy again, so the second one goes back in my bag, the triangular packaging carefully balanced point-down so the contents doesn't spill out.

I'm another two trips along the route when my second triangle comes in handy: a gift to a homeless woman. I know she's homeless because she has that been-down-the-coalmine look, the dirt of London ingrained into her skin.

She stands at the end of the carriage and as soon as she speaks I recognise her as "poetry girl" – the Victoria line beggar who recites a homemade poem before asking anyone for help.

Beggars are having to become more creative as the masses become more and more immune to them. The poem is also her way of saying "I'm human too". The irony is she's the most human person here: the rest are puppets.

The few people in the carriage with me are suddenly engrossed in the paper they are reading, or the piece of fluff they've just discovered on their clothes. Nobody wants to be rude; they just want her to go away.

It's not my sandwich that's the gift: it's me acknowledging her.

Her poem rhymes. It makes me think of Dr Laythe. In my first year at university he drilled it into us that any poetry that rhymed had better be good because it had to work far harder than any other type to be considered worthy.

He didn't have an issue with it per se, but would mark it down to preserve the reputation of the Creative Writing course at London South Bank University. I loved LSBU, but I loathed poetry and I loathed Laythe. I dropped his class at the end of first year.

I'm more of a classics fan. Particularly Shakespeare. And as Jaques said: *"All the world's a stage, and all the men and women merely players."* Well, I'm ready for my final exit, for the curtain to go down on my performance.

I'm ready to take my bow.

It's not until after 4pm that the carriage gets busy again. The same people who got in at least eight hours ago start to stream back on again, pouring their liquid bodies into the tiniest of gaps. The inadequately named "rush hour" will continue for at least the next three hours.

I lean my head against the plastic wall next to me, struggling in the heat of the additional bodies. My thin T-shirt is sticking to my skin, the moist fabric of my leggings clings to the backs of my knees, and my feet swim in the pools of sweat that have formed inside my shoes.

At Pimlico, on a journey back down to Brixton, an old

lady gets on, one that I'd call spritely but some way into her 70s if not a decade older. I make move to get up and realise I don't have the energy to do so. She looks horrified and waves me back down in my seat. The person opposite me gives up their seat instead.

The old lady is too old to care about the unwritten rules of the tube: she stares at me until she catches my eye. She gives me a sympathetic nod. I must look as shit as I feel.

I must be getting close. The waiting, the monotony of the journey, will soon be over.

I've been listening to the roar of the tube for hours. It is helping drown out the strange buzzing in my ears. I've never suffered from tinnitus before, but I'm making an educated guess that I am right now. It's one of the symptoms I'm expecting.

The train's roar lulls me, along with my robotic friend and her calming, reassuring announcements. With the noise and the warm air, I could easily fall asleep on here.

DUCKS IN A ROW

Zoe laid them out in a row. The capsules were half white, half blue: the caplets were standard white. She hadn't realised she'd not bought the same thing from Sainsbury's that she'd bought from Boots and Superdrug – just one packet of 16 from each to keep under the radar.

It was the kind of mismatch that irritated her, but thankfully did not damage her plans. And she was just glad not to be swallowing down the huge round Paracetamol her mother kept in the medicine cabinet. The ones she'd had to break in half to fit down her throat without bruising it; the ones that would make her gag on the bitterness as the raw edge of the break disintegrating as it touched her tongue.

She was pretty sure her mother bought those ones on purpose – to make sure you were in *lots* of pain before you asked for them. Well, Zoe knew there were types of pain that Paracetamol tablets *couldn't* touch – unless you took them in very large doses.

She opened up a bottle of Baron De Guers Picpoul De Pinet – also from Sainsbury's – and poured herself a very large glass. She took her first swig of wine, allowing the citrus and mineral flavours to flood her mouth before swallowing it down. She looked at the 48 tablets in a row in front of her and wondered if each one could represent something in her life that she loathed.

The second swig of wine carried the first two tablets: they represent her anger and her boredom. Zoe was permanently angry – and has been since she can remember. She was also bored. And bored with being angry.

Her boredom is fluid between the layers of her skin. A severe case of oedema, it builds up around her whole body, making her swollen with emotions. Sometimes it bulged up like a blister – and not one as easy to pop as the plastic-and-metal trays of blisters that had held the 46 tablets still in front of her.

A third swig took down the next two tablets, which Zoe decided were for anger and boredom too, because if she looked at all the times she'd not been happy in her life (and that's most of the time) anger and boredom are at the centre.

She swigged the tablets down two at a time, 24 gulps, until all 48 were gone and there was no wine left. And every gulp, every two tablets were for anger and boredom. She didn't have the mental energy to imagine symbolic references for them. No, she could leave that kind of symbolism to the people left behind.

She opened a second bottle of wine. With no tablets to

swig down with this one, so indulged in more leisurely swigs, letting each mouthful swim round her mouth before swallowing, each one cooling her oesophagus and fuzzying the edges of her brain.

If you take a Paracetamol overdose you go to sleep. And then you wake up. A lot of people don't know this. But Zoe did. Zoe knew it though. She was expecting it. She was counting on it.

And when she did, she carefully laid out her outfit for the day on her bed: a baggy grey T-shirt and black leggings. It was a ritual from her days as a child when her mother would do the same for her. Her mother would always talk about being prepared for anything. And part of that preparation was to think ahead. To get your ducks in a row.

To have your clothes ready before your shower. To get your tablets in a row. To have your plan in place before you swallowed a single tablet.

The house she'd shared at university had a cat (because they had mice) and laying out clothes was seen by the cat as an invitation to lie on them, so she'd temporarily curtailed the habit.

In the flat she now shared with Alison there were no mice, no cat, and she could smooth out her outfit in advance before jumping the shower, so it would be waiting for her when she got out.

Zoe had to turn the temperature gauge down before she stepped into the measly stream of water, the weak flow resembling the smattering of drips you'd get if you stood close to a wet dog as it shook itself down. She would turn it up again afterwards, so it was always in the right place for Alison.

As well as liking the shower a fraction hotter than Zoe did, Alison also liked it to pummel her awake – and complained constantly about it. Zoe ignored her. On the days she bothered using it, she appreciated the lacklustre flow.

Zoe had a strange relationship with water. She was perfectly happy to go swimming, but felt uncomfortable in her own skin the minute she stepped out of the water and back on to dry land. She would find herself stumbling, her legs seeming to jut out at strange angles as she made her way from swimming pool to changing rooms.

When she was younger, she'd wondered if she'd overdone the swimming, the stumbling being from tiredness. But she'd had enough lazy visits to the swimming baths as an adult, getting out after just a few lengths, to know that fatigue had nothing to do with it.

The post-swim shower was the only shower she ever enjoyed: her skin reconnecting with the water again. Showers at other times, when she started off dry, felt like an assault on her skin.

The morning after her special supper of wine and tablets, Zoe felt more awake than she'd anticipated. She'd slept far better than she expected. She wondered whether her deep sleep was a side effect of the overdose or the relief of being just days away from escaping her life for good.

Before she'd swigged a single tablet down Zoe had been pretty sure she wouldn't have any second thoughts. But she'd still predicted that niggling doubts would keep her awake until the early hours.

She was thankful she was wrong about the niggling doubts. She was even more relieved to be right about the second thoughts. Because the morning after was too late for either.

ZOE

I'm still sitting up, but my head is balanced against cold metal bars, not thick Perspex. And my legs are stretched out in front of me. This is not the tube; I'm in a hospital bed.

I've made it to University College Hospital, I just don't remember getting here. My head feels groggy. The ache in my left arm turns out to be from a needle inserted on the inside of my wrist, which is attached to a drip of water. I guess they've worked out I'm dehydrated. I wonder if they know why – if they've already worked out what's wrong with me.

Thankfully, it doesn't matter if they have, because I've already made sure it's too late. There's a window of opportunity to treat an overdose and I spent it yo-yoing up and down the Victoria line. Killing time. The time I need to make sure they can't stop me killing myself.

My bag is on the table next to my bed. As I wheel the table towards me, the woman sitting reading a few feet away from my bed looks up from her book. The look on her face tells me it's more than just a passing glance. I seem to have the NHS equivalent of a groupie.

I search inside my bag to check the sheet of paper is still in there. It is. It has the names and phone numbers of all the people I want the hospital staff to contact on my behalf, the ones I want to say goodbye too. Well, "all" is a bit dramatic. There are just two names and numbers on it.

And neither of them is my mother.

The Victoria line

In choosing the Victoria line, Zoe chose well.

Although London's subway service is called the "London Underground", most lines aren't fully under street level, with the Victoria line being just one of two with no stations above ground. (The other is the Waterloo and City line, also known as "The Drain", which is 1.47 miles long and serves just Bank and Waterloo stations.)

It meant Zoe didn't have to see the cloud clear up and the day turn into a gloriously sunny one, the kind of sunshine that breeds positivity − an emotional response that would seem at odds with her actions.

In the afternoon, temperatures reached a muggy 26 degrees, which would have felt more stifling than glorious for anyone working outdoors, but perfect for tourists able to sit in the shade and enjoy an unexpected picnic.

Those fortunate enough to have chosen Victoria Tower Gardens or one of the other few parks that line the Thames would have enjoyed the cool breeze off the river, which took the temperature down to a more comfortable 19 degrees.

What those unsuspecting tourists won't have known is the breeze they were grateful for would have been only marginally less dirty than the one Zoe felt rushing through the tube window each time her train left a station. Central London has an air pollution problem.

2 armbands

ALISON

I have no idea how to process this – any of it. Not only Zoe wanting to die, but her choosing the tube as her final resting place? Surrounded by strangers?

There's a junior doctor staring at me, waiting for me to say something. Words rush through my brain faster than any train on the London Underground, but none of them make the short route to my tongue. So instead I concentrate on staring back at him.

He's skinny, but seems surprisingly normal in comparison to the news he's just delivered. Considering his build, the long sleeve T-shirt he's wearing under his scrubs is probably to keep him warm in the cool hospital air. But it could also be a makeshift force field between him and his scrubs, to protect him from the emotional side of his job.

The hospital is the only place I've been today that hasn't been like a sauna – the tube, the office, the client meeting. But after the news I've just been given, I long to be anywhere else, melting on the outside not the inside.

I flex my tongue.

"The tube?" – it's all I can manage.

But it's enough. He was simply waiting for me to speak as a sign that I was ready for the next piece of information. He shifts forward in his seat, the way someone does when they want to be gentle, protect you, treat you like a child. I mentally brace myself – what could be worse than the news I've already been given?

"The overdose Zoe took was a serious one, and her liver is in distress, but she's very much alive. At the moment."

He waits for more words from me. I want to ask what he means by "at the moment" – is she still dying or not? I search the trains of thought hurtling through my head for the right words.

"But the tube?"

He doesn't know the answer. How can he? What explanation is there for such alien behaviour?

"A Paracetamol overdose is potentially a slow death. It can take a good few days, often a week or more. People take an overdose, pass out and wake up shortly afterwards, believing they've survived their actions. But often they are just at the beginning of their problems. So she might very well be relieved to be alive, not realising that she could have done irreversible damage."

I stare down at my feet while I let the words sink in. I look up at him again when the pause becomes uncomfortable.

"It will take a few days before we can fully assess the situation," he explains. "And the treatments we have don't always work. Unfortunately, we can't always offer a liver transplant to someone who chooses to take an overdose."

I wait for him to tell me how Zoe is one of the ones that's going to be saved.

"She's sleeping at the moment, but I can take you to her if you want."

I nod. He can't make me that promise.

The route to the ward is a tangled web of corridors and I'm grateful for a guide instead of a list of directions. It seems silly that a doctor is wasting his valuable time walking the route with me, especially as we do it in silence. Maybe this is his way of getting a break from the chaos of A&E. Or maybe he wants to me to avoid the natural chatter of the porters whose friendliness would seem insensitive in these circumstances.

On the ward, he leaves me in the care of a nurse rather than taking me straight to Zoe's bed, a curt nod in my direction to let me know his duty has been done. The nurse talks to me in soothing tones as she walks me over to Zoe's bed. There's a strange grey tinge to Zoe's skin, but she otherwise looks just as she does when she's crashed out on the sofa at home.

I sit in the chair next to her bed simultaneously wishing for her to wake up and sleep forever.

KARMA CHAMELEON

Alison was desperately trying to stop her bottom lip from wobbling.

When she'd come to London for her Open Day, she never actually made it onto campus. Instead of heading to London South Bank University – LSBU – she and Ruby had ended up on the south bank of the Thames, watching boats go by and nervously exploring the grand spaces and nooks and crannies of the Royal Festival Hall, not quite sure if they were allowed inside or not.

So when Alison arrived for the first day of term, she

struggled to take in the high-rise flats inspired by a child's Lego brick tower and the red concrete elephant levitating above an unloved shopping centre. She also struggled to find the university campus, expecting something more substantial than a mishmash of buildings along a main road.

Alison had chosen London simply because Ruby wanted to go to Central Saint Martins to study jewellery. She'd applied for all the courses in London where she could study English alongside Creative Writing. She'd not thought of the realities of studying there.

Alison had thought they could live together, so when Ruby explained each university had its own halls, Alison had been unnerved as well as bitterly disappointed. How many other strange rules were out there, waiting to trip her up now that she wasn't going to have Ruby to guide her?

When Ruby had pulled out of university altogether, saying she couldn't leave her mum, Alison had been devastated. But a tiny sliver of her was grateful, because it meant she could look for a Ruby replacement at LSBU without risking her new ally stepping on Ruby's toes.

But looking for this new sidekick would mean turning up on the first day by herself. And although she'd made it into the building with a sign on the door that included the enrolment details of her course, she couldn't trust herself to be in the right place. There were a few other students who'd also arrived early, awkwardly milling about like she was, waiting for a proper adult to turn up.

And then one did.

She looked too young for a lecturer, but was definitely older than the rest of them, and could easily work in the admissions team. Alison gravitated towards her, along with everyone else, from the hippy kids who looked like they'd slept in their clothes to the girls so dressed up they looked ready to go clubbing. They collectively stumbled over their words they sought reassurances that, yes, they were all in the right place.

Alison was astounded when this grown up joined the same queue she was in, filling in the same forms as the rest of them. This girl, who gave her name as Zoe Vickers, was very different from Ruby, but Alison instantly knew she was the perfect replacement.

The course was split into a number of tutorial groups. And when Zoe was whisked off one way, Alison another, Alison made it her mission to seek Zoe out at the earliest opportunity. But although she looked out for her during lectures, she didn't spot her. And the longer Alison went without seeing her, the more her memory of her faded to a vague image of an almost-adult.

Zoe was a chameleon to her, the perfect actress who could play every part. Each time what appeared in front of Alison was simply a pretty blonde girl with something ever-so-slightly missing from her facial expression.

It was the blank gaze that left Alison unable to remember that she'd ever met her before, never mind where. It was as if Zoe powered down into a holding position, only booting herself up when needed.

It was only when Zoe became animated that Alison's memory cells would fire up and she would realise it was the girl she'd been trying to find all this time. She would catch glimpses of Zoe on campus, her confident stride walking down Keyworth Street, her grin lighting up the room in the Students' Union, her raucous laugh being "shushed" in the library.

Each time she saw her, Alison would absentmindedly chew her thumb, scratching her teeth across the flesh, trying to detect the old scar of a lost friendship. And she would watch from afar. Too much time had passed since their first meeting and she no longer felt she could justify a nonchalant hello.

Her plan was to talk to her at one of their lectures, where she could sit near her accidentally on purpose, but she never saw her there.

Then, to Alison's amazement, Zoe chose to be friends with her.

It was a hard slog to get the friendship to the point where Alison felt she was a pivotal character in Zoe's world, but when Alison wanted to make a friend, she threw everything into it. And her hard work was rewarded in the second year, when Zoe suggested they live in the same student house, a barely habitable hovel in Camberwell.

Now they rented together in Brixton, a mere two miles down the road, but a completely different world. When they first moved in, the flat had been freshly painted in magnolia. The colour irritated Alison because it felt like a lie. It was one of those con words – a fancy sounding name that contained a sliver of hope it would *never* deliver on.

She'd gone straight out and bought a range of different colours – light teal, warm grey, rich olive – and repainted every room a mixture of feature walls and white ones. She promised Zoe she'd paint it back to dreary cream when they moved out if their landlord asked them to.

The walls mattered to Alison because magnolia was a lie, like vanilla.

"Strawberry or vanilla?"

Four-year-old Alison knew what strawberry tasted like and it was nice. But vanilla sounded magical – resplendent even, had that word been in her vocabulary. But when they brought it out, and it was just plain ice cream. Vanilla was a trick: a special word for something ordinary. Alison had choked back tears as she'd eaten her plain ice cream cone. Eating boring ice cream was far worse than not getting any.

Zoe didn't care about the colour of the walls: she'd been more interested in getting the slightly bigger bedroom – extra space that she hadn't needed at the time, but that would be used to store the items she'd rescue from the loft of her childhood home before it was sold.

The boxes of belongings were slumped together in an accusatory pile along the wall of Zoe's room until Alison bought her a Scandinavian-style sideboard as a late housewarming present. The untouched boxes were now hidden away behind smooth off-white doors, the perfect complement to the olive wall it stood in front of. It would not have worked as well against a magnolia wall.

Vanilla ice cream was the reason Alison knew she couldn't go it alone. She knew if she were part of a duo the other person would know vanilla was a trick. She needed a Scrappy to her Scooby, but without the scary adventures. A Penfold to her Danger Mouse, but without everything going wrong.

So when five-year-old Alison started school – and she was five already because her birthday was 2nd September – her first mission was to find herself her very own superhero sidekick.

And Ruby was the best sidekick ever. Until she wasn't anymore.

And then Zoe filled the gap.

ALISON

"Are you the next of kin?"

I can hear the hint of surprise in the nurse's voice. It's the same surprise I heard in my own voice when the skinny doctor told me it was my name and number on Zoe's paperwork.

No matter how old you are, how much education you have, how much money you earn, your parents are still meant to be there for you when it really matters. And I didn't look *anything* like the stereotypical significantly-older-grey-haired-lady-in-a-twinset she was expecting.

I nod. I'm doing a lot of nodding. After stumbling over so few words in front of the doctor, I don't trust myself to speak. I certainly don't want to get into a conversation about how Zoe's mum died last year, about how Zoe hasn't spoken about it since the funeral, about how she has ignored all the calls and texts from her dad and her sisters.

Under the circumstances, the fact she picked me as next of kin, and not Clare or Charlotte, is not too much of a surprise. I'm not sure if the overdose is a surprise or not. I should be reeling from the news, but instead I'm numb. I have just enough energy to slump myself into a plastic chair beside her bed and that's about it.

The nurse wants to check I'm the "Alison" on the piece of paper she has. I recognise Zoe's looped handwriting and it makes me ache for normality. My name and number are scribbled down, as are James's. I'm pleased to see mine are first – and simultaneously ashamed that I'm pleased.

"Where did you get that?" I ask her.

"Zoe gave it to me when they first brought her up from A&E. She was going to call both of you herself but couldn't face it."

"She was *awake*?"

I'm appalled the A&E doctor didn't mention it. I've spent the last 18 minutes staring at my best friend in a hospital bed assuming she's in a coma when in fact she's just asleep.

"They woke her up in A&E before bringing her to the ward."

"So James has been called too?"

"No, not yet. We needed to make sure the next of kin was called first. So I can leave this with you" – she hands me Zoe's scribbles.

The nurse wants me to call James. This is not what Zoe would want. And it's *certainly* not what I want. But before I can explain, she holds up the folder she has in her other hand.

The enormity of the situation – of my position of next of kin – descends on my shoulders. If all I have to do right now is stare at Zoe's sleeping mass in a hospital bed, I'm okay. But this nurse needs my attention, my help, something to do with paperwork and Zoe's details.

I'm not designed to go things alone. And the person I'd usually turn to is lying slumped beneath a pale pink blanket just a few feet away from me. I need to call for backup.

Oh God, I need Ruby. I just have no idea if she'll come.

3 swimming aids

TORI

"You're looking a lot healthier than I expected," I say to Zoe. I have no idea if it's the right thing to say: you don't get taught how to handle this situation in school. But I know from experience that you don't treat someone who's attempted suicide like they're no longer human.

And Zoe is looking far more awake and alert than I'd have predicted for someone who spent all yesterday on the tube, an overdose coursing through her blood vessels, flooding every organ, overwhelming her liver and her kidneys.

I note she's wearing a full face of make-up, expertly applied as usual, so complimenting how she looks seems shrewd – especially as I need to get her on side.

I know Zoe doesn't want me here, but I'm here for Alison. Thankfully, I was with her when she got the call from the hospital or God knows what state she'd be in. She was in enough of a tizzy to leave me in A&E while she headed up to the ward without me. I had to go to reception to find out which ward Zoe was on.

Alison wanted to wait by Zoe's bedside alone. But now Zoe is awake, I've stepped in to keep her company while Alison gets herself something to eat – I insisted on it.

I put my bag and jacket on the plastic chair and sit on the edge of the bed. The jacket is simply for show. In this heat nobody wears one, but we all carry one because it's an expected part of the corporate outfit.

My actions are watched by a woman sitting a few feet away. Whoever she is, she's not wearing a uniform, but she has a lanyard round her neck with an NHS ID attached.

The ward is an uneven T-shape and Zoe's bed is at one end of the crossbar. Not the most obvious place to have an impromptu break room. And she could at least *pretend* to give us some privacy.

I smooth down the front of my Phase Eight purple shift dress, glad that, on a whim, I'd dressed in an usually sober colour. Something like my Desigual block-print dress would have been wholly unsuitable for this situation. I don't understand fashion but I do like colours. And as it's the expensive clothes that are made from fabrics that feel good against my skin, I dress well by accident.

The end of the bed behind Zoe's head is raised, and she's propped up on a mountain of pillows, but she's still lower down than I am. I pull myself up straight to make full use of my advantage.

I take her right hand gently in both of mine, giving the equivalent of a bear hug from a distance. I notice her left arm has a drip attached. I want to ask if it's drugs for the pain or just fluids to ease the damage to her organs, but it seems uncouth, so I stick to my original plan.

"How has James taken the news?" I ask. I know he doesn't know yet.

She shakes her head.

"That badly?"

"He doesn't know."

I give her my best "confused" look.

"I asked Alison not to tell him, just to say that I'm in hospital. I want to tell him myself."

"*Alison* called him?" I ask. I already know this, but the situation is too perfect not to be milked. Alison and James cannot stand each other.

"The hospital called Alison for me – she's my next of kin. They waited until she was here and then asked her to call James."

"So…?"

I look around me as if expecting him to appear, even though Alison has told me he's not here yet. Zoe, trapped on the ward, is no longer privy to all conversations and it has put me at an advantage.

"Alison didn't call him until I woke up. She said she wanted me to be awake first, to check I definitely wanted him here."

I'm not the best at reading tone of voice, but I'm pretty sure I hear the irritation I'm listening for. She's annoyed Alison didn't phone James straight away. And now I have the perfect opportunity to get her to question why.

"Oh, that's very sweet of her," I say as if I'm hearing all this for the first time. I pause. I let go of Zoe's hand and stare out of the hospital window. The view is of a large metal generator that all but fills the tiny courtyard. I pretend it has captured my interest.

Then I drive the knife in.

"She needs to make sure she gets the timing right."

"Timing right?"

I pretend to be dragged back into the present, stepping

off the bed as if to distance myself from the thoughts I've just shared out loud. I smooth my dress down again, this time replicating nervousness I don't feel.

"Yes. To… to make sure James isn't here before you're ready to see him."

I see a flash of uncertainty in Zoe's eyes – she's now wondering if there's another reason behind Alison's delay. I feel a little guilty manipulating Zoe when she's obviously so low, so broken. But then she never accepted my friendship – and as she's not a friend, I don't have to protect her feelings.

"I don't have to head back to the office just yet, so I can look out for James when he gets here, makes sure he comes *straight* in to see you?"

Zoe gives me an uneasy nod. She's not enjoying having to rely on me from the prison of her hospital bed. But her neediness is apparent – and it's helping me sow the seeds that Alison might be waiting in the wings a little too eagerly to offer James a shoulder to cry on.

It's quite simple: if Alison is the target of Zoe's attention, I can fly under the radar.

A THICKER SKIN.

When Tori saw him, he hit her like a physical force. She forgot how to do the simple things like breathing and holding her body upright; her breaths became light and shallow, her body an awkward bag of bones. She knew who he was before he was introduced, but she wanted to enjoy the seconds before that happened, pretending that he might available.

"Tori, this is James. James, Tori."

And it was confirmed. The magnificent beast of a man in front of her was Zoe's boyfriend.

Tori flashed him her best smile, attempting to hold his

gaze, even though eye contact made her brain hurt, then looked at Alison, sharing the smile with her, so neither of them would know if those extra few seconds smiling at James were on purpose.

Zoe was running late, as usual, and Tori was glad – it meant the introduction was from Alison. If Zoe had introduced them, she would have used all the right words to *suggest* she wanted to introduce them, but in a tone that dismissed the idea as preposterous.

Tori didn't understand why they couldn't *both* be friends with Alison, but Zoe made it very clear she didn't want Tori around.

All through lunch at the Paternoster, between mouthfuls of the sweet potato quiche Tori had ordered just in case James was a vegetarian, she gave him sideways glances. With each glance, the food in her mouth would turn into a thick paste that she would have to try and gulp down with water.

The meal wasn't just physically painful: Tori had to endure the mental pain of watching James interact with Zoe, trying to understand what he saw in her – and trying to understand the mystical powers she held over not just James, but Alison too.

Zoe's humour was cold and cutting: she used the same mix of words and tone to deliver duplicity in every sentence. She aimed the jokes at everyone at the table, including herself, but Tori was aware that the one-liners with an extra layer of cruelty were always directed at her.

Tori was also keeping count and worked out she was the victim of a third of Zoe's barbs – higher than her fair share when split between four.

After lunch, as they stood by the door of the pub, Zoe gave Tori a rare hug, which caught her off guard, as it was supposed to. It was followed with a "So glad you could join us" and "Where do you get your train from?" – and that was it: Tori had been dismissed.

Not quite ready to leave, Tori delayed her departure by extending her goodbyes to James and Alison to the kind of ramblings that are perfectly acceptable in British culture but which, for the most part, she avoided as she found the awkwardness painful.

Instead of walking away, she shuffled as she pretended to battle with her coat. It meant she was close enough to hear Zoe chose the venue for after-lunch drinks for herself and James – and then hear her offer Alison the chance to "Join us for one" without skipping a beat.

Tori put a thicker skin on along with her coat.

"The Happenstance sounds lovely," Tori said with an innocence even Zoe would find difficult to question.

Her tenacity was rewarded with a steely glance from Zoe and an extension of the invitation by Alison. And so Tori got to spend the afternoon drinking Vignards and Earl Martinis, her glances at James becoming gazes as the gin and vodka took hold. And Zoe noticed.

TORI

I'm watching the back entrance to King's College Hospital, the one off the car park. It's unlikely to be the one James uses, unless he gets the train into Loughborough Junction rather than Denmark Hill, but I told Alison it's important we see James before he finds Zoe's ward himself.

For some reason Zoe is on an acute ward, not a psychiatric one, so he isn't going to get a warning in advance as to why she's in here. And although Zoe says she wants to tell him herself, I've convinced Alison we need to at least prep him for bad news. She has agreed and is covering the front entrance.

My phone rings. Alison.

"He's here."

"I'll walk through to meet you both."

I head back through the labyrinth of corridors painted in putrid colours and steer them both into Costa.

"Come on, we can get one for Zoe too: help her feel more normal."

They both agree: they are aware of Zoe's caffeine addiction as much as I am.

They stand awkwardly at the end of the counter while I order and pay.

I ignore them on purpose, focusing on the girl who serves me, her rich orange locks half-tamed by a messy plait, her skin so pale and colourless she could pass as one of the patients. She even makes Alison's ghostlike shade look normal.

She makes three coffees calmly and efficiently. Her harmonious actions soothe me. I want to spend the day watching her, not dealing with the fallout of other people's mess, even though I've made my name as everyone's go-to person.

I don't get much change from my £10 note, but sometimes you have to spend in order to gain.

I pass James one coffee, Alison two. I haven't bothered buying myself one.

"Zoe doesn't want us to tell you why she's in here," I explain to James.

"I know. Alison's already told me."

"*Told* you?"

"That Zoe doesn't want me to know – not why she's here."

"You realise it isn't good news though?"

He nods. I squeeze his arm. I choose the arm that has the coffee at the end of it so he can't escape my touch easily. While I'm practising physical contact, I don't always get it right, so I prefer a captive audience.

To James I say: "I'm going to let Alison take you to Zoe's ward as she knows both of you better than I do." Then I look at Alison and add: "I'll wait here for you; you can come and join me once you've dropped James off."

Alison looks at me gratefully. Armed with coffees, she and James head off to the ward. I want to be a fly on the wall in that ward, but I know I can make the biggest impact by not being there.

THE OFFICE FLORENCE NIGHTINGALE

Tori had two sets of drawers under her desk at work instead of the standard one. The second pedestal was stolen from the IT team after she overheard them boasting how they ran a paperless office. She'd coolly walked over and wheeled the drawers away, a "Well, you won't be needing these then" nonchalantly thrown in their direction for good measure.

The first set of drawers was used for typical work paraphernalia; the second set was what would make Tori the most useful person in the office.

The top drawer was packed to the rim with various painkillers, antihistamines, plasters, Lemsip (both blackcurrant and lemon flavours) as well as a healthy stash of pens, paper and envelopes to stop anyone ever needing to go downstairs to the official stationery cupboard.

The second drawer held packets of tights in different colours, sizes and deniers, ready for any ladder emergencies. Everyone got their first pair of tights free – and paid £1 a pair after that. Tori bought multipacks from Superdrug so the mark-up on price helped her replenish her stock of other items.

The tights took up two-thirds of the drawer, with the rest of the space given over to a random mix of make-up and perfume samples picked up from the local Debenhams at lunchtime. At the very back, there was a travel sewing kit, although it had not been used yet. The bottom drawer held a hairdryer, straighteners and curling tongs – each with salon-length cords.

Tori desperately wanted to be the person you turn to when you needed something.

When the plans were being drawn up for the office reorganisation, she'd fought to get a desk near the ladies, saying she wanted to be away from the windows because of migraines. The real reason was because it meant Tori was able to see who rushed in there close to tears, or who scurried in looking like a drowned rat. Tori would count to 10 and then head in there, ready to help.

Alison had been a Senior Brand Manager for three weeks before her first Tori-style emergency. Tori recognised the shaking, the rapid breathing. Nerves. This was not a job for the contents of her desk drawers: a little more subtlety was required.

Tori followed Alison into the Ladies, a hand over one eye, and walked straight to the mirror to fish out an imaginary eyelash. Alison was lost in her own thoughts, leaning on the edge of the sinks, giving herself a mental pep talk.

"I'm sorry. I've got an eyelash…?"

Five minutes later, after Alison has confessed her worries, they headed to a meeting room so Tori could be a practise audience for a big presentation. After the success of the real thing, Tori was rewarded with a weekly lunch date, which soon became twice a week and then most lunchtimes.

That was until The Happenstance.

Zoe had taken Alison to one side and although Tori didn't know what was said, she knew *something* was said. She felt a draught of cool air pass through the newly formed gap in their friendship as Alison cagily took a step back.

Tori knew she needed to find a way back from the edge of the friendship abyss. A story she could tell Alison. And when the idea came to her it simply fell into place and was pure genius. She just waited for the right moment, refusing to believe they'd never lunch together at work again.

Six weeks passed before the inevitable hiccup – the point where Zoe cancelled on Alison for James, like women always do – and Alison was itching to tell Tori all about it. Tori graciously accepted the invitation for drinks after work, a quiet table in the corner chosen, and a bottle of white to share between them, Alison's glass topped up more often than Tori's.

And Tori listened.

"… I don't get it. It's not like he's the faithful boyfriend type. He's collected a lot of notches – he's admitted it. And yet she thinks he's going to be a good boyfriend just because he's being honest about it."

"He won't be."

Alison stopped talking and looked at Tori quizzically.

Tori had laced the words with extra weight and Alison had noticed. If there'd been a spotlight in the venue, it would now be shining down on Tori. She had the audience-of-one she'd been waiting for.

She spoke quietly, making Alison unconsciously lean in.

"I had a one-night stand with him. I didn't know he was seeing someone at the time. Not Zoe, this was a while ago. But he definitely had a girlfriend at the time because she confronted me. It was awful."

"Oh…"

"Yes. At lunch, I kept staring at him to work out why I knew him. I'd blocked him out of my mind and hadn't twigged who he was in such different circumstances.

"Once I realised, I couldn't stop looking at him because I wanted him to work out who I was. I wanted him to be worried that I'd be able to tell my story to his new girlfriend. But he was oblivious."

Tori paused. And then she delivered her killer line.

"I know my behaviour upset Zoe, but I had to just let it go. I could hardly explain it all to her."

And with one perfect lie, embellished with the correct details, Tori went from Alison's embarrassing friend who letched over her friend's boyfriend to someone wronged by a man who was now seeing said friend.

As they left the bar and headed for their respective stations, Tori gave Alison an extra tight squeeze.

"Promise me you won't mention it to Zoe,"

The promise was made. Both women knew it wouldn't be kept.

TORI

I have to sit patiently for 12 minutes, but my wait is rewarded. Alison returns with a look of unease mixed with confusion. I pat the seat next to me. Alison slumps into it, defeated.

"She seemed mad at the coffee."

I hoped she would be. I'd told Zoe I'd keep an eye out for James, to make sure he went *straight* in to see her, but it now looks like my plans were intercepted by Alison who suggested they get a coffee together first.

The coffee says "Hey we sat down together without you

and you couldn't do anything about it because you were stuck in bed". It suggests to Zoe that her situation might have been discussed behind her back even though it's the *very thing* Alison promised not to do.

"Oh that's my fault, the coffee was my idea. I thought it would help."

Alison looks horrified.

"Oh no, I'm not letting you blame yourself. I thought it would too."

"I guess there's no way of knowing what's going on in her head at the moment," I say. "She's not exactly going to be thinking rationally."

I put my arm around Alison's shoulders and give her a sideways hug. Hugs, hand squeezes, arm squeezes – the NLP training I went on at work is paying off.

Oxford Circus

Oxford Circus is the busiest station on the underground network with over 98 million passengers per year. The entrances are exposed stairwells with no cover from the elements and the pavements surrounding them at the junction of Oxford St and Regent St are a swarm of people every rush hour.

It's what Zoe is reminded of when it comes to visiting hours as she sees a ridiculous number of people crowded round each bed, fighting for the few extra plastic chairs, nurses shouting at visitors who sit on the edge of the bed.

Zoe can't help wonder why her mother would always say "It's like Piccadilly Circus in here" whenever she or her sisters had more than one friend round. Surely it should have been Oxford Circus. (She was also faintly irritated when she discovered that neither of them were actual circuses.)

Zoe's bedside will be slightly less busy than any type of circus

– collection of clowns, tube stop or road junction – as she doesn't really want anyone there. She's only asked Alison and James to visit for their own sakes.

4 lifeguards

ZOE

"O beware, my lord, of jealousy; it is the green-ey'd monster which doth mock the meat it feeds on." – I can't help but reflect on Iago's words as I look from cup to cup to cup. James is holding one cup of coffee: Alison two. I'm assuming one of them is for me, but I can't help wonder if it was an afterthought, bought last minute while they stood in the queue talking about me.

Yes, James and Alison are the two people I wanted to contact when I first woke up in hospital. But they hate each other, so why do I get the notion they are colluding behind my back?

How long does it take to queue for coffee? To wait for them to be made? Long enough for Alison to fill James in on the basics – on *her* version of the basics?

Is he going to have to fake being shocked when I tell him why I'm in here? Or maybe he genuinely won't be shocked: maybe he had some inkling that the person he's been dating is so miserable and so angry that he's half expecting this.

Alison hands me the spare coffee, a hopeful smile on her

face. I can tell she wants it to make some sort of difference, and I feel guilty that it doesn't, so I do the overcompensating I always do and smile gratefully in return. I'm so used to filling the void with the actions people expect of me that it now happens on autopilot.

It's like every time Alison has a one-night stand. I know I'm going to spend the next day piecing her self esteem back together again while having to bite down the urge to tell her that pulling a random bloke while apoplectically drunk isn't the way to meet the man of your dreams.

And what did I get in return? On the rare occasion that I seek support from her, she complains that it's "okay for you" because I find empathy easy. I don't: I just find it no less difficult than any other hoop I'm asked to jump through.

It's like the time James took me to the ballet on a whim after he found out I was a fan. They were cheap tickets for a shoddy performance – dancers out of time with the music *and* each other, arabesques with wobbling legs. But I knew I was expected to love it for the effort he'd made, so I clapped enthusiastically and gushed afterwards about how wonderful it was.

For months afterwards, James milked the ballet visit every time he wanted something. I tried not to hate him for it – after all, my actions told him he had the right to.

The one-night stands and the ballet are examples, not isolated incidents. Each time I have to overcompensate to meet expectations, it's like I take another step out into a cool, dark lake. Yes they may be my best friend and my boyfriend, but the more time I spend with them, the less I want anything to do with them. And it's not their fault.

Now I'm in the centre of that lake, the water gently lapping over my bottom lip and into my mouth. I'm ready to stop treading water; I'm ready to drown.

I change my "grateful for the coffee" look into a pointed one – a cue for Alison to leave. I can tell she wants to stay, so I just stare at her, unmoving, a mental game of chicken, until she gives in.

"I'll, erm, wait outside," she says as she leaves.

"No need to wait," I tell her breezily.

I wait for the double doors at the end of the ward to close behind her before I put my coffee down. I haven't taken a single sip. Yes it will be better than the free muck they wheel round at break time, but I know its origins will leave a sour taste in my mouth.

"Did she tell you anything?" I ask James.

"No."

I raise an eyebrow.

"Well, just that it was serious, but nothing else. She said you wanted to tell me what happened."

"So not nothing" I think to myself – but I don't say it because I know it will sound childish and I want to choose my words carefully.

James is still standing awkwardly so I motion towards the plastic visitor's seat. I don't want James sitting on the edge of my bed, invading my space, as Tori did. He sits down.

"I took an overdose of Paracetamol."

"Fuck."

He sounds genuinely shocked, so I wait for my words to sink in a little, wait for him to look up at me, before I continue.

"I took the tablets yesterday, but I waited until today to come to hospital because the first eight hours are critical. That's the treatment window, the period of time when they can attempt to reverse the damage."

"You waited…?"

"I don't want them to be able to reverse the damage," I say slowly. The words "I want to die" hang in the air, unsaid. This is too much for James. I watch him lean back in his chair, increasing the gap between us, pushing the chair's flexible plastic back to its limits. As he pushes himself back with his feet, his force moves the chair back, scraping its feet along the linoleum. It's an old chair, its rubber feet long since worn away, and the screech it makes is an assault on my ears.

James is scrambling to get away, but I need him to listen.

"This is important," I tell him in my coldest voice.

He stills himself.

"I didn't want to just leave a note. I wanted a chance to explain why, and a note wouldn't do it. I knew a Paracetamol overdose would give me a window of a few days, before I died, to talk to you about it, to explain."

James tries to laugh, but it comes out as a wheeze, as if he's been struck in the chest.

"I'm here so you can get everything off your chest before you go? Is that it?" he asks, his voice filled with disbelief.

My head fills with anger.

"Look if you're not interested in hearing what I've got to say, you can always leave. You just won't be able to come back in a few days if you change your mind. Because I won't be here."

James has the decency to look a little ashamed.

"I didn't want to leave you wondering why, wondering if there was anything you could have done. I knew this way you'd have the chance to ask, so you wouldn't be left with any niggling questions. I wanted to make sure you could move on."

I realise I'm talking in the same slow way I've noticed the doctors talk to me.

"I thought of splitting up with you a few months ago so we weren't together for this, but I was concerned you'd blame yourself even more, blaming our break up as the final straw."

"Months ago? Just how long have you been planning this?"

I'm not going to answer that. I can't, because the honest reply is too much for a normal brain to process. Because there's not been a *single* daywhen suicide *hasn't* flooded my thoughts. I know that is something those without mental health issues just won't be able to fathom.

"Today isn't about me," I say instead. "It's about making sure you know I want you to move on."

"Move on?"

"Yes. Meet someone else, settle down, live a life."

"Meet someone else?"

"Yes, but…"

I pause. He looks up again.

"Anyone but Alison."

"Anyone but… *Alison*?" he repeats.

His mind is still playing catch-up, which is fair enough as I've just opened up my head, scooped out all the shit and dumped it on him.

As I wait for the cogs in his mind to whirr round, I rub my left arm. The drip that's meant to be making me feel better is making my skin itchy and stretched. And it's starting to look like I've got elephantiasis.

I notice James staring at my hand. I realise he's back with me.

"I mean it," I stress to him. "Anyone but her."

ELEPHANTS NEVER FORGET

Elephant & Castle was the sort of area of London that could intimidate even the not so easily intimidated. But Zoe refused to be shaken. After all, it was only buildings and people, just the same as anywhere else. And if they were going to build a university here, she knew it couldn't be *that* unsafe.

As a mature student, Zoe felt she should really be able rise above these silly first-day anxieties, so she walked along London Road and up the steps of the brown-brick curiously named Technopark building with all the confidence she could muster.

Whether she believed her confidence didn't matter because others did, watching her with their eyes wide, bottom lips trembling. She'd calmly told them that, yes, they were in the right place. It seemed she was the *only* person in the room that *didn't* need a proper adult to turn up and tell them they were right.

Zoe made a mental note of the names of those with vast, expansive eyes and wobbling lips, and of the ones whose faces crumpled when they discovered they weren't in the same tutorial group as her. She did this to ensure she could avoid them.

Although she didn't want to be ageist, Zoe was extremely wary about making friends with teenagers. She liked people who were independently minded, who were freethinkers, who were able to question her opinions when they were unsure of them, and most teenagers were not able to stand up to peer pressure. She wanted friends who were equals: 18-year-old lip-wobblers were disqualified.

As Zoe expected, these timid creatures glued themselves

to her and she spent the weeks that followed trying to extricate herself from the unsuitable friendships they were trying to form.

Well, all of them bar one: the one called Alison.

Zoe didn't know Alison was desperately looking for her. Zoe would see Alison scouring the lecture hall, but Alison's gaze would never stop on her face – not even for a moment.

During lectures, Zoe liked to withdraw into herself for an hour. She'd find peace in her own head, recharge herself, ready for whatever followed – a lively debate, a busy lunch, a bus ride home. Whatever came after the lecture would drain her and she would wish for another lecture and the chance to press pause.

Zoe had no idea the "serious mode" she reserved for lecturers made her look like a fluid, half-formed version of herself. She didn't know that to recognise her, Alison needed to hear the loud laugh or see the bright smile or strutting walk.

Zoe knew there was a chance Alison's face had been first-day nerves that had since faded. But she also knew "first-day nerves" should be called first-week nerves or first-term nerves – that 18-year-olds needed far longer than 24 hours to find themselves.

Which would suggest the look on Alison's face had been a silent, visual complaint about something else. And Zoe was curious to know what that was.

ZOE

"We are such stuff as dreams are made on, and our little life is rounded with a sleep" – Prospero is right: we barely make a mark.

So why do people fight so much to live such pointless lives? I'm *so* ready to die that I struggle to truly understand the fear other people have for it. I'm trying to be empathetic though. And I plan to wear less make-up each day, helping my features fade away, to help everyone prepare for my death.

I have one of those "naked palette" faces that makeup artists love; an incredibly versatile canvas which holds no character without a healthy coating of paint.

At school, everyone knows everyone, and I had the typical chubby cheeks of a kid back then. But in the world of work, you have many acquaintances, and I've noticed it take some people weeks to recognise me, to remember me, because I blend into the world as just another face.

I find it amusing that, as I start to talk, I get to watch their vague looks turn momentarily into ones of apprehension as they realise they should know me, and then into relief as they grasp how they do.

It's fitting really, because I have the same reaction to their lives, except my vague looks are the real ones and everything else is just me putting on a face for the outside world.

I'm perfectly sane. But suicidal.

There's nothing wrong with me in any other way as far as I can tell. I'm consumed by this overwhelming sense of loss. But I haven't lost anything. It's the only word I can think to use though, as my vocabulary just doesn't stretch far enough.

When I explain this to anyone other than psychiatrists they look baffled. But psychiatrists nod. I can't decide if that nod means they agree with me or if it's what they do to not alienate you, to keep you talking.

And that's the problem with psychiatrists. They never share their opinion. It's not lies as such, but there's a veil of dishonesty between you. You're meant to tell them everything about how you feel and in return they give you very little beyond nods and little white pills.

You never get to see the truths they share because their scribblings aren't for your eyes. I don't want *their* notes to define who I am after I'm gone any more than I wanted a note of my own to do the same. It's why I need to talk to Alison and James face-to-face, make sure my side of my story gets told.

At the moment, they're both too distracted with my looming death to listen to what I have to say. I know I need to give them time to process everything, but time is something I'm running out of.

Alison thought I'd wanted to die on the tube, for fuck's sake. She didn't realise I'd chosen it as a safe place to become ill. What I've not told her yet is that I did it for her. I didn't want her to come home and find me, to be the one to have to call the ambulance.

But going to hospital early was not an option, because of the window. So I needed to go somewhere where I'd be ignored until the right moment. Somewhere where my slumped body wouldn't be ignored, which it might easily be in a park or another public place. While I didn't want to get to hospital too early, I did want to get taken there at some point – for a more comfortable death.

There are quicker methods of death available – and ones that would offer a lot less pain and discomfort. But I chose this route for Alison and James's sake. To explain everything to them, but also to give them the chance to say the goodbyes I never got to say to my mother.

But they don't understand this yet, because they aren't capable of listening properly. They have no appreciation of my final sacrifice. And I'm not sure they've got the mental capacity to get there.

Maybe I shouldn't have said "anyone but Alison". Maybe they deserve each other.

5 lifebuoys

"I stand here with no right to ask
You sit there wishing your station had already past
Because if it had you'd not be here listening to me
Asking not for 'us and them', but for 'we'
We're all human at the end of the day
And I didn't want to end up this way
Now I have no choice but to ask for a hand out
Because at the end of the day I really have got nowt
So I offer the only thing I have – this rhyme
In the hope you see it as a sign
Of the human that's still inside of me
Who just wants a chance to live and just be."

RUBY

She finishes her poem and stands briefly at the end of the carriage that was temporarily her stage before shuffling between the two rows of seats, ignored by most.

I wonder how many times she's stood and performed it to an uninterested audience, carriage after carriage. I guess at many, many times from the mix of boredom and exasperation that she fails to keep out of her voice.

I realise it could also be the hundredth time that everyone else in this carriage has heard the poem, but I'm still shocked that nobody else puts their hands in their pockets.

I want to reward this homeless woman for attempting to connect with a carriage full of people who want to pretend she isn't there. I have no idea what an acceptable amount to give a homeless person in London is, so I guess at £2.

I fish the coins out of my purse and hand them over. I can tell from the slight flex of muscles on her face, a hint of surprise, that I've been generous.

Even though people earn more in London, it doesn't seem to matter; people here are just as protective of their own pennies.

She reminds me of the photos of me and Alison from Brownie camp, the ones where we'd washed our faces but missed our necks and ears, so the edges of us are covered in dirt, although it showed up much clearer on Alison's pale skin than it did on my dark brown tones. In those photos, the dirt is healthy a-few-days-playing-in-mud dirt. This woman is definitely not playing.

I'm always curious about the edges of things. I've felt I've been living on the edge of my life for too many years. And for this woman it's far worse: she's on the very periphery of society. She's standing on the edge of our world, her existence being lapped at by the sea. And when people gaze downwards, ensuring she is not within their eye-line, their waves of invisibility crash over her.

Our peripheral vision catches so much of what is around us. I used to believe its main tool was to make sure we weren't missing anything, but the older I get, the more I see it used as a tool to exclude.

How does she, in her position, find the strength to get up each day and perform her poem when just a few miles from here another woman – one with a job, friends, a boyfriend, a roof over her head, enough food to eat – lies in a hospital bed ending her own life?

BROWN OWL

A gaggle of mostly boisterous girls were standing on a tarmac no-man's-land between a scruffy minibus and a rundown church hall. Each girl had a rucksack and a sleeping bag.

Some had flashy sports rucksacks and brand new sleeping bags packed away in matching sleek bags; others had nondescript rucksacks and old sleeping bags rolled up and tied with rope or cord.

Both Alison and Ruby found themselves in the "others" again: the few misfits whose parents didn't realise that new stuff for Brownie camp was just as important as new stuff for school. For the hundredth-millionth time, Alison was grateful to have Ruby by her side, making sure she was not alone in her quest for survival.

Alison longed to be grown up. She looked at all the grown ups around her and even the rubbish ones like Miss Cleary from school had jobs. She liked the idea of being a Brown Owl, but wondered how someone paid for a house working only one night a week. If she were Brown Owl she would ban brand new sleeping bags.

On day two of camp (which was rows of old bunk beds in a converted church hall) the girls stayed up to tell each other ghost stories. They sat in a haphazard, elongated circle between the bunk beds, lights off, each person speaking lit by only torchlight.

That night one of the girls told a story about two boys

becoming blood brothers by pricking their fingers and mixing their blood, and how they were bound together forever, even dying the same death. Alison realised it was the perfect way to make sure Ruby never left her.

The next day, huddled in a toilet cubicle together, Alison unclipped her Brownie Promise Badge from her uniform, opened the fastening as wide as possible and bravely pierced the flesh of her thumb.

She pulled the pin out and passed it to Ruby. She waited for blood. Nothing. So she squeezed her thumb. To her relief, blood oozed out of the hole she'd created. Ruby held out her thumb and solemnly pushed the pin into her own flesh. Once her blood had also been squeezed out, they held their thumbs together, mixing their blood.

Alison sucked her thumb for the rest of the day. Not because it hurt, but because it comforted her to know that part of Ruby was inside her. That they would be best friends forever. That not even boyfriends could come between them.

RUBY

The hospital doesn't look very inviting from the outside. I hope for a better welcome inside. I'm here for me as well as for Alison. Yes, she needs me. And that's the main reason I'm here. But it means I'll also have the chance to find out why she threw our friendship way, to tell her how much she hurt me.

Of course I'm upset that she only got in touch because she needs me. But I'm also *glad* she did too. It means our friendship is still inside her somewhere: there might be something we can salvage.

When I see her I don't mention any of this – all this is for later. Instead, I envelope her in a huge hug.

She's filling me in on what's happened when we're interrupted by a haughty cough. I'm introduced to Tori, who extends a hand and offers a stiff handshake. Alison explains Tori was with her at work when she took the call from the hospital – unspoken words, that Alison wished she'd been alone, fill the air between us. Tori is oblivious to them.

Tori is wearing a rather formal purple dress that reminds me of the last time I saw Alison.

We'd both been bridesmaids for Becky's wedding. Not because either of use were particularly close to Becky anymore, but because Becky wanted 12 bridesmaids. She'd dressed us up in rich purple, asking Alison to get a tan beforehand so she wasn't too pale for the photos.

I'm still not sure what annoyed me more: spending the day putting up with being told I looked like a half unwrapped bar of Cadbury's chocolate; or the absurd orange streaky tinge that seemed to cling to Alison's skin and bruise her elbows and knees, all because someone else thought it okay to judge her for her skin colour.

The purple outfit, twinned with cropped hair that is styled within an inch of its life, looks totally out of place next to Alison's casual asymmetric-cut dress (probably an impulsive purchase from ASOS or Boohoo) and simple side ponytail to balance the look.

I'd spent enough time in hospitals to know that anything other than casual doesn't work, so I'd opted for a combo of T-shirt and jeans, smoothing over my days' old Bantu knots with a little Bee Mine Curly Butter.

Tori pushes her shoulders back, ready to take control of the situation. The purple dress must be some kind of power dressing. She fills me in on Zoe's situation, telling me what

Alison has already told me, but I nod along, giving the expected "hmm" type noises. Whoever this Tori is, she's a little unstable. It seems unwise to stop her mid-flow.

Tori's version of events doesn't include how hostile Zoe is being towards Alison over a cup of coffee, which is something I'm still trying to get my head round. I realise I need to meet this Zoe for myself to work out what's going on. So when Alison suggests I join her on the ward, I agree.

Tori assumes she needs to join us and Alison doesn't seem to be willing to bat her away.

When we get to Zoe's bed, the curtains are pulled round, so we have to wait. An awkwardness descends onto the three of us and we suddenly don't know what to do with our limbs. For some reason, planned waiting, like waiting for a bus, doesn't cause this kind of myopathy.

I watch Alison and Tori alternate between looking at the ceiling and looking at the floor, offering each other weak, watery smiles whenever their eyes meet. I'm breaking social norms – ignoring them both and staring at the closed curtains instead.

The curtains are pulled back from the inside and a nurse appears, dragging a monitor on wheels with her, lights still flashing numbers on the screen, blood pressure cuffs and cables making a bid for escape from the wire basket fitted just below the monitor.

It reminds me of the way the TV used to be wheeled into the classroom at primary school. TV at school was far more exciting than TV at home, even though the programmes were out-dated factual ones, fuzzy from being overplayed.

"Just checking her vitals," the nurse explains as she leaves. "You can go in now."

YOU CAN GO IN NOW

The nurse pulled the curtain back from around the bed and looked at the young girl, maybe eight years old, maybe a year or so older, who had transformed into a timid mouse before her eyes.

"It's okay sweetheart," the nurse said. "You can go in now."

Ruby wished Alison could be here, but Alison was still at school, no doubt cursing having to work through difficult sums on her own.

Ruby hated maths but she longed to be at her desk next to Alison's, the two of them struggling to understand what all the different squiggly shapes meant, while Miss Cleary droned on at the front of class not making any sense.

"It's okay," the nurse reassured her.

Ruby was hesitant – she could feel the presence of a force field where the curtain had been and she wasn't sure she was strong enough to step through it.

So the nurse gently guided her by the shoulders to the chair next to the bed, a chair that Ruby had to lift herself up onto, her legs dangling, not reaching the floor. The kerfuffle she made woke the person in the bed, who looked down at the fragile child in the chair and smiled.

And Ruby felt slightly less scared.

"Hi, Mum," she said.

6 armbands

TORI

We have to pretend we can't hear the conversation between Zoe and the nurse. Well, more of a monologue from the nurse with the occasional "hmm" from Zoe. We now know the nurse thinks Zoe is in some way special needs with the mental age of a five year old, because you obviously have to be that way inclined in order to try and top yourself.

We're no closer to knowing what Zoe thinks.

The idea that a slice of thin blue fabric gives a patient any degree of privacy is an embarrassing joke that we all go along with.

"You can go in now."

I watch as Alison introduces Ruby to Zoe. I'm not the only one watching. The same woman as before sitting in the chair by the wall and this time she's not even pretending to read. Are the NHS cuts so bad that they can no longer afford to have staff rooms in hospitals? Whoever this woman is, I wonder if she picks up on the same strange dynamic between the three of them that I do.

There's also a feeling of unease, which is mostly emanating from Alison. She's introducing Ruby and Zoe to each other in a way that suggests she doesn't want to, which is weird because she's the person who invited Ruby here.

I read fear on Alison's face, plus a hint of stubbornness. And then I get it: she never intended to let these two people meet.

There's a bizarre ritual attached to introducing friends: one that instils a hierarchy. Alison is making sure Ruby and Zoe both know they are both *her* friends first.

None of this is said out loud, of course. These social rules that everyone follows, the way people dance around each other never saying what they mean, annoy me. For some reason, this behaviour doesn't count as lying because *everybody* does it.

The look on Alison's face right now, I've seen this look before. It's the one someone has on their face when they don't want to share. I saw it on Zoe's face when Alison introduced me to her – it's how I know Zoe doesn't like sharing.

At the time, I'd stupidly thought the look *wasn't* on Alison's face because she was gracious at sharing. But now the look *is* on her face because she doesn't want to share Ruby with Zoe. Which means it wasn't there the first time because she didn't *care* about sharing.

The boundary between acquaintance and friend is not as thick as the blue hospital curtains and is invisible to everyone else on the ward. But it's definitely there. And I am on the outside of it. The only difference this time is that, with Alison, I thought I'd somehow managed to clamber over it.

I'm cross with myself for thinking this time was different. But I'm even more cross with Alison. She's not been honest with me about what our friendship means – if I can even call it that. People are usually very clear to me about how much they want to keep me at arm's length. But except for a few brief weeks when we didn't lunch together (which was all Zoe's fault), Alison hasn't been like that with me at all.

Looking at it with fresh eyes, I redefine my role from "friend" to "backup". I've always known I was below Zoe in the pecking order, but I'd assumed that was a best friends thing. And second place is better than nowhere. But now I've slipped to third and I'm not sure how far behind the other two I am.

Any shred of guilt I feel over the coffees, over setting Alison up to take the fall so Zoe wants me, and not Alison, to be there for James, evaporates. So I guess I need to thank Ruby for that.

Ruby. I'm not sure what kind of cruelty is it to name your child after a deep red jewel when they're brown skinned, but then other people's decisions rarely make much sense to me.

Zoe seems to be holding it together where Alison is concerned, which is annoying. After Alison came back to Costa all upset, I'd agreed to wait for James to find out what happened after she'd left him on the ward with Zoe. (I'd convinced Alison to leave. I'd made a point of telling Alison he might not be willing to be honest if she was there.)

When James told me about his "anything but Alison" incident I'd happily agreed not to be the person to tell her. You only get to play *one* role: if you're the messenger, you don't get to be the shoulder to cry on too.

Yes, I want James for myself, but I want Alison too.

When I offered – insisted – to accompany Alison to the hospital, it was so I could be there for her in the role Zoe would usually fill. And up until now, my meticulous planning has focused on being the person who offers one shoulder to James and the other to Alison. To be perfectly primed to step into the slot Zoe is about to vacate.

But now this Ruby girl has turned up, I'm no longer sure Alison will need one of my shoulders. So I need to find out who she is in order to work out how to remove her from the picture.

From the way Alison clings to her as they hug, I'd say she was someone from Alison's past. She's someone who knows nothing about London because she's not only turned up to the hospital in the scruffiest clothes (the sort you'd expect to relegate to wearing when doing odd jobs around the house) but she seems to think it's perfectly okay to walk round with her hair tied up in some sort of rollers.

I'm surprised she needs them as afro hair is already curly, but I daren't ask because I know I could be stepping on toes. I want to ask because wearing rollers looks like "cultural appropriation" to me – something black people accuse white people of all the time. It's exhausting.

More than asking her about her hair, I want to ask her about the marks on her cheeks. They can't be accidental scars because they're the same on each side. It's almost as if someone has decided to give her rosy cheek marks that have faded with time. Are they some kind of tribal thing? Or are they simply old acne scars? Does acne mark dark skin differently?

I'm curious, but I'm not going to let it distract me from the main task here – to use the time while Zoe is dying to walk away with as much of her life as possible.

Yes, Ruby, you may be from her past, but in the *present* version of Alison's life, I was here first. I'm sick of being second best. Sick of losing out. Well, I'm not going to let it happen this time.

HAVING WORDS

Eight-year-old Tori wanted to "have words" with her parents. That's the term they used when they wanted to talk to her about something serious. But when she said it, they found it funny.

It made her even more cross than she already was. She realised that sometimes adults were stupid and needed things spelling out.

"Maggie got the extra piece of cake."

Her mother nodded.

"Because she's the youngest."

"And Ellie gets to stay up half an hour later."

Another nod.

"Because she's the eldest."

"So what do I get?" Tori asked.

"Your father ferries you to and from gymnastics twice a week," her mother said in a stern voice.

But Tori wasn't going to fall for that trick. They'd used gymnastics in arguments before, so she was ready for this.

"And he takes Ellie to violin lessons, and he takes Maggie to soft play."

Her mother nodded again.

"Which are great examples of how we do things for all three of you. Different things, but it all evens out."

Except Tori wanted extra cake *and* a later bedtime. So things felt very uneven. And they stayed uneven through her teens. And it wasn't a surprise. "Parents" was always two adults, not three. So they should have only two children, not three. With three it's never balanced and someone always loses out. And it was always her.

Ellie shared the same love of music as their mother, while useless, pathetic Maggie could do no wrong in the eyes of their father – even when she did the same things Tori got in trouble for at the same age.

Tori realised she needed to strike out on her own. She planned to leave home as soon as she was 16 and move back to London, never forgiving her parents for moving to leafy Surrey when she was nine. However, she knew living alone would be daunting, so she wanted to get some practice in beforehand, getting used to navigating the world solo.

She started off by going for long, meandering walks. But Weybridge was a small place, and she soon ran out of places to discover.

So she started taking bus trips to the surrounding towns (preparing herself mentally for train journeys into London) even though she knew that not all bus journeys ended well.

TORI

In London, wine is the answer to everything. I don't know anyone who doesn't drink copious amounts. I hear people occasionally take a couple of days off drinking, or even a week, but I don't know a single person in the capital who could successfully accomplish Dry January – myself included.

So when the three of us leave the hospital together, it's natural for me to suggest going for a drink, to stop the two of them running off without me.

Ruby shrugs as she holds up her overnight bag, her way of saying "but I'm carrying this", convincing Alison to let them head to her flat first rather than straight to the pub.

Unfortunately, the route back to Alison's place from King's College Hospital is by bus. I'm not a fan of the bus. (Although I'm not sure we'd get Alison on the tube after today's events.)

I sit in the row of seats behind Ruby and Alison so I can

pretend to be in my own thoughts while still being able to listen. I want to see if I can glean from what is said why Ruby has been referred to as Flo.

The nickname hasn't been explained to me, which is an irritation. But asking why outright can lead to the awkward acknowledgement that the story isn't for your ears. So I need a way of asking without asking, by getting them to tell the story it relates to. I don't know what that is yet, but they could just need a nudge about how they know each other. And if that doesn't work, I need to find a way that makes them feel guilty so they have to tell me.

When we get to Alison's flat, I stand awkwardly in the hall while the two of them carry bedding from Alison's room into the lounge, sorting out some sort of temporary bed for Ruby. My place is such a trek from here and I know I won't get offered a temporary bed, so I need to convince them to go drinking in the centre instead of anywhere around here.

I hear movement. I watch Ruby head out of the lounge and into the kitchen and hear the rustling noises of someone searching for things in an unfamiliar place. Lots of banging doors. The tinkering of glasses.

"There's wine in the fridge, Flo."

I hear the fridge door open.

"Oh wine cow! No, two wine cows."

Now this I have to see. I head into the kitchen and have to strain to look over Ruby's shoulder to see what wine cows are because the door of the fridge opens the wrong way into the room. It's the sort of kitchen layout that would be infuriating to any sane person, but I still ache to live here.

There are two wine boxes on the top shelf, one white, one rosé. Each has a plastic tap poking through the cardboard like a forlorn udder. Ruby stands with the fridge door ajar while she tilts one of the wine boxes in order to read the information.

"Don't stand with the fridge door open!" – I want to scream this out loud, but the words just ring around inside my head instead.

You come out of your teens battered and bruised: "If you live in my house you live by my rules" and "If you don't like it get a job so you can live elsewhere". By the time you leave it's obvious your parents don't want you around anymore and you're questioning why they ever had kids.

I never wanted to live in their house and by their stupid rules, so as soon as I was old enough, I got a job and moved out. But the rules have followed me and I now find people standing with the fridge door open as infuriating as my parents did.

"Hurry up!" Alison shouts from the lounge.

"White or pink?" Ruby shouts back.

"Pink! And bring the cow biscuits!"

Wine cows. And now cow biscuits? They have their own language. Ruby's friendship is far more ingrained into Alison's life than I'd hoped.

Ruby carries the wine cow and cow biscuits (a packet of Fox's Malted Milk biscuits which have cows on the front) into the lounge. I bring the three oversized wine glasses – just as important but met with less enthusiasm.

The sofa is now made up as Ruby's bed, so it makes sense that Ruby sits on it at the pillows end, with Alison taking what will be the feet end. It's a sofa big enough for three people but they're lounging across it in a way that makes it just for two.

I'm left with the armchair in the corner – the seat I would have coveted as a child as it would have been Ellie's, but it sets me adrift.

The wine and biscuits are shared with me across the void of carpet, but the history, the in-jokes, are not. And I don't find out why Ruby is called Flo.

The Viking line

The Victoria line was almost called the Viking line as it passed through two busy mainline stations, Victoria and King's Cross — Viking coming from "Vi" and "king" the same way the Bakerloo line is "Baker" and "loo" after Baker Street and Waterloo.

The Victoria line seems more fitting, especially as there's now a Jubilee line and they'll be joined by The Elizabeth line once the Crossrail opens.

Getting the name right was important for Alison too. Ruby agreed to being called "Flo" from day one, whereas Zoe fought against anything other than Zoe, not even allowing Alison to shorten it to "Zo".

Tori and her sisters Maggie and Ellie all have two names — the shortened ones they use and their "official" names — Victoria, Margaret and Eleanor — that are rarely used. (And usually because they are in trouble.)

The only person Tori lets call her "Victoria" without sulking is Maureen, their old next-door neighbour.

7 swimming aids

ALISON

"So do you have a nickname for Zoe?" Tori asks me with a fake nonchalance that doesn't fool me for a second. "You call Ruby 'Flo' but I've only ever heard you call Zoe by her real name."

The minute we leave the ward, Tori pounces. It's like she can't help herself. I'm still reeling from Zoe's suicide attempt, and from seeing Ruby after all this time, and from introducing the two of them. And Tori wants to talk about nicknames.

I have the same feeling now as I'd had that evening in The Happenstance where it felt as if Tori were trying to absorb everything she could about Zoe and James. I'd freely shared stories and titbits of information, tongue loosening as we racked up the cocktails. A few things I shared came back to bite me, Zoe angry with me for being so free with stories about her.

That's when I'd confessed to her that Tori claimed to be an ex-shag of James's. (Although a tiny bit of me wasn't sure whether or not to believe Tori, it explained my behaviour and would help save my skin.)

When Zoe had demanded the truth out of James, he'd had to admit he had *no clue* who he'd slept with during his wilder days and was unable to deny Tori was one of them.

Although James's half-confession meant I escaped relatively unscathed, from that point onwards I'd been wary about saying too much of anything to Tori. I wish I hadn't been with her when I'd received the call from the hospital.

Well I wasn't going to let her do the same thing with Ruby. And if that meant sacrificing Zoe – who wouldn't be around much longer to hear about it – then so be it.

"At university we were always together, so people used to call us Maps after the A-to-Z map," I fib.

I can't tell if Tori believes me.

"After Alison and Zoe," I add redundantly.

I always babble when I lie. I prefer not to, but when I do, it's like I've turned the tap on in that part of my brain and false information and made up stories just come spewing out. I didn't have a nickname for Zoe, there's no way she'd have let me, but it was either make one up or tell her about Ruby's.

"A joint nickname?" Tori responds. "That's really sweet."

She smiles warmly at me and I twig what question is coming next.

"So did you and Ruby have a joint nickname back at school too? Or was she just Flo?"

Yep. Right on target. Another attempt to pump me for information about Ruby.

"I don't think so," I say. "Although I guess we might have had one behind our backs that we didn't know about!"

I laugh. The joke is a terrible one, but Tori laughs along – anything to please me.

"Talking of Flo," I say, "where on earth is she?"

I look round for Ruby – she's not in the corridor with us. I head back onto the ward and spot her standing by one of the windows next to the Nurses Station.

She has her head tilted to one side and one of the nurses is leaning in, looking at her face. What on earth are they doing? They're a similar shade of brown, so are they swapping make-up tips? Seems a bit of a strange thing to be doing on a hospital ward. But then if that's where you work every day, then that's where you swap make-up tips.

Ruby feels my gaze on her and looks over, embarrassed.

Ruby is wearing her hair in springy rosebuds. It's been years since she wore it in tiny braids with beads, but I get a twinge of disappointment each time I see her without them. I miss the clacking noise they used to make hitting against each other when she'd jiggle up and down all excited about something.

She says goodbye to the nurse and walks up to join us. She's brought the Whitstable air up to London with her, I'm sure of it, because I'm finding it easier to breathe when she's around.

As we head out of the hospital together, I'm busy working out how to shake Tori off, something I've not mastered yet. I want to get back to my flat with Ruby and without Tori.

Oblivious to this, Ruby is giving her take on the Zoe situation – and how she sees it as an outsider. Tori is pretending to listen while she simmers, obviously annoyed that I haven't shared the story about Flo.

Ruby and I have always been the outsiders. As you get older you realise there are more outsiders than you thought. Even if every school has just one or two outsiders, there are thousands of schools across the UK. That's thousands of outsiders you can make friends with.

And sometimes they decide to make friends with you.

CONFIRMATION BIAS

Zoe felt her skin prickle. She knew who'd just walked into the library before looking up. But she did look up; she *had* to, in order to send him a dirty look. She wasn't going to be intimidated by the course creep any more than she was by Elephant & Castle on that first day at university eight weeks ago.

A creative writing course was always going to attract a range of weird and wonderful misfits and it's one of the reasons Zoe chose it – in the hope that she's be in the majority for once, surrounded by people who didn't fit in.

She'd been faking her confidence when she'd first arrived, but it wasn't faked anymore: she'd shed the old Zoe and was wearing her newfound self-belief like a new skin.

Confirmation bias.

She'd come across the term during her Psychology A Level and now she was witnessing it first hand. If she were having a low day and didn't have the energy to fake her confidence it didn't matter any more. Everyone on the course already had her down as the confident, competent one, so they just adjusted this description and added words like "studious" to explain her periods of quiet.

What Zoe couldn't decide was whether being able to shift the type of person she was so easily was simply part of maturing, or whether it meant she was living a lie. And she didn't question the thought too much because she wasn't sure she wanted to know the answer.

Two weeks later there was a lighter air in the lecture hall

when the creep missed class – his absence making everyone feel better. And while they were filing out of the hall at the end of that lecture they were all asked to go back in again. There was a serious message they needed to hear.

A strangely corporate looking man stood at the front of the lecture theatre. His suit wasn't expensive or particularly well fitting, but it still gave him an air of importance because it said he had a job where he *needed* to wear one – and there aren't many of those at a university.

Mr Corporate explained that two female students have filed complaints against Carl Logan and the police have become involved. Zoe had never heard the name but instantly knew it was the creep.

Mr Corporate then explained that Carl had now been arrested and they were looking to see if any other female students had been affected. Nobody moved or said anything. So Mr Corporate asked for all the females in Carl's study group to stand up and come to the front so that he could talk to them in confidence.

One of those was Alison.

Zoe remembered the creep standing right next to Alison on their first day. And Zoe wondered whether Alison's crumpled face was a reaction to being in a group *with* him, rather than being in a group *without* her as she'd first thought.

The minute Zoe wondered if she'd misjudged Alison, she experienced confirmation bias again. Except this time she didn't know it. And to make up for avoiding Alison, behaviour she could no longer justify, Zoe decided to approach her and check she was okay after the Carl ordeal.

8 lifeguards

PRETEND, LIKE OFF THE TELLY

Alison was jiggling on the spot, hyperventilating. She could not believe it: Floella Benjamin was in her class. Alison was not a confident child, but the chance of meeting someone famous was too much of a lure and she went straight over to her.

"Floella Benjamin!" she squealed.

"No," Floella replied. "I'm Ruby."

"No you're not. You're Floella Benjamin, like off the telly."

"Oh you mean pretend!"

Did she? Alison thought about it and they did do a lot of pretending on TV.

"Yes!" she agreed.

"Then you can call me Flo," Ruby told her. "But nobody else can. Everyone else has to call me Ruby."

Alison agreed with this too. Floella Benjamin for just her and none of the other kids: they could only share her when she was on TV.

It was almost perfect. Alison wanted to be Floella herself. But if she couldn't be, then being best friends was the next best thing.

Alison's mum had laughed when she'd said she wanted to be Floella Benjamin when she grew up.

"You can't be Floella Benjamin because you're not coloured," her mum had said.

But that was exactly the point. She wanted to be coloured. The best bit about being Floella would be all the coloured beads in her hair.

Seven Sisters

Seven Sisters, a tube stop on the Victoria line, was named after a circle of elm trees that used to grow in the area. The earliest map showing their location is from 1619 although they remained an unnamed circle of trees in Page Green until 1732.

The original trees were replaced a number of times, with replacements being planted in 1852 and again in 1886. The last ring of elms survived until 1955. What's left of Page Green now is an unremarkable park, home to a circle of seven hornbeam trees – chosen instead of elms for their hardiness.

Seven Sisters is also the name of a set of cliffs on the south coast that are far more grand than the rather ordinary trees on a rather ordinary patch of land. But they don't get a station named after them.

Although seven sisters would have been lovely, Alison would have been happy with just one. So she decided to seek out surrogates instead. If only she didn't need to keep replacing those either.

9 lifebuoys

RUBY

Alison and I are both up early. I doubt she slept at all, knowing she's counting down the days to her friend's death.

I was perturbed by how effortlessly she replaced me with Zoe, but I'm feeling quite glad I didn't do the same. I've made only general friends and acquaintances since then. Being at my mum's bedside, and her being at mine, was enough for me without having to be there for friends too.

I'm up early because I never sleep well away from home. I could be in the most luxurious hotel in the world with a £5,000 mattress and I would still miss my own bed. Because I didn't fly the nest at 18, I never had to adjust to living, or sleeping, anywhere other than Whitstable.

I'm going to tell Alison that we're up too early to go straight to the hospital for visiting hours. This is strictly true, as visiting is officially 2pm to 8pm, but the Ward Sister said she could be more lax with us due to Zoe's situation. Thankfully, Alison doesn't know this.

Zoe isn't on a psychiatric ward. I wonder if we're getting

more flexible visiting hours because they have those on the psych wards. Or if it's because the Sister just wants extra help with a type of patient she shouldn't really be responsible for.

Zoe seemed normal, pleasant even. It made me wonder if the issue about the coffees was all in Alison's head. If Alison's train of thought is that Zoe doesn't care enough about her to stick around, then she might be ready to take everything personally.

I'm planning to take Alison on the Victoria line. After we'd finished the pink cow and moved onto the white one, she finally cried. At that point, Tori had the decency to leave – a quick glance in my direction to let me know she was going.

I wanted to talk to Alison about what all this meant. Up until now it had all been about Zoe. I hoped that after sobbing her heart out, she'd pour her heart out. But she sealed herself back up again, vacuum-packing her emotions.

So I made us barely drinkable cups of tea – cheap teabags directly in mugs with metallic London water poured on top – and we both sat there sipping at our drinks while she wondered how she could get to her job near London Bridge without using the tube.

To put her mind at rest, I fired up her laptop to check, finding the 133 bus route that was direct, plus a couple of others that meant changing at Elephant & Castle. Her eyes rolled when I mentioned that – she hated going to university there. It's one of the things she shared in one of the few letters she sent me. I know she blames me for it. But it wasn't me who got drunk in the concrete courtyard outside the Royal Festival Hall and refused to go to my Open Day.

Checking bus routes was only ever a temporary measure while she was drunk and emotional. I planned to get her back on the tube as soon as I could. A conversation I'm ready to bring up over breakfast.

"It's like getting back on the horse after you fall off. You have to do it straight away. The longer you leave it, the harder it will be."

Alison throws me a look. "They say never return to the scene of a crime."

"But that's only if you're the perpetrator."

The look is completed with a raised eyebrow. This is going to be harder than I thought. Alison used to do everything I said. When did she become so stubborn?

"Think about 9/11. It's like people going back to Ground Zero afterwards. It wasn't about the terrorists going back."

"Yeah, well, the terrorists were dead."

I sigh. Alison hears my frustration and gives me a sigh of her own – one of resignation. She realises I'm not going to leave this alone.

"Lots of people benefitted from going to the site of the Twin Towers," I say gently, "including those who'd lost loved ones there. I just think getting on the tube will help you face what's happened. And it might help you prepare yourself for what's still to come."

Alison's shoulders sink slightly. You can read a lot from someone's shoulders. It's the opposite of Tori's pre-monologue puffed up pose, and it tells me Alison is going to give in. Sunken shoulders also make it easier to hug someone, and I wrap my arms around her in a big bear hug – a momma bear hug.

We take it in turns to attempt to wash in Alison's pitiful shower. I know the rent on this flat is an eye-watering £1,500 a month, but that doesn't seem to get you decent running water. Alison has lived in London long enough to accept the place's failures as the way life is. Everyone I know in Whitstable has a shower that works properly even if it's just one attached to the bath taps.

I wonder if Alison misses feeling properly clean. As soon as you step out onto the main road, the air is thick with grime. Maybe that's why she accepts the shower as it is: she'd be fighting a losing battle anyway.

We decide to walk down Brixton Hill to the tube station instead of jumping on a bus, even though one goes by every few minutes. I'm a little nervous when one of the driveways we pass on the left has a sign up saying "HM Prison Service Brixton" but Alison is oblivious to it. Other than a couple of austere looking chimneys, you can't see the prison from the road – and for that I'm grateful. I'm less likely to have nightmares based on its proximity to Alison's flat if I can't visualise it.

It seems like a bleak place. Yes, the right-hand side of the road is green. But it is forlorn patches of dying grass spotted with a few trees. And there just aren't enough trees to stop it looking like an urban wasteland shadowing concrete blocks of flats.

After growing up in such a pretty place like Whitstable, I wonder if Alison has to put blinkers on to not notice how ugly her surroundings are now. On the way back, I'm going to insist on taking the bus.

Being in Brixton is going home to a home I've never had. I'm surrounded by black faces, many of which are several shades darker than mine. I'm at ease and intimidated in equal measures: I don't know if my blackness matches up here. There's an air of poverty, aggression and despair I'm not used to – you can smell it along with the spices and meats from the market stalls.

Everyone seems louder and more colourful than I'm used to. It's like the beginnings of a vertigo attack, when the world spins round me and everything becomes too intense and light becomes too bright. Except it isn't vertigo: I'm just surrounded by people with no volume control.

I'm used to this lack of noise awareness in kids on a badly timed trip to Canterbury that coincides with the end of the school day, when the kids fill the bus in noisy swarms. They have no idea how much noise they are making. And I have no idea how they haven't all gone deaf from the din that must constantly surround them.

We pop into the Starbucks by the station entrance. The staff recognise Alison, which surprises me − you hear all these stories about lonely London.

"They know you?" I ask as we leave and head down the steps into the station.

"I normally go in there with Zoe, who orders the largest coffee with two extra shots. The first time she tried to order it, they were like 'The largest already has three shots in it' thinking she didn't realise. But she insisted, and they made it for her.

"The next time we went in there, she ordered the same thing which shocked them because they thought she'd learn her lesson from the first time!"

I sip at my weak latte through the slot in the plastic top, the bitter coffee taste filling my nose as well as my mouth. I have a love-hate relationship with coffee: love the way it makes me feel; hate the taste. The bitterness works as a warning though, as too much caffeine gives me a headache. I can't imagine drinking five shots.

"Does she not get headaches?"

Alison shrugs. "She says not. I think she's addicted to the stuff because she barely goes five minutes without a cup. The coffee is always on at the flat."

Alison "hmms" to herself.

"What?" I ask her.

"That's been one of the weird things about her being in hospital: the flat smells strange. There's an 'old' smell that is usually covered by the scent of coffee."

I'd noticed the smell. It wasn't musty or damp, just odd. I'd put it down to the building being 1930s – at least I assumed the block was built around that time from the beautiful curved windows and balconies.

It is similar to the boiled-cabbage-and-garlic smell that permeated the halls at primary school even though neither regularly featured on the menu. Our school was a mishmash of rather grand old brick structures and rather more ordinary new buildings, but the smell was in all of them.

After making breakfast this morning, I'd purposefully burnt some toast so the charcoal could absorb the smell. Hopefully when we return later, the flat will seem a little more welcoming.

When we get down to platform level, Alison leads me to the front of the train. The further we walk, the more thinned out the passengers become until we reach a carriage with two adjacent seats free. We quickly claim them.

Alison puts her bag on her knee and adjusts it so it's pulled up towards her stomach. She then uses her knees to hold her coffee. I notice another woman is doing the same thing a few seats down. A strange London ritual.

We are going to ride the full length of the tube as Zoe did. Partly because it seems like the right thing to do; partly because I have no idea where we'd get off in order to go anywhere. Any sort of sightseeing would seem tasteless under the circumstances.

A few stops in and the train reaches Victoria station – the stop where the homeless poet got on my train last time.

I find myself looking round for her.

"Are you cold?" Alison quizzes me.

"No. Should I be?"

"It's just you're looking round. Zoe says she gets the shivers going through Victoria station, but I've never noticed any difference."

There's a tone in Alison's voice that suggests there's something more to it than meets the eye.

But then she shrugs it off with a grin – "But then I never feel the cold!"

All the pictures of us as kids have her in short sleeves when I'm in a jumper, or her in a thin cardigan when I'm wearing a coat. I can't ever remember seeing her wearing a scarf or gloves except on the windiest days in January or February where five minutes on the beach makes your face go to sleep like you've been to the dentists.

Alison has always been a slip of a thing and with her pale skin, people expect her to be physically fragile. With my larger build and darker skin I'm expected to be a little more hardy, which I'm not. But I definitely don't feel cold on the tube.

"A homeless woman got on here on my trip down, recited a poem. I thought maybe…" – I stop, realising that expecting to see her is a silly notion on my part.

But Alison nods in agreement. "Poetry girl."

"That's really strange, that you've seen her too."

"Although London is massive, I see the same people all the time. We do the same commutes, eat at the same restaurants, drink at the same pubs. All of us have our routines and most socialising is done in Zone One. Starbucks isn't the only place where I'm recognised."

I contemplate this new version of London where people know each other in the casual way they do in smaller towns. Is that how people survive here? By trying to make the same connections with people they would elsewhere?

As we pull out of Victoria station, I can't help but look out for any last chance of seeing the homeless woman. I catch a glimpse of an oval of navy blue tiles that house a white silhouette of Queen Victoria. It reminds me of the delicate cameo brooch Mum had permanently fastened to the lapel of her winter coat. It used to be her mother's and when I was little I thought it must be valuable – back when I thought all old things were.

Now I know it was more valuable than I'd ever imagined – but that the value is sentimental. The best kind.

GOOD LUCK CHARM

Whitstable isn't white picket fences, but it is white. Ruby noticed she was the only black kid in class, but did her best to pretend she hadn't. She worked hard and kept her head down. Alison, the palest girl in the class, was at her side for protection.

After a while, Ruby decided it was easier being the *only* black family in the street, the *only* black kid at school, rather than being one of a few. That way you just represent yourself – and didn't have to apologise for all the less respectable black families and less well behaved black kids.

That's what her mum said anyway.

Every day, when her mum dropped Ruby off at school, she would crouch down to give her a hug. Ruby would lean in to hug her on the left-hand side, so that the cool white carving of the old lady on her mum's brooch pressed against the side of her face.

Her mum often rubbed the brooch absentmindedly when she was thinking, and Ruby had decided it must be because it brought her good luck.

When Ruby was 10 years old, she got home one day to find her mum frantic. The pin on the back of the brooch was still attached to the fabric of her mum's coat, but the brooch itself was missing. Ruby had raced up to her room, grabbed her piggy bank and brought it down.

"I can buy you a new one."

Her mum gave Ruby the biggest, fiercest hug Ruby had ever received.

RUBY

I know now that the cameo brooch was the only thing she had left of her own mother, who'd passed away on the journey over from Trinidad. For years and years I had no idea, and then Windrush was on the news and everything about the boat ride came tumbling out of my mum's mouth, words banging into each other as she struggled to tell me the story she'd kept to herself for so many years.

Up until that point, my mum hadn't talked about her own mother very much and I'd always assumed, from what she'd said, that she had stayed in the Caribbean while my mum travelled over with her dad and brother. It had seemed odd to me at the time, but it was a different time and different decisions were made back then. And I'd picked up on a vibe from my mum that said "Ask no questions", so I'd always played dumb.

I kept expecting her to tell me about her mother one day (she called her "mother" even though she insisted I call her "mum") but she never did. The stories went untold. And I'd probably still not know the truth if it weren't for Albert Thompson.

Albert had come over from Jamaica with his parents in 1973 and had lived here ever since. It wasn't until he needed radiotherapy for prostate cancer that he discovered he didn't have the correct documents to prove he had the right to remain in the UK – and faced a £54,000 hospital bill if he went ahead with treatment.

After seeing the story on the TV news, she turned to me and said: "I suppose I should be grateful I was in hospital while Labour were still in charge."

But this story about Albert was about somebody without a passport or immigration paperwork. Surely my mum had those?

Then my mum broke down – cried real tears in front of me for the first time. And that's when she told me that she'd travelled over on her mother's passport and how what paperwork she did have had been in her mother's purse when she'd passed away.

My grandma was dead. She'd died before I was born, before my mum stepped foot on what she called "this cold, grey land". Without a passport or other papers, my mum had lived on the edge of life ever since. Just like the homeless poet.

And now, like Albert, it could affect her health. It gave me a second reason to pray that her Sarcoidosis would stay under the control of the drugs she was on.

Being in London means I'm worrying about Alison and some girl in a hospital bed. It's a welcome break from Windrush and all the questions it's thrown up about my identity.

Although I hadn't known anything about my grandma's death as a child, I'd still known the brooch was of upmost importance to my mum, so I insisted we head out to search for it. We scoured the streets of Whitstable that day, retracing the steps my mum had taken, but we never found the brooch. And she refused to take any of my pocket money to buy a new one.

So that's when I decided to make her one.

My mum used to do my hair for me. Allowing the hours to pass me by while she unravelled my braids, washed and conditioned my hair, and then fastened it back up into new ones was therapeutic. And I got the same meditative feeling from making jewellery.

I've replaced that brooch five or six times over the years, each time with something closer to the one she'd lost, the most recent version being carved from agate rock as her original brooch probably was. She accepts every one as if it is the most precious gift. And I love her for it.

At GCSE, I studied Craft, Design & Technology as well as Art, learning woodcarving and metalwork trades as well as honing my drawing skills.

The way GCSEs work is you have to choose History *or* Geography, French *or* Spanish, not being able to choose two subjects deemed to similar. But I wanted CDT *and* Art so much that I cried.

My mum was never the type to make a fuss, but she wanted to make sure I got the right education for me − to make her family's sacrifices worth it − so she'd marched into school to demand I be able to take the subjects I had a natural aptitude for.

While at college I started to build up a portfolio of my work in wood, stone, metal and glass. Although I wanted to get good grades too, the careers advisor had been clear that a strong portfolio was much more important when trying to secure that all important place studying Jewellery Design at the prestigious Central Saint Martins College − now part of University of the Arts London.

By the time I had to present my work at interview, I had an abundance of pieces to choose from. I presented a strong collection of 18 pieces, which I believe hinted at my natural talents as well as my dedication, as well as a photo album of other work. The careers advisor was right: I received a conditional offer of just two Ds.

Not going to Central Saint Martins broke my heart in the same way losing her brooch broke my mum's. But creating brooches for my mum has kept me going through my darkest times.

Instead of going to university, I built up my skills by devouring every book I could about various jewellery-making skills. I focus first on metalwork, initially working in the metals of my traditional education, then honing my skills with sessions working with Mireia Rossell in her jewellery workshop, until I could create a studio of my own in the small flat I rent round the corner from my mum's.

In the luxury of my own workspace I was able to experiment with carving different materials, producing work from pieces of abandoned oyster shells near the harbour, recycling sections of shell in my jewellery that had not been chosen to be recycled through the oyster farming process.

Rescuing discarded pieces of shell and breathing new life into them was cathartic. And these pieces ended up being droplet earrings or a pendant necklace instead of lining the seabed as part of the effort to re-establish oyster beds or being ground down to provide a calcium carbonate supply for imported oyster larvae to use in their shell-building process.

I liked to encase pieces of shell in silver to echo the metal oyster trestles that lined the intertidal area of the coast just west of the harbour. I would sometimes sit on the sea wall and watch the racks become completely submerged at high tide (but for the bamboo poles that marked where they were for swimmers and members of the sailing club) only for them to be slowly re-revealed as the tide went out.

Oyster larvae go through a metamorphosis similar to moths and butterflies, but instead of cocooning themselves and then breaking free, they remain in their cocoon – their shell – throughout their adult life. And in that way, oysters are more like humans, trapped in the worlds of their own making.

I don't know the heights I could have reached if I'd got to university, but I'm proud to sell my jewellery in a number of shops in Whitstable as well as running my own Etsy store.

At Green Park our train is held at the station. The muffled announcement by the driver explains there's a person on the tracks. I look at Alison in shock, but her face shows the same annoyance as everyone else in the carriage. There's also a lot of tutting. I wonder if I'd be the same if I lived in London. I hope not.

"I hope they're all right," I venture, not sure how Alison will react.

She looks a little embarrassed as if I've put her reaction in check.

"You become numb to everything here. If someone gets hit by a train, you don't get told whether or not they've survived. So you stop asking," she explains. "I can remember the first time my tube line was cancelled because of a jumper. The station staff were helping people plot new routes.

"When I got to speak to someone, the first thing I asked is was the person who'd jumped okay. The person I asked looked at me incredulously – I could tell they couldn't quite believe I was asking. But then that incredulousness turned into a knowing look that said 'you're new here, but just you wait'. And they were right. It wasn't long before I joined the crowds of people that just want to know how to get where they're going via a different route."

Without warning our train starts off again.

"I guess it was just a person on the tracks then, not anyone injured," I say, the relief coursing through my veins.

Alison looks at me sheepishly.

"They no longer hold trains while waiting for an ambulance to arrive if a person is dead. Body parts are collected up in black bags and stored in cupboards, ready to be assessed when the coroner arrives."

From the coffee/knee manoeuvre to body parts in bin liners, I'm being let into a private London club where you leave your innocence at the door. I don't know how to tell Alison that I don't want to learn the funny handshake in order to join.

London is a club I don't want to be a member of.

One under

Suicide is so common on the London Underground that staff have a term used for it: one under. The most popular suicide time is around 11am and the average number of deaths per year is around 52, averaging just above more than one per week.

Originally constructed to drain water, "suicide pits" have halved the number of deaths on the tube as they allow for trains to safely travel over a person on the tracks.

But successful jumpers are still common enough that a system has been devised to use cleaning cupboards to store bodies until an undertaker is available so the train services can get up and running again as soon as possible.

Although Zoe didn't jump in front of a tube train, she did get on the tube at around 11am. So her suicide attempt was perfectly timed.

10 armbands

ZOE

"There is nothing either good or bad, but thinking makes it so."

Denmark was Hamlet's prison; mine is London. I'm as much trapped in a role I don't want live as he was. The fact he's a character in a play and I'm living a real life doesn't matter – there's no point to either.

Whether it's a doctor on ward rounds or a nurse taking my blood pressure *again*, each one brings their own tactics of how to get to the bottom of why I'm here. They play good cop, bad cop, indifferent cop, and too-tired-and-stressed-to-care cop. None of them understand why I see life as a prison cell. And at some point, most of them stumble onto the fact that they see what I've done as "wrong". I have the same response for all of them.

"You said 'commit' suicide, liked you'd say 'commits a crime'. But suicide isn't a crime anymore, is it? You don't agree with suicide, and I get that. But the law is on my side. And I'm getting tired of having to defend my choices all the time."

It's the most innocent of questions that throws me.

"Do you know how many days you've been in King's?"

"King's?"

"Yes, King's College Hospital, on Denmark Hill."

"But I'm not meant to be in King's; I should be in London University Hospital."

There's a long pause.

"A member of London Underground staff found you on the train at Brixton. You were unresponsive. An ambulance was called which took you from Brixton station to here at King's."

Another pause.

"Why do you think you're in a different hospital?"

I shrug. I realise my reason – because it was announced on the Victoria line – will sound stupid.

I know it's my second day in hospital. But being in King's makes me uneasy. I have no idea what happened to me between falling unconscious and arriving here – and now that time is stretching out and I have no way of filling it.

I can't help but find it amusing that Hamlet's prison was Denmark and mine is now Denmark Hill. But I'm also a little sad that I have nobody I can share it with who will understand. I'm not just in prison; I'm in solitary confinement.

In between visiting times, doctors' visits, meal times and tea trolley visits, are the quiet times where the nurses are at their station and the mostly elderly patients snooze. My guard – or whoever she is – just sits, sometimes pretending to read, other times staring into space. Urghh. She gives me the creeps. Thankfully hasn't tried to engage me in any conversation. God knows how many times she's heard my "commit" suicide point.

So my main company in the in-between hours has been reduced to two clocks on the ward that tick out of time with each other, lining up their ticks every few minutes. One is slightly faster, but is out-ticked by the other's loudness. I listen as the faster clock takes over, only to be harmonised with the slower one a few minutes later for just a few ticks. I believe the whole process takes about four minutes, but find it difficult to keep track.

I'm the second clock. My internal clock ticks half a second out of time from everyone else's.

I'm in a strangely agitated state where nothing is right. I don't like it when I'm left to lie here with just the clocks for company. Intrusive thoughts buzz around my head like flies before being zapped to death on the ultraviolet tubes of my mind. But as soon as my visitors arrive I can't wait for them to leave. And each time Alison visits, she brings half the world with her.

Alison is so melodramatic, sobbing for the friend she's about to lose one minute, calm and dry-eyed the next. I think a lot of her tears are for herself – for being left behind. I think that's why she wants James. I need to speak to her about that. I want her to know that I know what her game is. The suicide, the hospital bed – they don't make me stupid.

Tori's insistence in being "helpful" and being there for me is exhausting. Urghh. I want to tell her to "fuck off", but it would be selfish of me – Alison wants her support.

And then there's Ruby.

I need to quiz Alison about this strange creature who has appeared from nowhere. While everyone else is faking being okay round me, she seems to be genuinely unfazed, and it's unnerving me. She's just here, existing, watching. She morphs into the background, along with my guard, and I can forget she's here until I hear her weird cough.

She's someone I vaguely remember Alison referring to in our first year at university, but nothing since then. I'd always assumed Alison's background was all sweetness and light; that her first foray into the darker side started with our friendship. But here's this person from her past who is totally unfazed by death.

I didn't realise they were still in touch. Ruby has certainly not visited the whole time I've shared a place with Alison, which must be getting on for four years now. Or something like that anyway. I'm not very good with the passage of time – whether it's seconds, minutes or years.

University was about spreading your wings, new experiences, meeting new people. Most people left old friendships behind, so nobody needed to know that I didn't have any real friendships to speak of from school or college. I got to start afresh.

I'm not very fresh at the moment. Hospital staff don't seem to monitor whether or not patients get washed and I haven't been offered any soap or towels. I'm still wearing the clothes I arrived in and I seem to be sweating more than I normally do – which I'm assuming is linked to my overdose.

I'm currently relying on the baby wipes I packed in the bag I prepared before I boarded the tube. I prefer to use them to clean my skin rather than using water, but the scummy feeling I get after a few days without washing properly is enough to make me brave having a shower.

I know I'm due a shower too because my eyes felt puffy this morning and were full of eye slugs. Baby wipes can only do so much.

It's a routine I've brought with me from home. When Alison first whinged the shower in our flat was rubbish, I just nodded along. She didn't know I used baby wipes most mornings, switching the shower on when I was in the bathroom so she'd hear the water flowing and assume I was in it. Assume I was normal. I'm not normal.

I know that a lot of people feel this, that they're not normal. But when you try and explain "No it's different for me" they don't get it; they don't understand that my version of not being normal isn't just social anxieties like theirs is. I don't know how I'm meant to feel about things and then sometimes I feel too much.

We used to go on wild nights out and I could never tell if I were enjoying them at the time. I'd have to wait until the next day to breakdown the night as a whole, to decipher my emotions. So it was easier to go along with everyone else when they say "What an awesome evening" and "What a totally blinding night" or whatever terms they use. I hardly go out clubbing now and don't miss it. Alison reminisces and I pretend to join in. I don't have any solid memories about any particular night; they've merged together and faded at the same time.

I stopped having weekly baths when I found myself lying with the water level to my eyebrows and bottom lip, the edges of my face completely under the water, wondering how easy it would be to go under the water and never come back up.

Lying in the bath was also a time where I'd be left with my thoughts with no distractions. Urghh. Back when I was a student, bath time would be when I'd muse over poetry or short story ideas. But work doesn't give you the same safe mental place to escape to, and I found being in the bath to be the place where I thought the most about death.

I also noticed that when I dragged myself out of the bath, my body would feel twice as heavy. There could be some kind of scientific phenomenon behind this, something to do with buoyancy or that we absorb water into our skin, but if would feel like a great weight bearing down on me as I attempted to rejoin the world.

SPACEMAN

Growing up, Zoe didn't have radiators in her house. She and her sisters used to get washed at the sink most days and would have a bath once a week, taking it in turns in the same water, Zoe going in after Clare but before Charlotte.

The idea was that the oldest got the hottest bath as younger children would like a cooler temperature, but the bath always felt too cold for Zoe's skin when she got in. And once the bath was run, that was it – her mother didn't top it up. It was never deep enough to lie in and get your whole body wet, so there would always be bits of body sticking out that would feel the draught of the house shifting across them. Whenever Zoe asked to have the bath "a little bit hotter" or "a little bit deeper" her mother would sigh and tell her that hot water was expensive.

Zoe was too young to know what a "mental note" was, but she made one anyway – about having deep, hot baths when she got married and moved into her own home. She would tell her husband that he needed to go out and earn lots of money for deep baths.

Zoe's mother was resourceful and would set up three sides of the old playpen as a fence around the fire, turning it into a makeshift windbreaker with blankets. Wrapped up in towels, Zoe and her sisters would curl up together next to the fire, their teeth chattering, listening to the gas hiss, the smell of the fire mixing with the spiced scent of baby shampoo.

It was one of the few times Zoe and her sisters were reduced to being three kids together, and they would play silly games much younger than their ages would dictate. It was after one of these baths when they were pretending to be spacemen, talking to each other in muffled voices through their towels, that Zoe shuffled round the edge of the playpen, disappeared, and returns holding a crumpled plastic bag. She shook the bag out and put it over her head.

"Look at me – I'm a proper spaceman now."

But her comments were drowned out by the shrieks from her sisters that had both parents running into the living room. Her father got there first. The bag was snatched off Zoe's head and she was met with a barrage of comments – "What an earth are you playing at?" and "What in God's name were you thinking?"

Her mother arrived moments later, filled in on the event by her father, Clare and Charlotte. She tried to make enough sense of the jumbled snatches to work out what Zoe had been up to *this* time.

"I have to watch you like a hawk!" Zoe's mother had screeched at her, her fear turning to anger.

A few years later, Zoe's parents talked about getting central heating, which Zoe decided must be like having a tube in the middle of the house with fire in it. She was really disappointed to find out they just meant radiators like at school.

Had Alison been there, she'd have told Zoe that central heating was a sneaky term like vanilla – something that promised exciting things but didn't deliver. That central heating was a lie.

ZOE

It's not just water that makes my skin feel strange. I don't like it when something brushes past you, like a cobweb. In my family, hugs were always proper hugs and it wasn't until I got to university that I suffered light touches and air kisses as a craze for being European swept across campus.

The area around LSBU – London Bridge and the South Bank itself – felt like my part of the city, especially as I'd grown up in Crystal Palace and got to know the south side of the river first. I also liked that south of the river was considered the underdog.

It hit me hard when there was an attack on Borough Market – three madmen driving a van into the crowds before jumping out and stabbing people. It's where we'd sometimes wander up for lunch at the start of term when we were feeling particularly flush and it had always seemed a safe and friendly place – something of a rarity in London. Maybe that's why they chose it.

Eight people died in that attack, that's on top of the five during the one in Westminster a couple of months earlier. I've always had an uneasiness that I couldn't quite place when I heard about terrorist attacks. I'm not sure if it's tied to jealousy: their time is up, why isn't mine?

It seems cruel that people who desperately want life, who cling onto it for as long as they can, end up dying, and then people like me have to take matters into our own hands.

Your time is up.

Wrong place, wrong time.

It's all about time.

Unfortunately, the time I have left includes visits from nosy medical staff. But the upside is that there's no continuity here, so I get to practice my responses to the same questions, honing them to perfection.

"Has someone talked to you about what's going to happen to your body over the next few days?"

Tempted as I am to joke "No doctor, I've no idea", the humour levels in the NHS are quite poor. So I stick to my script.

"Yes, I know. I've been told numerous times just how Paracetamol kills."

"It's a very slow and painful way to die," they will tell me, as if I hadn't spoken.

"Not slow."

"It could take days, maybe even a week or more."

"Yes," I say. "So not slow."

"Well…"

"Compared with the number of days I'd have to struggle through if I stayed alive, a week is fast."

"But it will be painful."

"As painful as life is?"

"You're in pain?" – this is always accompanied by surprise. I'm not on a psych ward, so this needs spelling out.

"A week of physical pain versus a lifetime of mental pain? It's not a difficult equation."

And then I get the "Ahh" of understanding. Except it's not understanding, because they are only grasping the mental versus physical bit, not the fact that the former could be worse.

I've tried explaining I don't care about the pain I face, but I get "the look" – the one medical staff give you when they don't believe you. I'll be adamant. But the more sure I tried to sound, the more sceptical that look would get.

"The lady doth protest too much, methinks."

Well actually, Queen Gertrude, I *don't* think.

It's quite simple in my mind. We're all going to die and whatever follows death (if anything at all) is what we all get eventually. I just want more of that and less of this, that's all.

I think it's unlikely that there's anything after this life, and that's fine by me – nothingness, no pain, is just fine. But if there is something, some kind of afterlife, then I hope my mother is there, peering down from the clouds, still watching me like a hawk.

All the chills

The Victoria line is kept cool via 13 ventilation shafts — more than double the original number. The newer trains on the line also use regenerative braking (returning power to the rails while the train slows) which reduces the amount of heat the process produces.

Some stations on the line have had air-cooling units and mechanical chillers installed, but not Victoria station, which uses a unique cooling system where groundwater under the station cools the platforms.

The system won a prestigious Carbon Trust Innovation Award because it uses an available and sustainable energy source. It was developed by a team at London South Bank University, where Alison and Zoe studied.

Although the system is very effective at cooling the platforms, Zoe isn't able to detect the air-cooling system from inside the train. Her shivers are mental ones.

11 swimming aids

TORI

I left the minute Alison started crying. I'm allergic to tears.

The only ones I can cope with are the insignificant ones, like the ones she shed when she was worried about her presentation, which I now fondly refer to as #Eyelashgate, although I've not told Alison this. Some nicknames are not to be shared.

The heat on the tube is not helping my headache, although my hangover could be far worse.

Alison's tears last night were a blessing in disguise because even though I'd been trying to pace myself, wine boxes – sorry, wine *cows* – make it much harder to do.

With bottles, you're able to check how full or empty they are, how many you've gone through. But the cardboard exterior of the wine box keeps your consumption hidden from you: you can drink more than you planned without realising it.

I like drinking to the point where the alcohol gives me a face massage feeling. Then I like to slow down so I can soak the state in. But if I reach this stage too quickly,

I don't notice it, and carry on drinking beyond it.

When I stood up to leave, I still had most of a glass of wine in front of me. But the swaying room told me not to touch another drop and to concentrate on getting myself home. So I left the wine in the glass undrunk.

I don't have the urge to down it any more than I need to clear my plate when I'm full. Why most people do the opposite confuses me as surely my way makes more sense.

The best thing about the wine cows is that they were already in Alison's fridge and so didn't cost me a penny. And I was able to get the Victoria line home and so didn't have to splash out on an expensive Uber.

I know from the mess my kitchenette is in this morning that when I got in last night I attempted to eat my way through all the food I own. *So* stupid. I can't afford to replace the food on my salary any more than I can afford so many calories to be consumed in one sitting.

But my midnight feast does mean this morning's hangover is a little less vicious than it should be.

Before heading down the escalator at Blackhorse Road, I send a text to my boss to let him know I'll be heading to the hospital before coming into work. I can't justify taking the whole day off even though I know he'd let me: he needs me there more than he thinks.

As I was leaving Alison's flat, I agreed with Ruby that I'd take the early shift at the hospital and that they'd go later. It means I get to be there for Zoe (so I can be there for James) without an eagle-eyed audience listening in to what I say.

I *refuse* to feel guilty about my plans to use Zoe to win over James. *She's* the one that made the decision to take an overdose. (And where she's going, she can hardly take him with her.)

I skip my usual coffee as I head onto the tube. I want to

be able to go via the hospital's Costa. I'm far too sensitive to caffeine to have two. I have no idea how Zoe manages to drink so much of the stuff. Really they should put coffee in her drip!

I don't notice the tube isn't moving until I hear the announcement from a weary sounding driver that we're "being held at a red signal to regulate the service". The windows in the tube are low, so I have to duck my head to see out onto the platform and for the roundel that will tell me where we are.

Seven Sisters.

I know how I'm going to win Zoe round.

ANOTHER SEVEN SISTERS

Tori loved the cliffs. They excited her because they made her so small and insignificant. She spun around and couldn't see another living thing except for seagulls.

She spread her arms and ran, flapping them and cackling with laughter, watching the seagulls rise up to escape her. She was a part of something bigger than herself. Something powerful.

She loved that nobody had built a fence along the cliff edge to make it safe. And she found it funny that the lighthouse was at the bottom of the cliff, in the sea, as if it too had sneaked off on its own, just like she had. The whole place was rebellious.

Up here, staring out at the Seven Sisters from her vantage point at Beachy Head, it didn't matter about her mother and Edie, or about how well she did at school, or whether or not she was any good at making friends.

It almost didn't matter about having to be in the top bunk. Almost.

She watched some of the seagulls resettle on the top of the cliff.

"Why can't Ellie stay at home?" she cried out to them – all but the bravest of them cleared the cliff again.

Tori was meant to get the second bedroom, the one Ellie normally got. But Ellie (who was now insisting on being called "Eleanor") had broken up with her boyfriend and decided to come on *just one more* family holiday.

What Tori wanted to know is if Ellie, sorry *Eleanor*, wanted family bonding so much, why wasn't she the one on the top bunk telling Maggie stories?

But when she'd suggested this to her mother, she'd been batted away with comments about her selfishness and how she reminded her of Edie.

Tori hated her mother's stories about Edie. They always painted their mother as virtuous while casting her mother's sister Edie in a bad light. Tori couldn't help feel Edie (who none of them had ever met because their mother was estranged from her family) got a raw deal.

The older Tori got, the more her mother's relationship with Edie seemed to fit within the realms of normal sibling bullying. Ellie had done similar sneaky things to her and in turn she'd done them to Maggie – although both of them were careful never to use the same tactics as Edie. God forbid you'd ever been compared to her!

Tori longed to meet Edie and hear the stories from her point of view – to hear how her mother wasn't the perfect daughter *and* sister wrapped up with a bow. She's started to make notes of the things her mother told her about Edie in the hope that she'd be able to use detective work to track Edie down. But until that happened, the only way to escape the stories was up on the cliffs.

The first time she'd slipped out of the caravan and caught

the bus from Eastbourne, she'd sat on the cliff edge for hours, staring out at sea, only moving when it started raining, keeping dry in the solitary phone box. A police officer on patrol had found her and told her she was "far too young to even be thinking about it". That's when Tori found out that around 20 people killed themselves every year by jumping from Beachy Head.

Pulling up to the caravan park in a police car had been painful. The fact that she wasn't in trouble didn't seem to matter to her mother though, who would refer to "the police incident" with ludicrous frequency.

"Was I cautioned? Was I in trouble? Was I arrested?" – it didn't matter how many times Tori asked, her questions always fell on deaf ears.

She knew another trip up to the cliffs came with the risk of the police finding her again, but it only added to the thrill. This time it was not the police who disturb her: it was a woman.

Tori found her difficult to age because she wore the sort of frumpy clothes mothers often wore that would age them at least 10 years, but guessed she was around the 40s mark. She paced up and down the edge of the cliff, her uncombed hair dancing manically in the wind.

Tori was 95% cross, 5% curious. While she didn't want this stranger in her space, she couldn't quite believe she might witness someone's last moments. It made her want to hold her breath until the woman made a decision whether or not to jump. Then the unexpected happened. The woman stopped pacing, turned on her heel and marched over to Tori.

"Do you have to be here?" she asked in a voice that very much said "leave now".

Tori's annoyance levels hit 98%.

"I've been here ages. Why should I move?"

"Because this is the spot where they check – so my body will be found and my family won't spend their days wondering what happened to me. They'll know; they'll get closure."

"Why do you care about your family?"

"What?"

"If you jump, you're leaving them. So why does what they think matter?"

The woman took a step back from Tori. She had that look on her face that Tori had seen too many times to count – the one where she'd said the wrong thing.

"You're the one about to jump," Tori snapped. "And you're looking at me like *I'm* weird. You're pretending to care about your family. But you're just thinking about you."

"This *is* for my family."

Tori was aghast. She'd assumed suicide was selfish.

"Haven't you left them a note?" Tori asked her.

She shook her head.

"If I wrote a note and then didn't... well, I'd have to go back home to the note. And that would be... too much."

Adults didn't make sense to Tori. Until now.

Her mother was always calling her selfish, thoughtless, because she did and said things without considering others. Being a grown-up meant considering other people all of the time.

"I can't leave," Tori said, quietly but firmly. "Because if I leave you might kill yourself. And then I'm being selfish because I'm not thinking about you."

"But I *want* to do this. *I'm* the one making the decision."

"I can't have your death on my conscience."

The woman sighed so loudly it sounds as if she's drained

her whole body of oxygen. Tori wondered how many people would be dead if you could kill yourself by sighing too loudly. Both her parents. Most of her teachers.

The woman walked back to the cliff edge. She started pacing again, head down so she didn't have to look at Tori. And then the pacing became pacing and talking. And the talking got louder as the woman argued with herself about what she should do.

The peace Tori craved was shattered and it consumed her, boiling over into anger. She did not come up here to watch some random woman shout at herself as she wore out the grass.

"Oh for God's sake," Tori snapped. "Either jump or fuck off."

The wind whipped at Tori's words, carrying them away from the cliffs, so Tori didn't know if the woman heard them. But seconds later, the woman ran at the cliff edge and jumped off.

TORI

I arrive at Zoe's bedside with two of Costa's distinctive maroon cups. I hold them up to Zoe, then put one down on her side table, not forcing her to take it. It's the gesture that counts – I don't need her to drink it.

"I hope you're not mad at me for bringing coffee," I joke, grinning.

She smiles back, so I know it's okay. But it's the reminder about the "James and Alison" situation I want it to be.

I'm glad it's Zoe that's dying, not Alison. Out of the two I prefer Alison. And this way I can get a boyfriend out of it as well as a best friend.

Today I've gone for a more relaxed outfit of AllSaints

grey slacks and a fitted dark grey top from Zara – an office take on "lounge wear" and something that will be fine for work while not raising too many eyebrows here. My purple dress earned me too many stares and bemused looks. When doctors walk round in what look like glorified pyjamas, I suppose it's not a surprise.

I'm psyching myself up to share my "confession" about the time I planned to kill myself on Beachy Head, to bond over our shared experiences. People judge me for telling lies. They don't understand I need to tell them in order to connect with people. And this might be a whopper, but it will die in a few days along with Zoe.

And it should be enough to get Zoe on my side so I can be there for James.

I wonder where he is. Alison and Ruby aren't visiting until later. But as much as I want to see him, I don't want him to interrupt us.

"James not here yet?" I ask.

Zoe frowns at me. I wonder if I've been too direct.

"I sent him a text – told him not to visit."

"But I thought it was Alison you were angry with, not him?"

Zoe's frown deepens – she's only just twigged that I know. She must realise we're talking about all this behind her back, surely?

"Alison mentioned it," I explain. "It's why she's not visiting you until this afternoon. I told her to give me a chance to talk to you first."

Zoe's frown turns into a look of complete surprise. I'm not sure which particular part of my comment she's reacting to, but I decide it doesn't matter, so I bluster on.

"Once you're gone, she's the person left behind who's dealing with all of this," I point out.

I've wanted to say that for ages. Nobody else will. Zoe needs to realise she's made a mess of things. I'm not suicidal, but if I were, I'd make a better job of it than this.

"I said I'd come this morning and point this out to you, to give you some time to think about it before she visits later – and that hopefully you'll cut her some slack."

Zoe gives me a brief nod. I read it as permission to continue.

"It's the same with James. They'll both have to pick up the pieces. There's a chance, well, that they're going to need to lean on each other – no matter how much you don't want that."

Zoe picks up her coffee and sips at it. She's not shouting at me, so I'm telling her things she already knows. I mirror her behaviour, taking sips of my own, a weak "just one shot" Americano with lots of milk – the coffee for people who don't drink coffee.

"Alison says you took Paracetamol so you could say goodbye to both of them, to help them move on. But what you're doing at the moment is making it worse for them."

"I know I am," she says quietly.

Fuck. I did not expect *that*. What I'd planned to say next won't work now. The cogs in my brain are freewheeling.

"It all made sense in my head," Zoe says, "but it doesn't make sense to them. Neither of them will listen to what I've got to say. It's like I've decided to kill myself, so I'm obviously not sane enough to have an opinion."

Zoe runs a finger through the coffee that has spilt out onto the lid. I watch her like it's the most riveting thing I've ever seen as I have no idea what I'm meant to do or say.

"They're both walking round on eggshells, like I'll do something stupid if they say the wrong thing. Like what though? I'm already dying!"

She sighs – it's as heavy as the one from the woman on the cliff top.

"You're the first person who's actually said what they think."

Wow. I don't need my Beachy Head story to get her onside – I've managed it by accident. And I'm back knowing what to say. Thank fuck for that.

"I've already spoken to Alison," I lie (I haven't, I spoke to Ruby). "She's coming in this afternoon and will hopefully be more ready to listen. So let me speak to James. Let me get in contact with him. Explain that you want to give him time to get closure."

I can see Zoe is considering it, so I carry on sipping my coffee, leaving a silence for her to fill.

"Okay," she relents. She puts down her coffee and picks up her mobile phone.

"I'll give you his number so you can get in touch with him."

It takes strength in every fibre of my being to *not* dance around her hospital bed with glee. I'm getting his mobile! Woo-hoo!

"That sounds like a good idea," I say in a calm voice after taking a second or two to compose myself.

Once I've typed James' mobile number into my phone, I want to run off and text him, but it seems a little insensitive, especially as Zoe has just praised me for speaking the truth. To try and calm some of my nervous energy, I sit in the plastic chair by Zoe's bed. I don't need to adjust the hierarchy by sitting on her bed today.

I have that internal washing machine feeling. The one I get when I start to warm to someone at an inconvenient time, usually when they're unexpectedly nice to me. I shake if off because it doesn't matter. One, Zoe is dying, and that's her fault not mine. Two, once she's gone it won't count as stealing her boyfriend.

I get ready to dig deep into my reserves to find some small talk that will pass as acceptable under the circumstances. Thankfully, an old lady enters the ward pushing the drinks trolley: having someone to observe makes small talk easier.

"She's livened the place up," I venture.

Zoe rolls her eyes.

"The patients love her. It takes her so long to get from the kitchen to the ward the tea's already cold, but nobody cares."

"A break in the monotony of the day?" – I've already worked out real hospitals are not as exciting as the ones on TV.

"It's the attention. We get five minutes with a random doctor; nurses are rushed off their feet. She's the only person who sees us as humans, not patients."

"I've noticed some of the staff can be a little abrupt," I say, not adding "with you".

"Some of them reserve an extra layer of coldness for me," she says. So she has noticed.

We watch the tea lady go from bed to bed, handing out teas and coffees, spilling them a little as she lifts them onto side tables. She seems familiar, but I can't place why.

"You've got posh coffees already," she says to us when finally she reaches Zoe's bed. "So I'm guessing you won't be needing one from my trolley,"

She's talking to both of us, but directs her comment to Zoe – as she has done with every patient, making them the centre of attention. Her voice sounds familiar too.

I check out her name badge: Maureen. Do I know any Maureens?

"Maureen?" I don't realise I've said it out loud until she turns to me, a quizzical look on her face.

Then her face lights up, the sun shining out of every pore.

"Victoria? Is that you?"

Wow. It's my parents' old next-door neighbour.

As a reply I stand up and hold out my arms ready to embrace her in a hug. She obliges, folding her now fragile body into my arms. She's tiny, almost birdlike. Her frailty scares me. Zoe wants to die, which is fine as it's her choice. Maureen feels like she's far too close to it.

"It's Maureen's girl," she says to Zoe.

Ellie was mummy's girl, Maggie was daddy's girl; I was Maureen's girl.

"You two know each other?" Zoe asks.

Why is Zoe speaking? Can't she see that *she's* on the other side of the invisible boundary this time? The washing machine feeling has stopped.

"My family lived next to Maureen growing up," I explain.

I don't offer anything more. She doesn't need to know any more. But Maureen, being typical Maureen, takes over the story.

"I loved having a house full of children, even after my own had grown up and flown the nest. A lot of kids aren't interested in us oldies, but Victoria and I always got on, didn't we, love?"

Maureen was widowed young and her children had grown up and moved away. She loved company – said it stopped her rattling around inside her house. She'd bribed us with cake and biscuits until my mother "had words" with her about spoiling our appetites. But I was glad because it meant Ellie and Maggie stopped going round. And I got her to myself.

"Well," Maureen explained, addressing Zoe, "Victoria had a bit a tough time growing up and I lost my Eric quite young, so I think we became friends in spite of the age gap because we saw a sadness in each other."

Zoe looks at me and I see something new. Something I *never* get to see. Sympathy.

I don't need to tell my Beachy Head story to get James's number – I already have it. But now I *want* to tell it. I *have* to. Because sympathy is the most powerful drug and I need another hit.

12 lifeguards

ZOE

James is holding my hand. His warmth seeps into me and it's making me unclean. Urghh. Every ridge in his epidermis grates like sandpaper. His sweat coats my hand in slime.

He's here because I asked him to come. I got Tori – or *Victoria* as the lovely tea lady calls her – to contact him specifically to come in so we could talk. But now he's here, I don't want him to be.

I'm musing the fact I never twigged that Tori was short for Victoria. I guess she never featured high enough on my radar for me to give it any thought. But it's fitting she has a new name for the new side I now see.

There's a glint, a sheen, to Tori that gives the impression of her being a mean girl. The way she was able to tell me to cut Alison some slack – you don't speak to dying people like that, whether it's self-inflicted or not. But now I'm wondering if the shards of ice inside her are her way of coping with a mean life.

I have a feeling she told James that he needed to come

straight away, because he's here within half an hour of her leaving. Tori and nuances do not go together.

Unfortunately, thinking about Tori is not enough to distract me from James's touch. I long to get out my baby wipes and clean him from my skin.

We were never touch-feely as a couple. Never held hands. So I know the James at my bedside isn't *my* James. That this is going to be pointless.

I'm grateful he's not holding my left hand, as the skin is more sensitive than usual after the drip in my wrist leaked into my tissues. My elephantiasis. The nurse whose drip failed was full of apologies but they don't touch me. It wasn't on purpose so it doesn't matter. My elephant hand is now only slightly puffy, but it is still swollen enough to warn people away from touching it.

My new drip is now at my right elbow, keeping my arm straight. So I can't pull my right hand from his without admitting the fact that I'm awake. My only option is the "harrumph" turn in bed – the one you do with so much noise and so much fuss, it's too much to be fake.

I turn restlessly and noisily onto my left side, attempting to take my right hand with me. But my lack of movement at my elbow and my slow turn is not enough for me to loosen his grip. As I move my hand across the front of my body, his hand comes with it.

So I concentrate on slow, steady breaths in and out while willing for him get bored waiting for me to wake up. I pray to the God of Costa to call out to him to buy yet another coffee to keep him going while he waits. Their hospital café must make a killing from its captive audience.

It's not the first time I'd feigned sleep. And yesterday it delivered bombshell.

THE CONFESSIONAL

Ruby quietly leaned over the bed to check if Zoe was asleep. She was. Good. Ruby wanted to talk to her, to explain, to tell her things, to say "Thank you" and to apologise. But she didn't really want Zoe to say anything in return.

Talking to a slumped body in bed would be like an empty confessional at church where there's no priest to hear you and absolve you of your sins. Ruby wanted to pull the curtains round Zoe's bed to afford them some privacy, even though she was aware the rough blue fabric would be a poor substitute for the strong wooden confessionals in her mum's church.

"I'm really sorry your life has been so tough that you've decided this is your only solution," Ruby started, hesitantly. "I want to say 'thank you' for bringing Alison back into my life. The situation is shitty and I'm embarrassed to be gaining from it. But I also thought it might be some comfort to you that something good had come out of it all.

"Alison stopped being a friend of mine years ago. She went away to uni and that was that. I was out of her life. I mean I technically saw her about 18 months ago at a wedding. This girl Becky from school wanted lots of bridesmaids and we both got roped in. But it was awkward and we didn't really get the chance to chat properly.

"I gave her space at the service thinking we'd catch up afterwards, but we were on different tables. We'd been inseparable at school and the only way Becky would have split us up like that is if Alison had asked her."

Ruby sighed – and managed to catch her breath, turning the sigh into a noisy cough, a cough that was followed by a number of stilted smaller coughs as she tried to get her hacking under control.

"And I saw her again last year, out on the beach during

the storm. The beach is the best place for storm watching. She didn't see me and I wasn't sure how she'd react if I approached her, after how she'd been at the wedding. So I decided to pop in to see her mum, something I still did from time to time, ready to stumble upon Alison by accident.

"But she wasn't there. And as we chatted, it became clear her mum didn't know anything about Alison's visit down either. I found it really difficult not to tell her – I felt like I was lying to her. Since Alison moved out, her mum has been on her own.

"I need to talk to Alison about why she cut me out of her life. I can't do it right now, not with all this going on. But I'm glad we're in touch again so I finally get the chance to ask."

ZOE

I'd known about the wedding. It was at some posh priory in Essex – and Alison had been relieved she didn't have to head home. But I didn't know about her trip to Whitstable – the very place she's always taken great pains to avoid.

When did Alison go to Whitstable? How had she managed to leave London and go storm watching – if that's actually a thing – without me knowing? Why was she sneaking around behind my back? Lying to me about going on holiday? Sharing coffees with James?

I'd wanted to see the coffees they shared as innocent, even after Tori implied Alison was getting ready to make a move on him. I told myself I was being ridiculous, imagining things, because Alison wasn't like that. But now I'm not so sure. Because if your best friend can lie to you about a trip home to the place she hates, then she can lie to you about wanting your boyfriend her herself.

But *how* do I ask her any of this? *When* do I ask her any of this?

Ruby is right. It's all about timing.

I still need to tell Alison and James how I feel – what I couldn't put down on pen and paper – but every time I see them it's not the right time. I realise I'm going to have to *make* it the right time though, because I don't have a lot of it left.

I need to tell James everything now, while he's here, even if it means I push him into Alison's arms.

I also need to free my hand.

So I start yawning and make what I believe are typical rousing-from-sleep noises. He lets go of my hand.

I reach for the baby wipes – I can't help it. I wipe my face first, before using it to casually wipe my hands. My actions are not nonchalant enough. James stares at my hands, then his own, then pointedly wipes his own hand on his jeans. I suppose that serves me right.

"Thank you for coming to see me."

I sound absurdly formal. But it seems to fit the circumstances.

"Texting you telling you not to come, that was unfair of me. So thank you for coming back. I appreciate being able to say what I couldn't put in a note."

"Which is what exactly?" – there's a coolness in James's voice that matches my formality.

"I don't like people," I explain. "Any people. Including you. But not just you. *All* people. And I tried. I *really* tried to like you. But I couldn't."

He stares at me, stoney-faced.

"I know it sounds clichéd, but it's not you, it's me. I *can't* like anyone. I just *don't* work like that. I have a best friend and a boyfriend and both of you have been loyal and caring."

I pause. When I took the overdose I had no idea that they'd both be capable of being disloyal.

"And yet everything I've given back has been fake. I thought if I *tried* to feel something towards you that it would happen. But it didn't. And I didn't want to be fake — didn't want to fail at the very basics of being human.

"It made me so depressed. And then I felt angry at feeling depressed. And that's when I realised that's all I feel: depression and anger. That's it. Nothing else.

"And *that's* why I decided to kill myself — because I can't live with just depression and anger. I can't keep faking everything else.

"But I couldn't write all this down in a note, about being fake, without explaining it. Because on paper it just sounded wrong."

Wow. I've said it. I've actually said it.

James starts speaking and I miss what he has to say, I'm in such a daze. I have to ask him to repeat himself.

"Have you said any of this to Alison?"

I shake my head.

"She's not here until later."

He stands up slowly and backs away from the bed. He wipes his hand on his jeans again for good measure.

"Then don't," he says. "Don't say any of it. She deserves better."

13 lifebuoys

BUILD YOUR OWN LIFE

When they were seven years old, Alison and Ruby decided they were going to be primary school teachers and started collecting old bricks so they could build their own school. They adored joining Alison's mum on trips to B&Q in Swalecliffe because she would let the two of them wander off. They would walk round deciding on how they would decorate their school. Their shopping list included glittery wallpaper, *Thomas the Tank Engine* bins and elephant-shaped lights.

As teenagers, their trips to B&Q were without any parents, but the aim was similar – to decide how they would decorate the flat they would share when they first moved out of home. Their shopping list included shabby chic butterfly bedding, a full-length rustic-style mirror and star-shaped fairy lights.

Shortly after they'd finished their A Levels, and when they'd discovered they'd be in different halls in their first year, Alison made a sneaky solo trip to B&Q to buy a box of star-shaped fairy lights, ready to give them to Ruby as a housewarming present.

But the lights were never given to Ruby and the unopened box has instead followed Alison across London, taking up home at the bottom of a plastic storage tub shoved into a dark, unloved corner underneath her bed.

ALISON

I'm glad Ruby suggested the tube trip. Not for the trip itself: but because she did it for me.

I've always thought of Zoe as Ruby's replacement. But although Zoe can be fantastic fun, there's an angry edge to her that I'm constantly afraid of wakening. I've been living on eggshells for years and didn't even realise it until I was back in Ruby's company.

I want to thank her, so I suggest we get out at Victoria on our journey back − so I can treat her to lunch. Up on the main concourse, I scan for somewhere that's not too busy. We spot Costa, look at each other and both cry "No!" at the same time.

We share a grin and Ruby gives me one of her all-embracing hugs.

It's weird to feel good emotions.

I miss the uncontrollable laughter that was always commonplace in Ruby's company, when we'd try − and fail − to regain our composure with careful shallow breaths, blowing air out through pursed lips, a single comment from my mum about the two of us being ridiculous enough to set us of again.

I hope we can get back to that.

I remember there's a Leon upstairs in the food court. I know what I'm going to order − the Sweet Potato Falafel Hot

Box and Fresh Slaw – because I have the same thing every visit. But Ruby needs to check out the menu, having never been before. She goes for the Moroccan Meatballs and Baked Fries. I know before she tries one that the fries are going to be a disappointment.

I surprise myself by enjoying my food. I'm starving after struggling to eat at breakfast. After my main course, I manage a chunk of banana bread washed down with a cup of English Breakfast tea.

I can't face coffee.

Ruby checks her watch and signals it's time for us to get going. On the tube back to Brixton I chew over my own thoughts. I'm envious of Tori being in work, escaping all this. I was annoyed with her the other evening for her questions about Ruby, but I was being unfair. Dumped in the middle of an old friendship, her questions were normal. I just don't have any mental space for normal right now.

Zoe is dying. I'm sure once she's gone I'll wish I could have just one more day of her friendship. But right now I'm wishing she could die quickly. Because each day I have to see her in hospital is a tiny bit of me dying too. When we get off the tube, I suggest we walk to the hospital instead of jumping on the bus. I need more time before I see her.

I know the back roads, so we walk up by Brixton Rec, the ugly brick leisure centre of the old Brixton, and Brixton Pop, with the pop-up bars and food hall of the new. Ruby noses curiously at the latter. When this is all over, I hope Ruby will want to stay long enough to explore. I want to make new memories here to paper over the old ones of my visits with Zoe.

We cut through at the far end of the foreboding Southwyck House – known locally as Barrier Block.

"When I first saw it, I though it was Brixton prison," I tell her sheepishly.

"What is it?" – I hear the horror in her voice.

I can see from the way her mouth hangs open that she's seeing the same oppression I did – the zigzag of bricks, the miniscule windows. She has the look on her face everyone has when they see this place with new eyes.

"It's council housing."

"People *live* there?"

"Spend five years here and you just accept that not all of London is the city the tourists see. Not all of it can be as nice as the South Bank," I add pointedly.

Minutes later and we have Victorian terraces on both sides. They're tired round the edges and some need more than just a lick of paint to sort them out, but I hear Ruby exhale slowly – a sigh of relief that we're back somewhere familiar. It's not until we're pushed out of our comfort zone against our will that we realise just how amazing normal and familiar can be.

As we get to the junction, the no.35 bus passes us. Ruby throws me a look – it says "We get the bus next time, okay?" It reminds me of my first day at university, when every building was scary. Of course Ruby wants the safety of the bus.

The rest of the walk to the hospital is uneventful, except for the police tape around another council estate – this one made up of low-rise blocks. The tape blocks the pavement on the left side of the road completely. We're on the right-hand side, but Ruby wants to cross over to ask one of the police officers what's going on.

"They can't tell you anything."

But she either doesn't listen or doesn't believe me, so I wait on the pavement while she crosses over. A minute later, she's crossing back towards me, shaking her head in annoyance.

"It's probably gang related," I explain. "They don't tell

you anything when it's that. But the tape is out, so it means somebody died."

The tape is as effective as hospital curtains.

I see the same look cross her face that she wore on the tube when I told her about them scooping up body parts from the tracks. She's going through all the mental hoops everyone goes through when they first move here, when you wonder to yourself how anyone lives like this.

We're on Coldharbour Lane and about 100 yards from where I lived during my second year at university. The house was a dump and we had nightmare neighbours, but Camberwell is on five different night bus routes and has 24-hour takeaways. It's strange that I have some fond memories of what to an outsider must seem a daunting place to be. I long to stay outside and chat with Ruby about my university years, all the madcap things we got up to, but we've reached the hospital and I owe it to Zoe to go inside.

Today, Zoe's ward is the same but different. The staff have changed shifts, some of the patients have changed, but the weary air, the peculiar smells, they stay the same. What's different is that, today, I feel awkward about seeing Zoe. I can tell from her face that the feeling is mutual.

Zoe being Zoe, she cuts straight to it.

"Tori came to see me this morning."

I know the shock is showing on my face. I look at Ruby and she has the decency to look embarrassed and a little ashamed.

"Sorry," Ruby says to me. "I told you there was no morning visiting so we could have the morning off and Tori could visit first. And so I could get you back on the tube."

"Tube ride?" – Zoe sounds intrigued.

"Ruby thought going on the Victoria line would help with, you know, all this," I shrug.

"Ah yes, *Ruby*," Zoe says sweetly. "One of the people visiting me that I *don't* know. Is there any way you could maybe wait somewhere else?"

Ruby shifts uncomfortably.

"I'm okay," I tell her.

"I want to talk to you about James," Zoe says as soon as Ruby has left.

I can't think of anyone I'd rather *not* talk about.

"Okay," I say instead.

"I know you've always been awkward round him," Zoe says to me. "But I always assumed it was because you didn't like being the third wheel, not because you fancied him."

The world slows. Yes I am awkward around James. But it's not because I fancy him. Eww. Anything but. I have the perfect explanation as to why, but by the time I found out they were dating it was too late to say anything. And it would seem cruel to tell her now. I'd be ruining their relationship.

"And now he's saying that you deserve better."

"Better than what?"

"Now, why would he see you as deserving if the two of you can't stand each other?"

James can't stand me? I thought he was indifferent.

God I need to focus.

"I don't know what James thinks of me because I don't spend any time talking to him about me – or about *anything* for that matter."

"Except for me."

I'm not going to go there.

Whatever is going on in Zoe's head – the paranoia that comes with dying maybe – I don't have anything I can say that will make her believe me. I have no way of *proving* I don't fancy him.

"I don't like James," I say – which I've said a million times before. "I give you my word."

My reward is a look of hatred, of scorn, of pity.

She's dying and *she* wants to pity *me*. Wow.

Our friendship is toxic. I don't understand why I've never seen it before. But now I do, I'm glad she's going to hate me – it means I'll be free from the grip of her friendship.

Whatever her reasons for choosing a slow death, I don't want to hear them. So I turn on my heel and head after Ruby.

PEACOCKING

Alison and Zoe had gone for drinks at Be At One on Greek Street. It was one of their favourite haunts because of the 2-for-1 cocktail deals. It was an easy place to miss if you didn't know it was there: an unassuming doorway at street level, but one that leads to a massive basement bar.

London was as flooded with as many Be At One bars as it was Leon fast-food places. But unlike the identikit Leons, each Be At One was different and everyone had their favourite. Zoe liked Greek Street because it was large enough to offer the possibility of male talent. Alison liked it because Zoe liked it – and she had a better night out when Zoe was in a good mood.

Alison also liked it because she could "hide" in the bar's dim red lighting. And because the lighting made Zoe marginally less stunning and evened out the playing field a little. (Although Alison preferred not to admit this to herself.)

Zoe and Alison always sat on one side of a booth near the bar so they both could have a good view of anyone who came up to buy a drink. If Zoe spotted anyone she liked, she'd give them lots of eye contact. The brave ones came over to talk to her. The cocky ones sat down the other side of the table uninvited.

One of the brave ones introduced himself as James. He was the typical peacock, strutting round with his tail in the air. He waited to be offered a seat (passing the first test) and was resilient as well as charming, managing to lure Alison into the conversation as well as chatting to Zoe. So when Zoe needed the loo, Alison wasn't too apprehensive about being left alone in his company.

"You're really funny," he told her.

Alison felt herself flush with pride. When she hit her alcohol sweet spot, she became the quick-witted one, landing all the one-liners.

"But your mate," he said. "She's stunning."

Alison's world crashed down around her. The "funny" compliment was just to butter her up because this guy wanted Zoe. To cover her hurt, Alison took too big a mouthful of her cocktail, the acidic liquid burning harshly as it sloshed down her throat. It was a difficult mouthful to swallow, never mind keep down, and some of it made its way back up, bringing the taste of sick with it.

"So I'd like to ask your mate out. Because, well, she's gorgeous. But you. You're different. I fancy you."

James leaned in towards Alison.

"So how about just one kiss between the two of us while I'm still single? Before kissing me would be cheating on your mate."

Alison leaned back into the corner as far as she could go, pressing herself up against the squeaky fake leather covering the booth. She couldn't get far enough away from him, so she covered her mouth with both hands, making it clear just how much he's not going to get to kiss her. Relief coursed through her body when she saw Zoe heading back to the table. James picked up on it and pulled himself away from Alison.

Once Zoe was sitting down again, James gave her all his attention, ignoring a relieved but annoyed Alison. She glowered at him, wanting him to leave, but if he noticed, he didn't let on. When she and Zoe left at the end of the evening, Alison was relieved that James was not coming with them.

It was a couple of weeks later when, over glasses of a beautifully honeyed Gewurztraminer at The Wine Parlour, Zoe confessed she'd been out on three dates with James.

"I didn't want to tell you in case it didn't go anywhere," she told Alison.

"Why? Because I'd try and stop you?"

"He told me that you hit on him, so he wanted to ask me out discretely. He waited until you went to the ladies to take my number. And I kept it from you afterwards so not to embarrass you. I only wanted to tell you if I had to."

Alison was annoyed in so many ways. That James lied. That Zoe automatically believed him. That Zoe had let her bitch about James on the journey home and not said anything, all the while planning to see him again. That Zoe was ruining her favourite wine at her favourite venue with this conversation.

"I didn't hit on him," Alison said in a calm, measured voice. "He gave me the creeps. And he picked up on it, which is why he gave you his number in secret."

Zoe gave her a sideways glance. The one thing Alison was known for more than her drunken one-night stands was her honesty.

"Well I'm telling you about it now because I like him. And he's not creepy. Which you'll find out for yourself when you meet him properly."

Alison stared at her in disbelief.

"I have to see him again?"

Alison and Zoe didn't introduce each other to flings – it wasn't worth the hassle. So an introduction meant Zoe and James were moving onto something more serious after just three dates.

Alison knew it was too late to tell Zoe the kiss story. Because Zoe's brain had been living in James's version of what happened for weeks – long enough for it to become the truth. So anything Alison said would now sound like tit-for-tat, even though it was the truth.

"Well it's going to have to wait as I've got my training course coming up," Alison said.

"You didn't mention any training course?" Zoe sounded surprised.

"You didn't mention any dates," Alison snapped back.

Two days later, Alison packed for her "training course", making sure Zoe saw her work outfits folded on the bed, ready to go into her suitcase. What Zoe didn't see was casual clothes Alison had piled up on the chair in the corner – the stuff she was actually taking.

Alison rarely took time off work, saving holiday for when Zoe decided on a whim they should go away for a long weekend. It meant her boss was used to her asking for time off at short notice – and said "Yes" to her mid-week request just as easily as he had all the times when she'd asked to take a Friday or a Monday off work in order to head to Prague, Budapest, Madrid, Brussels.

When the train stopped at Whitstable, Alison had to resist the urge to jump off and rush straight to Ruby's house. But she couldn't go there, because they hadn't been friends in years and because, after the stuff with Zoe and James, the risk of rejection from Ruby was too much to bear.

Instead she stayed on one more stop until Chestfield & Swalecliffe station and walked the half-mile to Seaview caravan park, juggling her wheelie suitcase and the bag of food she'd bought at Victoria station. It was close enough to summer for the caravan park to be open, but enough outside of the main holiday season for caravans to be available for last-minute bookings – and for them to be cheap.

It wasn't until she reached the reception and was greeted by two members of staff giggling over something, their warmth spilling over to her side of the counter, that the stresses of London, the ones Alison couldn't shake on the journey down here, started to dissipate.

Alison's caravan was in row "K" in the farthest set of caravans from the reception area. It was a happy accident because it meant she was close to the beach and a decent distance from the noisy entertainment block she wouldn't be using.

To get to her caravan's front door, she had to go up brand new steps and through a gate onto a fenced decking area complete with outdoor table and chairs. This was much better than the caravans she remembered from her childhood.

After her parents separated, Alison had lived with her mum. So her dad insisted on taking her on holiday two or three times a year. As they lived by the sea, they'd head inland and stayed in places near forests and lakes. Alison remembered them as being awesome holidays right up until the day she was too old for them, but the caravans had been quite dingy.

She put her shopping away in the fridge and cupboards – fresh rolls, sliced ham, sliced cheese, a massive bag of Peanut M&Ms and two bottles of pinot grigio. After The Wine Parlour, she couldn't face honeyed flavours.

Next was a shower – she wanted to wash away the grime of London, and any thoughts of Zoe and James with it.

The shower room was another pleasant surprise. The walls were a plastic mould, like the ones for jelly, only this one carved out the shape of the shower and a set of shelves. It was a clever way to make a decent space out of a tiny section of caravan – something the average London landlord wasn't that good at. Alison had seen too many badly designed flats that were the result of houses being carved up without any real forethought.

She turned the shower on expecting a dribble not too dissimilar to the one in her Brixton flat. But after an initial splutter, a strong jet of water swooshed out of the showerhead. She stripped off and climbed in, laughing at how ludicrous it was that a shower in a caravan park in the middle of nowhere could be better than the one in her outrageously expensive London flat (as every flat in London was by default).

It was a glorious feeling to be able to stand there and let the water pummel her awake.

The shower put Alison in a good mood – and not even realising she'd forgotten to bring a towel in with her could ruin it. Instead she squealed as she ran naked into the bedroom to wrap herself up in one.

After her shower, she headed to where the caravan park met the sea wall. She stared out at the familiar. The sea looked like someone had done a really poor job of colouring it in, using a mix of blues and various shades of green to patch it up after their navy felt-tip pen ran out of ink.

Off to the right, Alison could see the stranded end of the old Herne Bay Pier. The structure had been designed to be long enough for passenger ferries to use, the far end reaching deep enough waters – the navy blue felt tip. But when a storm destroyed the centre of the pier, the pier head was left isolated. As a child, she'd thought they'd left it there because they planned to rebuild it, rather than it being "a waste of taxpayers' money" to knock it down.

Alison turned left, heading towards Whitstable. She daren't go as far as the actual town centre because she risked bumping into someone she knew – and that would mean having to visit her mum, which she just couldn't face right now. But she wanted to go as far as Tankerton Slopes and drink in the memories of all her happy afternoons there.

The scruffy café at the top of the slopes was still there. Alison popped in for a takeaway cup of tea and took it to a nearby bench.

While sipping her brew, Alison watched the hazy sun cast its faded yellow glow down the slope, over the rows of beach huts with their Technicolor stripes and then over lazy waves that left shiny sea-washed pebbles behind. She watched a couple of terriers interrupt the calmness, tearing up and down the slopes at such speed that they went careering across the pebbles and into the sea.

Her summer crowd – a group who rubbed along together when school was closed because of their proximity to each other, but who wouldn't be seen dead with each other during term time – used to hang out here. They'd ride down here on their bikes then lie them down, strewn across the grass, their bodies scattered amongst them, a tangled mess of bike frames and youthful limbs.

They'd talk about racing down the slopes on their bikes – just as the duo of dogs was doing now – but they never did. Even at that age, although not totally aware of their own mortality, their brains were advanced enough to be apprehensive about the pain they might experience if the dare went wrong. Self-preservation always kicked in.

ALISON

Something has made Zoe think I'd want James for myself. I thought it was clear that I couldn't stand him, but now she thinks that's jealousy – that I've been jealous all along.

I'm trying to work out what that "something" is.

It has occurred to me that I'd know if I'd stayed on the ward. But I wasn't willing to listen to Zoe spew a torrent of abuse at me. My self-preservation kicked in. So now I'm left to figure it out for myself.

In the beginning, I'd desperately wanted Zoe as my friend and had to pinch myself when she decided to claim me. I repaid her by taking Shakespeare as one of my course options and agreeing to move into a crazy house share in Camberwell. Those things were Zoe's choices and I simply followed.

Could that be the something? That she kept those first few dates with James a secret because she wanted something that was just hers, something I couldn't try and claim as mine too? And now that she's dying, she thinks I'm finally going to get my chance to?

14 armbands

RUBY

Alison's whole body slumps when I tell her the next day that we're going to visit Zoe. I know if she doesn't go back, it will be one of those things she regrets later on.

We risk Zoe asking us to leave, but if we don't go, we won't know, so we need to take the chance. Once Zoe is dead, there will be no more chances. And so any such regrets could turn to guilt and eat Alison up until there's nothing left of her.

But getting Alison to visit Zoe again is as much a selfish act as it is a selfless one. Yes, I don't want Alison to have to go through any kind of guilt associated with this. But I also don't want *me* to have to go through Alison going through any kind of guilt. I know I'd be the person she'd lean on.

We might not have seen each other in years, but we've slotted back into our old friendship as if there were never a gap – and a little too comfortably for my liking. Alison is back in the role of needing me. I realise she absolutely needs me right now, but it means there's no space for me. And if that's the case when all this is over, then I need to be ready to walk away from this friendship.

Since hearing about my mum's Windrush journey, and how she had to cope with living in a strange land while grieving for her mother, I've developed a harder outer skin that's a good match for its darker tones. I used to accept the fact that my skin colour put me in the minority, which meant working hard for everything that just landed in the laps of other people. But I accepted it because I understood we were working towards a position of equality. But now there are people like Albert Thompson and everything has changed. All these years later, there *is* no acceptance.

My mum married a Nigerian man who gave me the surname "Adebayo". My surname is apparently difficult to spell and to pronounce. I'm often told this in an accusatory tone. It's a tone I no longer accept.

They met while working in the same factory, but I don't know much about their lives before they moved to Whitstable because that was all before my time, my mum remaining tight-lipped about her whole past in order to bury the hurt from losing her mother.

I'm glad she wasn't as reticent about my own childhood. I have some amazing memories of my dad, but I'm not sure which are real and which are the embellished stories my mum has told me mixed in with the few photographs we have of him. In today's selfie culture it's difficult to imagine that just a generation ago, many people didn't have cameras. The few photos of my dad are very formal – a far cry from the jovial man I remember and the one that my mum paints for me.

But now, since Albert, I am learning more stories about my roots and they fill me with a mix of pride and hurt: pride at how my family has coped; hurt at how little it seems to matter. I have to be careful to keep my rage under wraps because I don't want to upset my mum. She believes the rough times she went through were worth it because I don't have to. She accepts all the injustices she's faced, but I want to rant and scream at the sky.

I was swallowing it all down for my mum. And now I'm choking it back for Alison – and for Zoe and for Tori. But once this is done, I will be screaming my anger from the rooftops whether anyone who calls themselves a friend is listening or not.

SLOWLY UNDERSTANDING

For Alison, Ruby being a different colour was something that dawned on her slowly. First she learned that "coloured" was another word for brown skin, just like "white" was for pink skin – although hers wasn't pink all over because she had freckles and strange blue lines that belonged to Wayne.

It was when they were playing on the beach and they kicked off their flip-flops that Alison first realised there was something wrong with Ruby's feet.

"The brown's come off!" she exclaimed.

But Ruby laughed and said the bottoms of her feet were always pink, just like the palms of her hands and underneath her fingernails.

"You don't have Wayne's lines though," Alison said, pointing to a crisscross of lumpy blue lines on the underside of her wrist.

Ruby looked at her own wrist and, sure enough, although there were lumpy bits that you could squish if you pressed them, they weren't blue.

Ruby's mum was ill, so she spent many weekends with Alison and her mum. Alison's mum used to refer to them both as "her cheeky little monkeys" until some old lady in the supermarket gasped and suddenly it wasn't okay anymore.

Alison didn't understand why, but Ruby did. She was able to tell her that monkeys were brown and that you weren't allowed to call brown people things that were also brown.

With each year, Alison would learn more things that were different for Ruby just because she was brown – including the latest thing you were called if you were brown. When they were younger, people called Ruby "coloured", but as she got older, they started calling her "black".

RUBY

I get ready slowly and methodically, gaining peace and calmness from the rhythm of my routine. My Bantu knots are now beyond saving, so I take them out, freeing my bouncy curls. The change in my appearance will no doubt garner looks from Tori – or the Toribot as I've secretly named her. Well, she does seem obsessed with nicknames.

As an adult I have learned to own my blackness, so Toribot can look all she wants: today I will not be having that conversation.

Although I'm sleeping in the lounge, I've taken to getting ready in Zoe's room, using her bed as makeshift storage for my things. She has set up a mirror leaning against the window that is perfect for making sure my skin is as close to flawless as I can get it.

I carefully apply Varama Cover Cream to my cheeks to hide the patches of redness. Afterwards I still have areas of skin that are noticeably raised if I stand in the wrong light, but I have become an expert at applying camouflage make-up, so the differences in skin tone have vanished.

Now I'm dressed and ready, I check on Alison. She's sitting in the lounge, a mug of tea clasped in her hands. She looks lost. Exhausted. She used up all her energy ranting about Zoe and James last night.

I take the tea out of her hands.

"Why don't we go and get breakfast at that Burnt Toast café in the village?"

Alison had mentioned it when she caught me burning some to hide the musty smell in the flat. She'd suggested going there – but as with anything she suggested, the words "once this is all over" were silently added. However, she needed a boost now and it was the only place I knew to recommend back to her.

"We can walk down to the village to get some fresh air, get our appetites up," I say. I pause – "but *then* we're getting the bus."

She grins at me. Thankfully, the promise of a decent breakfast is enough to get Alison moving and out of the house.

Each time we walk down Brixton Hill, I'm less intimidated by my surroundings: the concrete blocks of flats seem less foreboding, the traffic less noisy, the shops less scruffy. I'm becoming desensitised to its ugliness far quicker than I expected. This must be how people cope living here.

I was looking forward to seeing the old bit of Brixton, so I'm genuinely disappointed to discover Brixton Village is not the same as any of the "old town" areas I'd explored on holidays abroad. Instead of meandering through higgledy streets too narrow for cars, we end up in an indoor market.

We grab a table that is "outside-but-inside" – outside the café itself but in the busy walkway of the indoor market. We sit on wooden stools either side of a wooden slatted table,

Alison letting me have the seat with my back to the café so I have the better view.

She points to the elegant silver Dualit toaster taking pride of place on our table – "So this place lets you decide how you want your toast done."

"Oh, so the name of the place comes from the fact it has more burnt pieces than the average café?"

She smiles. "I've assumed the same thing."

"Isn't the whole point of eating out to get someone else to cook for you?"

She shakes her head – she's thought about this before and dismissed it.

"It's like those places that bring out a hot stone and let you cook your own steak. On the one hand they're silly gimmicks, but on the other they bring the customers in."

While we wait to be served, I take in my surroundings. Although not as pleasant as sitting outside, the high ceiling is made of clear corrugated plastic, which means the place is bathed with morning light.

It's nothing like the narrow streets of Madrid or Rome I'd hoped for, but it still feels as though we're on holiday. There's a full orchestra and sounds to lose yourself in too, from the Middle Eastern sitar music competing with soulful reggae coming from neighbouring stalls, to the women cackling outside the flower stall. It's a welcome lift from the stress.

This is the sort of place to bring Anthony Bourdain to. He's an advocate of peasant food and the simple dishes eaten by the poorer inhabitants of different cultures. And what could be more peasant food than toast?

He's my favourite TV chef and I prefer places like this to the kind of overly worthy eatery that would suit Jamie Oliver (think healthy and devoid of any fun) or the avant-garde establishment that Heston Blumenthal would frequent.

We're not having toast though. Alison has bullied me into trying their pancakes with bacon and maple syrup. The mix of salted and sweet doesn't appeal to me at all, especially not for breakfast, so I order a large freshly squeezed juice to help it go down.

The bacon comes smothered in syrup, not on the side as I'd expected. I realise I'm just going to have to tuck in and hope. And it's perfection – right down to the sharpness of the fresh strawberry pieces that stop the syrup from being too cloying. I try to steal myself a few minutes away from the reason I'm up in London so I can enjoy the food.

After scoffing the crisp pancakes and all their gorgeousness, Alison insists we have cappuccinos. The coffees brought to our table are beautifully steamed. I wonder if Zoe is able to appreciate something like the perfect coffee? I'm all too aware of how easy I find it to enjoy the simple things in life. But I don't want to ruin breakfast with my sentimentalities, so I swallow down my thoughts along with my coffee.

Our escape from reality ends all too soon and we head to the bus stop. A tiny part of me is considering suggesting that we walk just to delay the inevitable hostility from Zoe. Zoe or Barrier Block? Barrier Block, please!

Zoe took Paracetamol because she wanted a chance to say goodbye to Alison – and at first I assumed this was meant to be a gesture of love, of friendship. But with each visit I get more nervous that the goodbye is tainted with some kind of poison of its own. I can't share these thoughts with Alison though: it's been difficult enough to get her to the hospital as it is.

We do our usual stop at the Costa on the way to the ward, getting just Zoe's coffee as we've already had our own, the barista behind the counter nodding her recognition and starting on Zoe's rocket fuel coffee straight away.

As we leave Costa, we bump into Toribot.

"You've got coffee," she says, "that saves me getting any."

Toribot joins on the walk to Zoe's ward, using the time to update Alison on office gossip. I walk a step behind them, taking in Toribot's glamorous outfit.

Although not to the purple dress standard of that first day. She's got on a silver blouse that I want to say is made of silk, but it seems more structured than I'd expect silk to be. It's quite low cut and reeks of money – this is definitely a label item.

She's coupled the blouse with wide-leg black trousers that cling to her nether regions before flaring out, giving the illusion of being slutty and demure all at once. I'm assuming that's the intention. And either she's wearing the world's thickest mascara or she's got false eyelashes on. Who wears those to the hospital?

"Have you got an event this evening?" I ask Toribot.

She looks confused.

"No. Why?"

"Oh I thought…" I signal that I'm referring to her outfit.

For the first time since I met her, I get to see Toribot off guard, to see her overly perfect robotic mask slip a little – to see a hint the real Tori underneath. And then I twig. If the outfit and the make-up aren't for tonight then they're for the hospital. So is this all for James?

"We've been here most of the morning," I lie – Alison shoots me a confused look, I throw her one that tells her to stay quiet.

"But we haven't seen Zoe's boyfriend yet. What's his name again?" I ask, innocently.

"James" Tori says – and it's Tori, not the Toribot, that answers, her voice barely containing her longing, her neediness, her lust.

I take the maroon coffee cup from Alison's hand and pass it to Toribot.

"Can you take this in to Zoe?" I ask her, "I need to speak to Alison for a minute."

I can tell Toribot wants to stick around to hear whatever it is I've got to say to Alison.

"Please" – I say in a voice that is telling her, not asking.

"Is something going on between the Toribot and James?" I ask Alison as soon as the double doors to the ward swing shut behind her.

"Who?" she asks.

I start to blush. My brown skin is light enough to show it, so I'm grateful for the camouflage make-up that will hide it. I grin back, pretending not to care I've been caught using the nickname.

"You haven't answered my question."

"Oh nothing's going on," Alison assures me. "She can't stand him. He's an old one-night stand from years ago, so she finds him uncomfortable to be around."

"So is that what her outfit is for? Because she 'feels uncomfortable'?"

Alison "hmms" – she's not convinced.

"Did you not notice the way she said his name?"

Alison rewinds the conversation and replays it in her head. The whole world rewinds with it, the air in the corridor floating past our ears, the sounds around us reduced to a whirring, like an old cassette player running out of power.

I know she hears it – the lust – in Tori's voice.

"Could *she* be the reason why Zoe thinks you're after James?" I ask her. "I know you've got this theory she thinks you automatically want everything she's got. But that on its own wouldn't be enough, surely?"

"It could be," Alison says, sounding hopeful. But then her shoulders drop. "It doesn't matter though. I've always been awkward round James and I've never really explained why. So it serves me right if she thinks I'm jealous."

For all her faults, and Alison has as many as the next person, she doesn't have a jealous bone in her body.

"But Zoe *knows* you. There's no way she's going to think you're jealous unless she's been given a hefty push." I give Alison a you-know-I'm-right look.

"Maybe," she concedes.

The door of the ward swings open. We fall silent, checking it's not Toribot. It isn't, it's Latoria – the Ward Sister who always asks me about my skin.

"What are you two doing out here?" she asks.

"I'm trying to convince Alison here to ask Zoe some tough questions. I think someone else has tricked Zoe into thinking Alison is after her boyfriend when she's not. And I think Alison should ask Zoe about it."

"And I know I can't," Alison says, "even though I want to. Because there are things you don't say to someone who's dying and that includes accusing them of things you have no proof of."

"Oh sweetheart," Latoria says to her. "Has nobody told you? Your friend isn't dying."

15 swimming aids

ALISON

Ruby and I wait in the ward kitchenette while Latoria, the one I think of as Ruby's nurse, asks Tori to leave, telling her Zoe needs to have tests.

I wait for the ward doors to close behind Tori before I walk up the length of the ward to Zoe's bed. She's pretending to be asleep.

"I know you're not asleep," I tell her. "Latoria has just been down here to ask Tori to leave. It was so I could come and talk to you."

Zoe rolls over and opens her eyes. She's unimpressed. She powers up the end of her bed so she's sitting up. She views me warily.

"No Ruby?"

"No, just me."

"Oh. I'd come to the conclusion the two of you were inseparable."

Her voice is dripping with every negative emotion she can muster.

Coming to the ward each day to see her has been surreal because although I've been supposedly watching my best friend die, in many ways she's already dead.

I look at her and I can no longer see the Zoe I know. The person in bed in front of me bears no resemblance to the friend I made half a decade ago. It's as if, when she took those tablets, she switched off her soul, and even though she's no longer going to die, she hasn't switched it back on again.

I'm not sure it's even worth saying my piece any more. But it's the reason I'm here, so I take a few deep breaths, try to compose myself. As I search my brain for the sentences I'd planned out, she starts talking again.

"You see, I was going to suggest that Tori take my room in the flat. But it looks like you're lining Ruby up for it. Don't worry – I haven't said anything to Tori about it."

With everything going on, I haven't even thought about the flat. It's like we're a couple going through a bad break-up and she's the one thinking about all the practical things while I focus on the emotional ones.

"Erm, I'm not sure Ruby is looking to move to London. And me, well… I, erm, I'm not sure I want to stay in the flat. Erm, so maybe you want to stay instead?"

"*Erm*," she says, copying me. "If you haven't noticed, I'm in hospital. Dying."

Oh fuck. Nobody has told her.

"You're not," I say.

She looks totally flabbergasted.

"What?"

"Well you're in hospital, obviously – that much is true," I babble. "But you're not, erm… you're not…"

"I'm not dying?"

I nod, my eyes directed at the floor. I don't want to be the person giving this news to Zoe.

"How – the – actual – fuck – do – you – know?" she asks.

"Latoria just told us."

"Who?"

"The nurse who got Tori to go away. Ruby and I were in the corridor and she came out because she'd finished her shift. Ruby said I should say some things to you and I said I couldn't because you were dying. And she said you weren't."

We've been joined by a stern looking woman in her 50s. She's wearing the same uniform Latoria had on – the dress that's a darker shade of blue.

"Hello both of you," she says with a calm voice. "I'm the Sister looking after this ward today. You both seem to be a little upset?"

Zoe lifts her right arm to signal to her drip.

"What's this for?" she asks. "This drip. What is it for?"

I hear the anger building in her voice. I'm relieved she has turned her attentions towards the Sister and away from me.

"Is it, as I was led to believe, to make me *more comfortable*? Or is it to stop me from dying?"

Zoe's voice carries across the ward. Other staff pause in their duties and patients who've looked on death's door for days suddenly have the energy to lift their heads off their pillows to look over. The Sister calmly pulls the curtains round Zoe's bed, cocooning the three of us in blue fabric. Although they are completely useless at giving us any privacy, they have the desired effect – Zoe calms down a little.

"Your drip contains Acetylcysteine," the nurse explains. She twists the bag of clear fluid round on its stand so Zoe can see the label.

"Acetylcysteine is what we use to treat a Paracetamol overdose. It's the drug we use to try and stop your liver from failing. And it will make you feel more comfortable as it starts to work."

"But I waited the eight hours," Zoe said, exasperated.

Eight hours? Of course, the whole point of her tube journey. So why has the treatment worked?

"The first eight hours are crucial," the Sister explains. "It's much harder to successfully treat an overdose after that point. But we will still give every patient the treatment in the hope that it does still work."

Zoe is white with anger. Her words come out as a growling whisper.

"If I'd known, I would have refused it."

The Sister looks at me, parts the curtains a little so there's a gap, and ushers me out. I stand the other side of the fabric wall, unable to move.

The Sister speaks very calmly again, but this time there's a hint of condescension in her voice: "The reason you ended up on an acute medical ward and not the psychiatric ward is because you didn't refuse treatment. Had you done so, our A&E psychiatrist would have had no choice but to section you under the Mental Health Act in order to ensure the right treatment was given to you."

Fuck.

When I'd turned up on that first day to see Zoe, I was shocked she was on a normal ward. When I'd enquired, the nurse I spoke to said Zoe had been assessed as posing no danger to herself or others. She'd *just* tried to kill herself, so this sounded like bureaucratic nonsense to disguise a lack of suitable beds. But now it makes total sense.

Except she *isn't* as sane as they think she is, because it turns out she had *no idea* she was being treated: she thought she was being left to die. I back away from the curtains – I don't want to still be here when they open again.

All the litres

An astounding 47 million litres of water are pumped from the London Underground network each day. There's considerably less fluid in Zoe's drip, but to her, every drop is far more significant.

The real fluid in her drip is matched only by the metaphorical fluid in her head, which is swimming with a million and one different thoughts.

Her main thought — the one she keeps returning to — is how to reverse the damage she's just done to her cause in order to convince hospital staff to discharge her. Zoe wants — needs — to be away from their watchful eyes so she can get her suicide right second time around. And this time it will be quick and painless.

16 lifeguards

ZOE

The Ward Sister is still staring at me. I think she's waiting to see if I have anything more to say. She's just told me I could have been sectioned. I have no words right now.

I've had a sense of uneasiness since I discovered I'm in King's and not the hospital near Warren Street – the one I've forgotten the name of. Countless members of staff had spoken to me by the time I found out and none of them had bothered checking I knew which hospital I was in.

So this Sister can say whatever she likes about me agreeing to my drip, I didn't know it was a treatment because I thought it was too late to treat me, and the nurse that put the first drip in – the one that failed – had been no forthcoming about its contents than anyone had been about my location.

"Life's but a walking shadow, a poor player that struts and frets its hour upon the stage and then is heard no more."

Except I'm now expected to stick around for Act Two. Well no thank you. I've played my part and now it's time for me to bow out. How on earth I get myself out of this hospital and back home to my supplies is another matter.

Ironically, I'm no longer waiting to die, but waiting to get well enough to leave so I can kill myself properly this time. Thankfully, I won't be factoring in the needs of other people second time around so it will be quick and clean.

"You've still not explained why nobody told me I wasn't dying. I've been here three days and I've only just found out."

"We've only just found out," the Sister explains. "Your latest bloods came back just before shift change – so the results were left for my team to share."

Oh. So up until today I *have* been dying.

Convinced the conversation is over, the Sister pulls the curtains back. The ward was carrying on as if they hadn't just witnessed my whole world come crashing down. And true to form, when things get tough, Alison is nowhere to be seen.

Well I need to do *something* to get myself out of this mess.

"I want to see someone from the psych team," I call after the Sister. She nods that she has heard my request and heads to the phone.

It's after 6pm and this is the Tory fucked up version of the NHS, so I know there's no way any psych is going to be down here until tomorrow. That gives me time to compose myself and come up with a plan.

DO IT YOURSELF

Before Zoe went shopping for Paracetamol, she took a trip to B&Q. Her visit was very different from the meandering ones Alison and Ruby used to make.

She jumped on a bus to make the trip to the closest store

in Tulse Hill. Anyone who loves London will tell you that you can buy anything there. What they will fail to mention is that it might include a trek that's the equivalent of travelling to another town if we were anywhere else in the UK.

The trip to Tulse Hill wasn't too painful. Zoe cut down Brixton Water Lane and caught the bus by the large Sainsbury's – where her special shopping trip would end.

Her DIY shopping list was short – plastic tubing, a strong clear plastic bag, a ball of twine – but that didn't mean it was easy to shop for. Zoe had the diameter of the tubing she needed, but not necessarily what it was ordinarily used for. And asking a member of staff for assistance would lead to the obvious question of "What do you want it for?" – and Zoe didn't want to have to answer that.

She found a suitable solution in the gardening section. Not standard hosepipe as that would be too big, but special micro hose that came with all sorts of special garden watering paraphernalia. She instinctively balked at the price, which she found amusing, realising her brain was still set in "alive human being" mode. Money was going to be no use to her once she was dead.

The plastic bag was even harder to source. The only bags were ones similar to those in a supermarket, black ones for bins, green ones for garden waste. She was able to find plastic sheeting of many thicknesses and colours, but none of them clear. It had to be clear. She knew from her childhood that she was capable of putting a plastic bag over her head, but she instinctively knew it needed to be clear – that she needed to be able to see out.

Suitable clear plastic was elusive until she found one as the wrapping for a travel blanket. She opened the packaging up, unfolding the blanket, pretending to size it up for a passing member of staff, before putting it back on the shelf not in its bag. She then freed the plastic bag of any labelling, folded it and put it in her shopping basket.

And finally twine. That was easy to find.

Before heading to pay, Zoe stopped at the main paints aisle and picked up paint booklets for both Crown and Dulux, positioning her folded plastic bag between them. When it came to paying, Zoe put the hose and twine down on the counter and then moved the paint booklets from basket to shopping bag. The woman behind the till didn't bat an eyelid. Whatever exhilaration shoplifters experience when they steal something, Zoe didn't feel it.

With her B&Q shop done, Zoe jumped back on the bus and back to Sainsbury's, where she headed inside to the multi-service collection point and tapped in her code for her Argos order: a 0.4-cubic-metres helium canister.

She calmed herself with long deep breaths, preparing herself for the overly friendly staff member that always gets positioned at this sort of counter, where complaints and returns are dealt with alongside Click & Collect.

The girl who brings her Argos order out to her – and Zoe thinks the term "girl" is fair here as there's no way she's older than 16 or 17 – has the eager air about her that Zoe was worried about. It makes her take a step back. Zoe is the only person at the counter, but the girl reels off a long order code loudly as if announcing it to the shop. Zoe holds out her mobile phone to show her order details, confirming the code.

"Here you go," the girl said, handing the canister over to Zoe. It is both lighter and heavier than Zoe expected.

"There's a note here from the stockroom to check you realise that the balloons are sold separately. To make sure you know you've only bought the helium."

Zoe looked at the girl and held her gaze.

"I don't need balloons."

ZOE

The face of the girl in Sainsbury's still makes me chuckle to myself. I didn't mean to sound so ominous, but it was an instinctive reaction to her chirpiness.

I wonder if she Googled "uses for helium" when she finished her shift, although there's a chance that I was long forgotten by then. She's part of the social media generation: something gets five minutes and that's it. Nobody gets their 15 minutes of fame any more – that's far too long.

On the Monday morning of Mental Health Awareness Week, the #MentalHealthAwarenessWeek hashtag was trending on Twitter. I looked through some of the posts and there were *so many* people just piggybacking onto the hashtag with inane rubbish – anything to be noticed. It meant they were clogging up the feed of those people who had something useful to say. By Wednesday, the hashtag wasn't trending at all. Urghh. Never mind a whole week of awareness; Twitter couldn't manage three days.

I slept really badly for the first time since I was admitted. But I still need to attempt to look focused and in control, so while I'm waiting for the on-call psych to turn up, I'm going to shower and make myself as presentable as possible with the clothes I have available.

It means asking a nurse to detach my drip, otherwise I can't take clothes on and off. This is no mean feat as nurses are not only busy but look at me suspiciously when I request it. I now understand why.

Free of the drip stand, the first section of tube dangling aimlessly from my arm, I head into the shower room. I'm glad I packed flip-flops in my supplies because it means my feet don't have to touch the discoloured tiles on the floor.

I hang my wash bag from the door handle by its strings.

It's not the cleverest of designs because for the strings to be free to be used as handles, the opening to the bag needs to be ruched closed. The two-string-loops mechanism for closing the bag is very simple though and it's what I've replicated, with twine, on my suicide bag. Together with a helium canister and roll of hosepipe, it forms part of the perfect suicide machine.

I'm now angry with myself for not using it first time round.

I should have just written everything down in a note and not cared how it affected Alison of James, or if either of them had unanswered questions.

The other reason I opted for Paracetamol is because it meant Alison wouldn't have to find me, my dead body strapped up to a helium tank, plastic bag over my head. I know what it's like to have totally fucked up mental health. And while I might not be able to love Alison the way a friend should, I couldn't bring myself to do anything that could fuck hers up too.

The shower is adequate in both temperature and flow. The towel is not. It seems incapable of absorbing any moisture. I take a wad of paper towels from the dispenser and use those instead. I dress myself in the cleanest of my clothes, and then head back up the ward to my bed, sitting on top of the blankets. I know I could be in for a long wait, so I pick up my phone and read up on everything I can find about mental health in the NHS.

I'm still staring at my phone screen, pretending to engage even though the screen has long since gone dark, when one of the nurses comes over to let me know the on-call psych is here. I look up and see the psych standing by the Nurses Station. The psych doesn't come over to my bed themselves though – oh no, they are *far* too important for that. Urghh.

It's part of the unspoken hierarchy of the hospital. So while she stands there doing *nothing*, one of the nurses has to stop whatever useful thing they were doing in order to come and get me.

I give both the nurse and the psych a tight-lipped smile. I can't manage anything more – and I think anything more would be rather strange under the circumstances. The psych nods when introduced to me, hands remaining firmly clasped. If she's not willing to shake my hand, to feign normality, then I've got my work cut out. I don't catch her name – not that I need to. If she's not going to treat me like a human being then she gets the same in return.

We go to what's called the Quiet Room. It's opposite the offices and kitchen at the top end of the ward, so it's anything but quiet.

On-Call Psych motions to the sofa, so I sit. She follows suit, but in one of the plastic chairs.

"I want to make a complaint," I say. I've decided how this conversation is going to go and I'm controlling it from the beginning.

"Can we just take a step back," she says – it's meant to be a question but her tone has none of the necessary inflection. She's stating we're taking a step back.

"A step back from where?" I ask. "I've asked to speak to you so I can complain. You say take a step back like *you* organised this conversation and I'm trying to ambush it."

On-Call Psych is suitably rankled.

"When I came into the hospital, I was put on this drip. At no time was the contents of the drip explained to me – which is clear in my notes, I might add.

"So I've spent the last three days preparing myself mentally for death and at no point has anyone – not a single member of medical staff – discussed with me the fact that I might not actually be dying. You're a psychiatrist so you must have some idea as to the mental turmoil this has put me through.

"And the way I find out is because one of my visitors tells me. And I want to be angry that the Sister in question was happy discussing my health like that. But I can't be angry at them because I'm too grateful – as it's the only way I found out."

On-Call Psych takes a moment. It's one of those irritating pauses they do.

"Well I can't speak for all the hospital staff –" she begins. I cut her off.

"I'm not asking you to. I'm not asking you to do *any* speaking. I'm putting in a complaint and I want it to be investigated. Someone on *your* team made the decision that I didn't need to be on the psych ward. And because of that decision I've not received the mental health support I need."

On-Call Psych reaches into her bag for a file, opens it and leafs through scrappy notes until she finds a clean sheet of paper.

"I'm going to make notes about your complaint," she explains. "And then I'm going to take it to my superior for it to be reviewed."

I pretend to calm down at this suggestion, allowing her to go through all the points I've raised, making sure all the details are recorded. When she *thinks* she's finished, she stupidly closes her file.

I stare at the file. At her. At the file. At her.

"Is there something else you wanted to add?" she asks.

"Yes there is," I say before delivering my *pièce de résistance*. "I feel betrayed by the staff of this ward, and of this hospital. So I want to be discharged."

Her eyebrows shoot up for a split-second before she

composes herself. I'm guessing she's an on-call because she's newly trained: she hasn't reached the full psych poker face stage yet.

I then get the infamous psych nod – the one that says "I'm not agreeing with you, I'm agreeing with your right to ask" – and says she'll talk to her boss about this too.

"Can you write my request down in your notes?" I ask. "I want it recorded that I asked during this session."

She opens her file back up again, searches through for the notes on me and adds some scribbles to the bottom. I have no idea what she's written: she's already perfected the doctor handwriting that stops anyone from reading their notes upside down.

"How long will it take for you do get back to me?" I ask, adding, "I'm obviously very upset and don't feel safe *or* protected on this ward and don't want to remain here."

Her poker face fails again – what I've just said hits the nerve I wanted it too. I'd found the words "safe and protected" mentioned on a forum during my internet search.

"I'm going to speak to them now," she tells me.

Her voice is shaky, I'm sure of it. And I'm guessing that's why I'm dismissed back to my bed with an arm-wave, because she doesn't trust herself to speak. I leave the room as causally as possible as if I'm unaware of the abruptness of her dismissal. Then I lie on my bed simmering, waiting for a response.

A mere three hours later On-Call Psych reappears. This is the NHS equivalent of the speed of light. I know the person with her is her senior because he stands by the Nurses Station while On-Call Psych comes over to my bed. I make her work for it, pretending to be too engrossed in my phone to hear her speaking to me from the foot of my bed while she collects my notes.

I wait until she's at the side of my bed, gently touching my arm to get my attention, before I acknowledge her presence.

It's a shame the nurse this is all for is not here to witness it, but it's still satisfying to level out the playing field a little. I'm a little concerned our next conversation is going to be two against one, so I need to get all the levelling in that I can.

Thankfully, I've managed to fit in another trip to Costa this afternoon, so I have some coffee to help me through this. I go through the collection of Costa cups on my table, lifting each one and giving it a gentle shake, to find the one with something in.

While I'm going through my paper cup collection, On-Call Psych heads back to the Nurses Station and hands my notes over to her boss: Mr Big Guns. Coffee in hand, I climb off the bed and follow them both to the Not-Very-Quiet Room.

I listen to Mr Big Guns waffle on about hospital policy, ensuring patients get a high level of care, blah, blah, blah. Urghh. Well, I only half listen – and make no effort to conceal it. I don't want him to think he's getting one iota more of my attention than he is. I'm making it clear that I'm waiting for him to finish with the politics so we can have a conversation.

"Your colleague here," I say, nodding towards On-Call Psych, "asked me if I regretted what I've done. It's not about regretting it at this stage. It's gone beyond whether I regret it or not," I explain. My speech is measured. I try to make myself sound earnest. "When I first came in, I thought I was going to die, so I was in that mindset. I've only just found out I'm not, after *three days* of lying round waiting for death to arrive."

It feels far longer than three days. I find time difficult to measure at the best of times, and that's when I have varied days. Here I get to lie in bed and wait for mealtimes, wait for visits I then don't want. Every day is the same day. I am trapped in a Bill Murray nightmare. It might be only day four today, but it feels a lot longer.

"This isn't about me saying 'Yes, I want to live' or 'No, I don't want to'; this is about me attempting to come to terms with the fact that nobody told me that I might do. Not a single doctor on ward rounds bothered to ask how I felt about the fact I wasn't going to die."

I pause. I can hear my voice getting tighter. I need to take a breath.

"But what about the members of the psychiatry team who came to visit you?"

We've been in this room since forever, and it's the first question Mr Big Guns has bothered to ask me.

"*What* visits?" I ask.

Mr Big Guns opens my file. He flicks through my notes. I don't speak. I want him to see for himself that I've had *no* psych visits since being discharged from A&E.

"Ah," he says eventually. "It would seem that a member of the A&E Psychiatry team you saw felt you were stable enough not to have daily visits, so you were set up for request visits only."

The way he says "A&E Psychiatry team" suggests they are nothing to do with him. The way he delivers their decision suggests he disagrees with it.

"Request visits? And how was I meant to know I could get those? The only reason you're here now is because I wanted to complain – I didn't know anything about request visits."

I add this last point before he can suggest that me demanding to see someone equates to me asking for a request visit. I stare at him. He concedes with a half nod.

"So," I say, my voice calm again, "I guess telling me about request visits should have happened during the same conversation where I was told about the contents of my drip."

He snaps my file closed.

"I understand why you don't want to be on this ward," he says, and I know there's a massive "but" coming as he's conceded this far too easily. "But I'm not happy to discharge you right now."

He looks at me for a response. (On-Call Psych might as well not be in the room.)

"I understand that," I reply, "But I'm not happy being on this particular ward."

I purposefully mirror his language.

"Moving you would be difficult," he says.

"But not impossible," I reply.

Another half nod from him.

"I can't trust anyone on this ward," I explain. "Rounds staff aren't honest with me and nursing staff talk about me behind my back. Being on this ward is *negatively* affecting my mental state."

He sighs a deep sigh.

"As I've said, I'm not sure you're ready to be discharged from hospital, but I understand why you don't want to be on this ward. However, moving you to another ward is not an easy job. So I suggest we speak again tomorrow and we can either discuss a discharge plan or, if I don't feel we're ready for that, I will put in for a ward transfer for you."

This conversation has gone as well as it could. I knew I wasn't going to get discharged today, but I'm one step closer. There's no way they're going through the expense of moving me to another ward unless they absolutely have to, especially as I'd be marked as damaged goods – a patient being moved because of a complaint. Nobody would want me.

I give him one of his half nods.

Mr Big Guns shifts in his seat, which spells out to On-Call Psych that the meeting is over. As she stands up, so do I – I'm not being dismissed by her like last time. As the two of them mutter and faff with their notes, I squeeze past them and leave the room. It's only as I do this that I realise they'd sat down in a way that created a barrier between me and the door.

I'm exhausted. But I need to find some extra energy from somewhere: there are so many interim things to sort out. One thing I definitely need is clean clothes. If I'm going to convince Mr Big Guns I'm ready to leave then I need to look less dishevelled each time he sees me.

It means I need to speak to Alison.

17 lifebuoys

ALISON

I'm pleased to receive a text from Zoe asking me to bring in some fresh clothes for her because it means I have permission to visit. Well I *say* she asks. Typical Zoe, she just *informs* me that she requires my assistance.

I head to the hospital by myself. I don't go via Costa. I have my "serious" face on and I'm not going to let caffeine-related small talk derail me. Also, no free coffee will say everything to Zoe about the mood I'm in and how much shit I'm willing to take. (And the bag of clothes I'm carrying means I'm not technically turning up empty handed.)

My outfit isn't to "Tori purple dress" level but I've made an effort today. Even though I'm not yet ready to face work, I've dressed as if I am – giving a signal to Zoe that now she's not dying, the rest of us have to get on with things.

According to Tori, my boss is "making noises" about me still not being back at work. I'm ignoring her comments about this just as much as I'm ignoring my boss. So much has shifted inside my head over the last few days, I can't contemplate going back to work and dealing with the mundanity of it all.

I shove thoughts of Tori and work to the back of my mind and walk purposefully down the length of the ward. When I make eye contact with Zoe, I give her a tight smile – it's not what I planned, it's simply all I can manage.

Now Zoe is no longer dying she's used up her fair share of attention. For three days she was at the centre of everyone's thoughts. But now it's my turn.

"I need to talk to you," I announce when I reach the end of the bed. I'm not planning on getting close enough to give her even a perfunctory squeeze hello – and I'm holding her bag of belongings in front of me like a shield to protect me from having to.

"Not about when I'm getting out of here," she jokes.

It hasn't occurred to me that she'll ever leave the hospital, that I'll have to deal with Zoe back in the real world after all of this. But I have to ignore these thoughts – I need to keep myself on course.

"I have something to tell you that I've not told you before. It's not a confession as such, because it's about having never told you something. I've never set the record straight because I couldn't find the right time."

I pause.

"It's about James," I add.

As soon as I realise she's about to speak, I cut across her – "and it's not what you think."

I stay standing to talk to her. I don't want to sit down and get comfortable. There's nothing comfortable about this.

"When we met him on that night out, he told me he wanted to ask you out because you're stunning. But he thought I was funny and I'm the one he actually fancied. So he wanted to kiss me while you were in the ladies to work me out of his system."

Zoe looks a little stunned. She's used to being the one everyone fancies.

"Then, for some reason, you decided to start seeing him behind my back. I have *no idea* what he said to you to convince you to do that. And his story that *I'd* asked him out? Why would you believe that when you know I don't ask guys out? I get drunk and take them home."

I check out every inch of Zoe's face looking for some sign that she's starting to see the James situation from my point of view. I hate confrontation of any kind and if she misses any of this there won't be a rerun. From the uneasiness on the edges of her face, some of it is sinking in.

"And whatever it was he said to convince you, it damaged our friendship. Because you decided to trust *him* and not me."

I've been practising what I'm going to say, but that wasn't part of it, and it's not until those words fall out of my mouth that I realise I've been thinking them.

"And do you know what really hurts? He had a one-night stand with Tori. *Tori* for fuck's sake. Yet you *still* held onto the belief that I'd asked him out and he'd turned me down just so you could carry on going out with him."

I feel guilty for being so mean to Tori. But there's something so otherworldly about her that it's easy to believe she's never had a boyfriend, that she's never made that sort of connection with another human being. If James is willing to sleep with her then, I'm sorry, but there's *no way* he's going to turn me down.

"I don't know what to say," Zoe says.

Well, that's a first.

"But up until now, you've accepted that I can't stand the

guy. But then you end up in here and you get this crazy idea that I'm using the situation to hit on him again. What? Just because Tori thought it was a good idea we get you a coffee first? Going to Costa before coming to see you is somehow betraying you?

"Because you never go to Costa" – I wave a hand at Zoe's side table, which is littered with maroon takeaway coffee cups.

"But you were dying and needed James to be there for you. So I accept the fact that my *supposed* best friend was going to die hating me just so her idiot boyfriend could comfort her in her last hours."

She winces at the word "supposed" – although it's obvious to both of us that our friendship has been distorted completely out of any recognisable shape.

"But now you're not dying. And I want to know if James knows."

"No he doesn't."

"Good. Because I want you to get the truth out of James once and for all."

"And how do I do that?"

I've piqued her curiosity. I see a glimpse of pre-hospital Zoe.

"I want you to ask him to come and see you. And I don't want you to tell him you're going to live. Let him still think you're dying and tell him that clearing the air with me is important, like a dying wish. Tell him you *know* he asked me for a kiss – and ask him to admit the truth."

Zoe's face is a mixture of horror and awe.

18 armbands

TORI

I'm back beside Zoe's bed. Annoyingly, I couldn't share my confession earlier because Alison and Ruby turned up. And then the nurse told me Zoe needed tests; that I should come back in the afternoon.

It's just given me more time to perfect my story. I've been thinking about why people choose Beachy Head. It's because the world feels both vast and empty at the same time. You're reduced to being an ant on the landscape. Your lack of significance is spelled out to you – it makes it easier for you to jump because you realise how little you matter. I know all this from being up there, from watching that woman jump.

Usually when you jump you do so alone – or I'm assuming you do anyway. The time to be by yourself, and to be so small, is part of the process. And why the woman I watched kill herself was angry I was there.

Witnessing someone jump, having to use the phone box to report a death, waiting for the police to turn up – and the ambulance too, although I have no idea what they thought they were going to be able to do – it gave me a feeling of what it would be like to be the person ready to jump.

I'm pretty sure I understand the process this woman went through enough to explain it to Zoe as my own thoughts. It's not empathy as such, more just understanding. I'm not able to put myself in her shoes – and the idea that people are truly capable of doing that is nonsense. But understanding is enough, and it's something all good liars must be able to do.

I don't think she heard my final shout. And if she did, her death is still not on me. No adult can blame a random teenager for their final actions. (Not that she can, seeing as she's dead.) I've had to carry her death with me all these years and that is *almost* as if I was up there ready to kill myself.

The worst part of that day wasn't looking down at the beach and struggling to see the essence of something that was once human. It wasn't calling the emergency services and being quizzed as to why I was there and what I saw. (I told them I saw movement on the cliff edge when I was about 100 yards away.)

No, the worst bit about that day was the hysterical show my mother put on for the police officers when she came to pick me up from the station. It was the second time I'd been brought down from the cliff top by the police. And she obviously didn't believe the "I like going up there to clear my head" any more than they did.

From that day, until my mother got bored and found a new drama to consume her life, I was treated *as if* I'd been contemplating killing myself. So I have a good understanding of the whole process, especially the bit where people treat you differently afterwards.

All this flashes through my head as I sit next to Zoe's bed. She's looking healthier today, but it could just be the clean clothes. For the first time since she arrived, she's not in black.

I take a deep breath and she looks directly at me.

It's now or never.

"I have a confession to make."

SAYING THE WRONG THING

Tori watched her mother arrive at the police station and take centre stage. Tori doubted there was anyone in the whole station with any doubt whatsoever that her mother wasn't actually "mother of the century". Tori hoped the officers sitting round sifting through paperwork and drinking congealed tea hadn't fallen for her mother's act. Her mother was an okay mother: not the worst, but definitely nothing special.

Watching her mother, Tori made a mental note to always be low-key with any stories she needed to fabricate in the future – histrionics made the truth seem less likely. Although this particular mental note couldn't help her right at this very moment as she'd already said the wrong thing.

A female police officer had given her a cup of hot chocolate from the machine in the hallway without asking her what she'd like, just assuming Tori was too young to want to drink tea, which irritated her. She then asked her lots of questions about what she'd seen and how quickly she'd called 999.

Tori was frankly getting a bit bored with it all because it was the same questions over and again. In her frustration, she snapped, the same way she would do at school if a teacher had put her under too much pressure.

"What do you want me to say? That I was there when she killed herself? That I spoke to her? Or that I planned to kill myself only I didn't because I saw her jump? Is this what you need to hear in order to stop asking me the same things? Because I've already given you my answers and you don't seem happy with them."

The female officer reacted as if Tori had slapped her across the face. She stood up and left the room. Left on her own, Tori assessed the room. No tape recorder and, from what she could tell, no cameras. So whatever she said wrong in her rant she was pretty sure it hadn't been captured.

Tori knew at this point that the best response was to go quiet, to withdraw, to wait until her parents showed up – as she would do in school after any outburst. So she waited. And after watching her mother's bizarre performance in front of the police officers, she watched her mother being taken into a side room very much like the one she was in.

A few minutes later, her mother swooped in and scooped Tori up in her arms, before storming out and screeching as to why her *poor* daughter had been left by herself at *such* a difficult time.

Tori watched the female officer try to take her mother to one side again, but her mother was having none of it. No, she wanted answers right now, here, in the centre of the station, not in some quiet corner where the needs of her daughter could be pushed to one side.

Tori recalculated her mental "mother assessment" and decided that her mother probably scored higher than "okay" after all.

TORI

"I have a confession to make."

Zoe nods.

"Beachy head," I let the words sink in, know the connotations attached to them will fire up in her brain, prepare her for what I'm about to say, just in case she thought my confession was anything else.

"So passé right," I say with a half-laugh.

"Why Beachy Head?" she asks.

"It was near where we holidayed."

"And why didn't you jump?"

Her eyes bore into me.

It seems an obvious question to ask and yet I'm still shocked by her bluntness. In fact it's the *very* question I would ask. But I would get shunned for doing so. Where's the pretence of having a superficial conversation?

Other people aren't meant to do this. Unless they are parents, police officers or counsellors. And they do it when they don't believe your story. I haven't even told mine yet!

Have I overstepped too far too many times? Does that mean I don't get the benefit of the doubt now? Is she really questioning my story before I've even told it?

Thankfully, I have the right ammunition: I have details; liars are vague.

"It was really windy," I tell her. "And I wasn't sure if I jumped that I wouldn't be blown back against the cliffs and somehow not make the drop. The last thing I wanted was to survive and be injured, maybe paralysed.

"My parents didn't know where I was. So if I'd made it part way down, I could have been stuck on a ledge for hours, or days even, waiting for the police to show up, maybe dying a slow death from dehydration. I wanted to be dead, but I didn't want to go *through* death."

It *had* been really windy and after the woman had jumped, one of the reasons I'd needed to venture to the edge and look down was to make sure she'd made it all the way to the beach – that she was a "splat" on the ground as she'd hoped, rather than trapped part way down, injured but very much still alive.

"Did you write a note?" she asks. I guess she's curious about this because she didn't.

"No. I didn't – in case I couldn't go through with it. That would have meant returning home to the note," I explain, stealing the woman's story as my own.

"But why Beachy Head? Why *that* spot? Miles of cliffs and yet you choose the same spot as everyone else?"

I know how to answer this – I asked the woman who jumped the same question.

"Because it's patrolled. My body would be found and it would bring my family some level of closure. And as I didn't write a note, it would be the only closure they got."

"But why no note?"

"Because I didn't know what to write."

This last point makes sense to Zoe.

"Putting it down on paper – that's the tough bit," she says, sighing.

Phew. I seem to have Zoe back on side.

"So what happened next?" she asks.

"It started raining, so I stood in the phone box waiting for it to stop. And that's when a police officer spotted me," I say, pulling from a different memory. "They insisted on taking me back to the caravan we were staying in and my mother was hysterical. Didn't let me out of her sight for a year."

Zoe smiles wryly. "I should be grateful I don't have to worry about what my parents think."

"They're both dead?"

"My mother is. My father, well, he might as well be."

Wow. Lying about planning to kill yourself is one thing.

But going through with it and *not* telling your father? That's something else.

"Oh, so did you write a note for him?"

A black look descends across Zoe's face.

"You didn't write a note, did you?"

"No, but —"

"And both your parents are still alive?"

"Yes, but —"

"So why is this any different when it's just one parent?"

How have I gone from being on the same side as Zoe to being her combatant again in so few words?

"Because of this" — I wave my arms around to signal her being in hospital.

"This?"

Oh my God, this is hard work!

"You're a talking dying person. When someone is dying, people travel across the country to rush to their bedside, to say goodbye. You've decided to give that gift to Alison and James, but not to your father."

"So…?"

"So that's why I asked if you left him a note. Because he's not here; just Alison and James."

"And you and Ruby."

"And me and Ruby?"

"Yes you and Ruby, both of you, at my bedside *without* an invitation. Why *are* you here?" — I can hear her pointed look in her voice.

"I was with Alison when she took the call. So I came with her to the hospital."

"And?"

"And what?"

"Well, *where* is she? If you accompanied Alison?"

"Well, that wasn't today."

"So if you're not here to *accompany* Alison, why are you here?"

My throat is so dry I wouldn't be able to speak any words if I had any to say. I can hardly tell her I'm here because I want Alison and James for myself. Better I pretend not to know why I'm here.

"Seriously, why are you here?"

"Why am I here?" – I hear a deep voice behind me answer. It's James. I've *never* been so happy to see him. "Because you sent me a text."

"James!" I gush. I throw my arms round him. I feel him freeze under my contact but I don't care.

"Thank God you're here," I whisper to him.

I pull away from my hug.

"Well it looks like you two have a lot to chat about," I say brightly, giving both of them my best smile. "So I'll leave you to it."

I cannot get off the ward fast enough. I'm not sure I want to tell another lie ever again.

TELLING THE TRUTH

The counsellor Tori is sent to questions everything Tori says more than anyone has ever done in her life before. At the beginning of the first session, she told Tori that their sessions together were a "safe space" where it was okay to say whatever she felt, that she needed to work through her feelings in order to come out the other side of what she'd seen.

But the counsellor *didn't* want the truth: she wanted to hear what she *expected* to hear. And after one or two false starts, where Tori started to hint at how she was feeling about the who episode (or more, how she *wasn't* feeling because she didn't really *feel* anything), Tori went back to saying what she thought people wanted to hear.

At first, Tori told her that she'd looked down onto the beach, but the counsellor seemed horrified she'd be that curious, so Tori adjusted the story and explained that she meant that she looked down in her dreams, that she had a recurring dream where she looked down and saw the woman's body on the beach.

The first thing the police and the ambulance crew did when they turned up was to look down onto the beach, so Tori *failed* to see why this was unusual behaviour. But she'd learned a long time ago that asking *why* her behaviour wasn't okay was deemed far more freakish than the behaviour itself.

So with each shocked look, Tori adjusted the story, just as she adjusted the version of herself she showed to the world. She thought it strange that adjusting the story counted as lying, but adjusting herself was considered good social skills.

But Tori couldn't adjust the contents of the story enough, or fast enough, to stop the counsellor "having words" with her parents.

TORI

Not only did James offer me the most beautifully timed escape route, but it's now perfectly feasible for me to loiter in the hospital grounds waiting for him to come out under the pretence that I'm checking he's okay. Well, that bit isn't a pretence – I want to know if he's okay or not. And I want the answer to be "No".

The most obvious place to wait is Costa, but I cannot face yet another coffee (and I refuse to part with good money in return for a teabag in some hot water) so I decide to wait outside. The front of the hospital ends abruptly on the main road. Land is expensive in London and they've built on every last morsel.

The pavement out the front is narrow: there's no space for loitering. So I find myself an awkward corner outside A&E and wait for James to appear. I don't have to be particularly patient as I see him coming out of the main exit around five minutes later. I wonder if the brevity of his visit is a good thing or not – and it seems like the perfect opener.

"Wow, that was quick," I say as I reach him.

He seems surprised to see me. Was waiting for him not the social norm here?

"We have less to talk about each time I visit," he says with a shrug.

Hmm. I know fewer words being spoken and having less to talk about are not the same thing. And the mood Zoe is in, she can say *a lot* in five minutes.

Weirdly, I've talked to Zoe more in the past few days than she's ever entertained before – although I ran out of my extra minutes today.

"But she text you? So she *wanted* to talk?"

"Yes she did. But it's like the 'Zoe show' in there. With each bombshell it becomes more and more about her – and not the people this is *supposed* to be for."

Bombshell? Some sort of fight? I have to know what this is about.

"Pint?" I suggest.

It's the perfect gambit. And he accepts.

He directs us through a side street that takes us via the hospital car park to a pub that someone decided to paint bright yellow. The colour is a misnomer: inside it's a typical

London hipster pub. Very little has been spent on most of the décor: the crumbling concrete floor and disintegrating bricks are the perfect juxtaposition to the one wall of luxurious wallpaper.

A hipster pub unfortunately means overpriced beer, even for London. And the seemingly clever names above the door are often at the expense of a decent wine list. Normally, I'd take one look at a place like this and push to go elsewhere, but there's no way I'm giving James an opportunity to change his mind, so I mentally prepare myself to suffer Chardonnay with lemonade.

It turns out they have a proper wine list which even includes a viognier, so I indulge myself.

Is this a good omen?

He pays for the first round after ordering a pint of Volden Summer for himself. Someone else paying is lovely, but makes me feel uneven. Hopefully we'll be here long enough for me to buy the second round and my equilibrium can be restored.

I can't tell if he's paid automatically, so used to being with his girlfriend, or if it means the barriers have shifted. Why can't people just *say* why they are behaving in a particular way, you know "I thought I'd buy the first round seeing as we're friends now" or "Oops, I'm so used to buying the first round because I'm usually with Zoe".

Why are we expected to guess?

James chooses a table on the side of the pub with wallpaper. I'm relieved. The "deconstructed" side of the pub has chunks missing from the plaster. Just looking at it makes my skin itch.

"So what happened in there?" I ask. "You know, the 'Zoe show'."

He winces.

Damn, I shouldn't have added that last bit. I said it to build a sense of camaraderie. But it seems that *he's* allowed to mock her, but I'm not.

"Just Zoe being Zoe."

I'm not happy with his non-answer. But I'll take that over him defending her. I need to get him to talk, so I sip at my wine, hoping the silence will break him.

"What about Tori being Tori?" he asks.

What on earth is that meant to mean?

"What have you been up to?"

Do I thank him for the translation?

Usually, I love talking about me. But not right at this minute.

"Oh you know, the usual."

He takes another mouthful of beer. He's waiting.

"Lots of internal events on at work that I'm overseeing, which is keeping me busy. And I've just been fitting that around visiting Zoe."

"How come you're visiting Zoe? I didn't realise you two were close."

Have they been talking about me?

"I had a period of feeling suicidal when I was younger. I felt it might be helpful to Zoe to have someone who understood."

I've replayed my conversation with Zoe over and over in my head. I've just given James the answer that failed to materialise in my brain under Zoe's spotlight.

"Oh, she didn't mention that."

So they *did* talk about me. Should I be flattered?

"She probably felt it to not be her place. It's not the thing one goes around sharing."

I'm grateful she didn't. Admitting to feeling suicidal at

some vague point in my past is a much easier lie to live with than the one where I sat at the top of a cliff and considered killing myself.

"Agreed. There are some conversations that shouldn't be shared."

This is like talking to the Cheshire Cat, all these riddles.

"Does that include your latest conversation with Zoe?" – I risk asking outright because I cannot abide any more of the sidestepping.

"Yes it does," he replies.

We go back to drinking in silence – but this time I'm grateful for it. With the conversation going round in circles, I'd rather just enjoy my wine, the rich flavours like popping candy, waking up my mouth. I'm enjoying the resulting brain lubrication too.

"That's going down quickly" – he gestures to my glass.

If there's one thing I loathe it's those drinking alcohol judging others for drinking it a fraction faster.

"I feel like I've earned it," I say, my voice slightly harder than I intended.

He takes a few large gulps of his pint.

"Me too actually," he grins.

He's forgiven.

"I think I drank too much the night we ended up in bed together though," he admits. "I can't really remember anything about it."

While I'm relieved James is such a tart he can forget who he's slept with – because it means he covered my lie – I have no intention of having to fabricate a whole story. Not after the Beachy Head mess.

"I think we need another drink for this," I say, grinning.

I need James to have more than one beer swishing round

his brain so I can be vague on all the details – where we met, where we ended up, what happened during the deed itself, what happened the morning after. He needs to leave here no more clear of the events of our evening together than he is now.

It's a shame we didn't walk up to the Stormbird, famed for its super-strength drinks they recommend you purchase in thirds. But I make the best of the situation by buying James the strongest beer they have on tap – a 7.5% Hepcat Double IPA – ignoring his request for another pint of Summer. (I'm annoyed the aptly named "Souls of Mischief" is just 5%.)

When I put his drink down in front of him, he frowns at the unexpected amber tone of the liquid.

"The Summers off," I lie.

It takes him a few sips to adjust his palate, but soon he's drinking as if it were water. And I talk generally about what it's like to pull in a city as big as London, watching for his pint go down before we get on the specific topic of me and him.

The extra juice in his second pint hits the spot and soon he's up ordering a third round, passing his glass across and asking for "whatever he had last time". The barman signals to the correct pump and I nod.

The irony of the situation doesn't escape me. I'm not getting James drunk so I can take him home and sleep with him; I'm getting him drunk so I can pretend I told him about the time that I did.

He reaches peak drunk part way through pint number three – that point where your brain and mouth no longer work together and where everything is hazy. He starts saying things as soon as the words pop into his head, rather than processing them first. (Something I do without the alcohol.)

"I think if I had the chance to kiss you again then I'd remember our evening together," James says, letting out something that's half way between a snigger and a giggle.

As we've been drinking, he's been shifting his chair closer – and he's now sitting next to me, not opposite.

I decide that I'm not going to kiss him, but that if he kisses me then that's different.

And he does.

I can taste the bitterness of his drink and his lips are puffed up from the boozing too, but once I've adjusted to the sensations I'm not expecting, it's a kiss worth melting into. It's only the shout of "Get a room" from one of the lads on the next table that pulls us apart. James looks at me lustfully before something switches in his brain and his look of desire is replaced by one of horror.

"What the fuck am I doing?" he asks.

I reach out to touch his arm, but he shrugs me off. That's fair enough: he's feeling guilty. I know I just need to guide him through it, make him see that it's okay.

"Hey," I say softly, "Don't be too hard on yourself. It's an emotional time for you at the moment – for both of us – and we're bound to act out of character."

I try the arm again, and although he tenses, he lets me.

"Zoe is dying. How on earth are you meant to process that?" I ask, before answering, "well, I guess this is one way."

"She's not though."

"What?"

"Dying. She's not dying."

"What?" – it's like all my other words have evaporated.

"That was part of today's bombshell: she's going to survive."

I'm reeling.

Not just from the kiss. The kiss is bad enough. But I need to make sure James *never* tells Zoe about it because she'll tell Alison. And Alison will hate me for it. And with Zoe back on the scene to reclaim James, I'll be left with nobody.

Oh fuck.

Fully automated

When it first opened in 1968, the Victoria Line used an automatic train operation system, making it the world's first full-scale automatic railway. Once the train doors closed the driver simply had to press two "start" buttons — and as long as the track ahead was clear, the train would drive itself to the next station.

The original system was replaced in 2012 with a more sophisticated automatic train operation system, which has increased the capacity on the line from 27 trains an hour to 33.

Tori wished people ran on systems similar to the one in place on the Victoria Line. She would love to be able to press "conversation" buttons and for the conversation to flow as soon as the path was clear; to press Friendship and Relationship buttons and for the people chosen for those roles to fall into place.

19 swimming aids

ALISON

"He told the truth" – that's all the text from Zoe says, but it's enough to make me crumple to the floor, weeping. I had no idea how much I'd been carrying the burden of the unsaid issues between us until they were out in the open.

Ruby hears me crying and comes rushing in to comfort me, shushing my attempts to tell her why, insisting that I cry it all out of my system. Only once my sobs have turned into ragged breaths is Ruby willing to look at the phone screen I'm shoving in front of her.

She reads the screen and smiles.

"Do you want to go back in and see her?"

I shake my head – the thought seeing her twice in one day makes me weary.

A weight has been lifted off my shoulders, but when I look around me I'm not sure what it's left: the weight had become central to our friendship. I still haven't processed Zoe's suicide attempt either. When Zoe stares back at me from her mountain of pillows, the person behind her eyes is a stranger.

I've always liked facing life as part of a duo. And right now Zoe is the thing I'm facing and Ruby is firmly back in the role of wing commander.

Ruby has made lunch, but I can't eat, so I just pull at the crusts on my sandwich and sip my tea, letting Ruby's chatter keep me company.

"I wonder if we'll see James at the hospital?"

"No we won't."

Ruby looks surprised I'm so sure.

"Because we're not going."

"He might be there if they're still trying to work things out," she says, ignoring my comment. "Now that she's not dying, everything has flipped."

It hadn't occurred to me that Zoe would want to stay with James.

"Do you really think she'd want to carry on seeing him?"

Ruby shrugs. "The only way we're going to find out is if we go and see her."

"Okay, fine!"

I've somehow managed to talk myself into another visit.

When we leave the flat I stop resolutely at the first bus stop. I don't care the bus from Brixton Hill to the hospital isn't particularly frequent: I have no capacity for faffing.

Ruby's chatter continues for the length of the journey. I'm grateful. Silence would let me go down the rabbit hole of thoughts. Listening to her tell me about another shop in Whitstable that has agreed to sell her work stops my head from exploding.

Once off the bus, I match my breathing to our matching footsteps as we approach Zoe's ward. But then my footsteps are solo. Ruby has stopped. She's talking to Latoria – the nurse who told us about Zoe. I can't fucking believe it.

The mental explosion Ruby's chatter was keeping at bay erupts.

I storm over to them.

"Really?"

I choke on the word. I'm so upset and so angry that Ruby can't just keep in step with me as far as Zoe's bed. I don't think I'm asking too much. The nurse looks at me with a mixture of concern and bemusement.

"Someone doesn't have to be in one of the beds to be a patient here," she explains in a musical lilt that I place as Jamaican. "I'm just checking up on how Ruby's flare-up is doing on her cheeks."

Ruby's cheeks?

I stare at Ruby's face. As I move from side to side, the harsh strip lights highlight a raised area on each cheekbone that would be fitting for rosy cheeks on a cherub. As I lean back again, the light no longer casts a sheen across her face, and they disappear.

The nurse points to a similar raised area on the back of her own hand – only hers is also red and look brittle, as if they would crumble if touched.

"We've been comparing lesions. I don't get to cover mine at work because of hygiene regulations – although sometimes the reactions I get from patients suggest they think I have a hygiene problem!"

I stare from cheeks to hands to cheeks. Except for the colour, they are similar.

"What *are* they?" I ask.

"Sarcoidosis," Latoria says in a voice that implies I should know this.

Sarcoidosis. I've heard that term before.

"Your mum?" I look at Ruby.

She nods, but averts her eyes. She won't look at me – as if looking will tell me things that she's kept from me all these years.

"It's far more of a concern for black people," the nurse explains, dragging me out of the thoughts that flit around my head like butterflies – ideas about what Ruby has been hiding, memories of visiting Ruby's mum in hospital, of Ruby staying over at mine yet again, of my mum setting up the Z-bed permanently in my bedroom, clearing a space in my drawers so some of Ruby's clothes would fit.

"When white people get Sarcoidosis, they eventually fight off the infection. But those of us from the Caribbean and certain parts of Africa, when we get it, we can't. When we get Sarcoidosis it's for life. And sometimes it kills us."

So just as I find out Zoe is not longer dying, you tell me that Ruby might be?

"When?" I ask. "How long have you known?"

The part of my brain that's not obsessing about Zoe is whirring at 100 miles-an-hour trying to work out what this all means. How ill is she? Could she be dying? Is this why Zoe's death hasn't fazed her?

Ruby won't look at me.

"If I carry on standing here I'm not going to have any break left," the nurse says, her voice thick with forced joviality. And that leaves just two of us.

"Your cough," I say.

It's a dry hacking cough. Not such a big deal in itself, but serious when it's a symptom of Sarcoidosis.

"Yes, my cough," she responds.

We fall silent as the million things that need saying zip back and forth between us silently, building a wall between us.

"I don't know what to do," I tell her. "I don't know what to say."

20 lifeguards

Of course you don't know what to say,
When it's not your problems you shy away.
Of course you don't know what to do,
You can't put yourself in anyone's shoes.
You just don't understand empathy,
Such as why I didn't go to university.
I couldn't go because of my health
But you could only think of yourself.

RUBY

I think this but I don't say it. We're about to have the conversation I've been waiting to have ever since Alison got in touch and I'm not going to ruin it by stamping all over it just because my emotions are running high.

"It's why I didn't come to university," I explain. "I used my mum as the excuse. I was scared if I told you I was ill that you'd drop out of university too. I didn't want you to do that."

She starts crying.

"You should have told me. Instead you deserted me."

"I deserted you? You deserted me! You fucked off to university and that was it – no letters, no phone calls, no visits. Is that why you did it? Why you cut contact? You were deserting me because I deserted you first?"

"I'm *never* first," she sobs.

"What?"

"I had you, but then you put your mum first. So I worked really hard to get Zoe. But then she put James first. It's never me. Why am I never first?"

"People *do* put you first. I'm here aren't I? I came up to London the minute you called me, even after you ignored me for *five* years. People put you first all the time – you're so used to it you can't see it. You come across as so fragile that people are naturally protective of you. People put you first all the time – just not *all* of the time. And it's the times they don't that you notice.

"You're right though, I didn't put you first when I didn't go to university; I put *me* first. I wasn't well enough to be away from home. And I needed my mum there – she was the only person who understood what I was going through. I'm *allowed* to put me first.

"And I put you second. I *lied* to you about staying home for my mum, didn't tell you I was ill, because I wanted you to be able to go to university without feeling guilty."

She looks subdued.

"I know it might sound harsh, Alison," I say softly, "but anyone would think it was you in the hospital bed, not Zoe. You've got me here, you've got Tori here –" Alison throws me a glance "– okay you might not be thrilled she's here, but she's still here for you.

"Zoe chose Paracetamol so she could say goodbye to you. I thought that meant she had something specific to say, but it could just mean that she wants you there. I don't know. I don't know her."

She shrugs.

"You're meant to be her *friend*," I stress. "Pinprick or not, you're meant to be there for her when things get tough. You two need to have a *proper* conversation. And While I'm not sure what that entails now she's not dying, she knows the truth about James, so you have somewhere to work from."

I take a deep breath.

"And I can't do this for you," I add.

She looks at me wide-eyed. That look doesn't work on my any more.

"You need to go and have that conversation with Zoe now. Just the two of you. And I'm going to head back to the flat."

I put my hand out for the keys. She reluctantly hands them over.

SOUNDING THE ALARM

High Street was the main high road running through Whitstable town centre. At its western end, where Alison and Ruby's primary school was, it changed into Oxford Street. And about 100 yards down the road from the school, the train tracks crossed over the road via a bridge. The trains that headed east, out towards Margate and Ramsgate, passed through without any fanfare; but those that headed west, towards London, sound their horns.

As kids, Alison and Ruby had noticed only *some* trains blew on their horns, but they were in their final year of primary school before they sussed out it was only trains travelling in *one* direction that ever bothered. Curious as to why, the pair investigated – and discovered that about 50 yards west of Oxford Street there was a pedestrian-only level crossing. The trains were sounding their horns to make sure people had time to get out of the way.

After Ruby was diagnosed with Sarcoidosis – the same condition that was eating away at the life of her own mum – she used to walk down and stand by the metal gate in front of the crossing. There was a sign from the Samaritans urging people who may be suicidal to get in touch, but Ruby didn't need it. She liked it there because she liked standing *so close* to death. It signified how fragile life was: how it could be taken from you in an instant.

Each time Ruby heard of a death on the crossing – there was one around once a year – it would make her muse about her own mortality and how she was happy to still be alive. She *needed* the crossing as a reminder.

In 2015, Ruby found herself standing on the tracks. But it wasn't an attempt to kill herself. She had a placard in her hands and she was campaigning to keep the crossing open. Three out of the four most recent deaths had been suicides – people who needed this crossing as much as she did, but for the opposite reason.

In some ways they were her kindred spirits. They stopped her feeling quite so alone.

Without Alison by her side, Whitstable was all Ruby had left. She would walk as much as her health would allow, wandering down Joy Lane to Seasalter beach in the dark. The road's dim streetlights made the area seem *anything* but joyful, particularly the strange graveyard of neglected ice cream vans half way down the road. Each time she visited, she would venture further into the field they sat in, daring herself to look into the windows of the most decrepit.

They weren't particularly scary – but Ruby needed them to be.

Late at night, what little light there was from Joy Lane would cast an eerie glow across the houses and over the water behind them. The only other light was from the offshore wind farm over towards Herne Bay, the warning lights transforming the beautiful sweeping angels into red-eyed demons.

Ruby wondered if the sweeping arms of wind turbines cause enough turbulence to create tornadoes on the other side of the world. She liked the idea that Chaos Theory was real because it meant life wasn't worth planning. And if a butterfly flapping its wings could cause a storm, then imagine the damage a whole wind farm could cause?

The walk to Seasalter was one of Ruby's favourite walks during the day too, but on these occasions it would be to gawp at the grand house announcing themselves via a curved gravel driveway or an overly conspicuous burglar alarm. These people, the rich ones, were as far removed from her as Alison was.

It was an area where the wooden "to the beach" signs (the ones hung with forced nonchalance from pieces of distressed rope) were replaced by 3ft high sailboat replicas that loomed from large stairway windows (windows whose main use seems to be to showcase said sailboats).

At the far end of Seasalter, the train tracks sliced a wound through what was otherwise the perfect upmarket neighbourhood. Even though Ruby knew the tracks where there, she would allow the rush of each train to surprise her.

During the day, this far from the harbour, the offshore turbines were so far away you had to squint to check they weren't a figment of your imagination. Out here, they felt as out of her grasp as Alison was.

On the walk back from Seasalter via the beach, the path

played a trick, curving away from the beach and cutting through the middle of a scruffy caravan park that Ruby was always surprised to see. She knew it was there – her surprise was that it was *still* there. She knew one day she'd get here and the old caravans would be replaced with the plastic-coated scaffolding that announced a postmodern build was in progress.

Regeneration. Apparently it was happening because "half of London" was moving to Whitstable. But it didn't feel very London to Ruby. And it certainly hadn't brought Alison back.

It was a stupid place to build really. The row of four-storey terrace houses that were already here, their chocolate box colours a nod to the nearby beach huts, were permanently covered in scaffolding as their owners attempted to fight back at the sea air eating away at their homes.

The walk out to Seasalter by road took Ruby past the Rose in Bloom pub. She would think about all the drinks she and Alison never had there. They hadn't been able to appreciate the serenity of a secluded pub garden when they were younger. And they'd not been friends since.

Ruby hadn't been for a drink there with any other friends either. The ones she'd made since Alison had left were mostly superficial ones connected to the gallery-style shops and boutiques that stocked her jewellery to sell. Friendships that could manage one or two rounds in the local in the evening but were never strong enough to venture out of the comfort zone of the high street.

Whenever she did the walk to Seasalter, Ruby would glance up at the old fingerpost road sign on the corner of Canterbury Road. The one that informed her that London, that Alison, was just 55 miles away.

RUBY

I was already in my pyjamas when Alison got back from the hospital. I could tell she wanted to talk, but I told her I had a headache and needed an early night.

I was drained mentally and physically – and just couldn't face another gossiping session until the early hours. I should have been out like a light, but I struggled to get any sleep.

I wake up early, even though I'm still shattered. But I accept it's time to get up.

I miss my teenage years when I could languish in bed for hours, snoozing in and out of sleep, allowing a whole morning to pass, not getting up until the time on my alarm clock was "pm". My body doesn't let me do that any more.

I head into Alison's bedroom to see how she's doing. Her bed is empty. I listen out for her useless shower but can't hear it, so I pad along down the hall to the bathroom where I'm met with an open door and yet another empty room. The lounge is currently my bedroom, so the only room left is Zoe's room.

Even though I've been using Zoe's mirror to do my make-up I'm overwhelmed with a sense of uneasiness about venturing into her space. I knock on the door, not wanting to catch Alison unawares. There's no answer, so I open the door slowly, peeking round it. Another empty room.

I do another circuit of the flat.

Where the hell is she?

There's something unnerving about being in someone else's flat when they're not there, especially when you don't have a key so you're effectively trapped inside until they return.

I now regret not talking to Alison last night. Has she gone

back to the hospital without me? Am I going to be stuck here by myself all day?

The lounge is a decent size, but the room feels smaller, the walls closer. I decide to open the windows only to find them sealed shut. I know I'm being ridiculous, but I can feel the panic rising in my chest. I can't describe just how relieved I am when I hear keys working their way through the three different locks on the front door.

Alison wearing a red dress I instantly recognise. It's one of her "feel good" dresses – something she wears when she's making a statement to herself. The red dress eases my anxiety away. Whatever the reason for her early trip out of the flat, it's a good one.

She holds pieces of orange cardboard out to me. I take them. They are train tickets. Day Returns. London Stations to Whitstable.

"We need a day for us, away from Zoe," she says. "I tried to think of somewhere we could go in London, but nowhere would work. I realised we needed to escape London."

Escaping London. Thank God.

I don't argue. I simply get ready while Alison makes breakfast – cinnamon and raisin bagels that she'd bought on her way back from the station. She toasts them under the grill so they don't need to be squashed into the toaster. She lavishes them with butter and plonks them down on the lounge table alongside big mugs of tea.

After breakfast we head out, walking in an easy silence down towards Brixton station. There's a determination about Alison today that I know it's her trying to make amends. She knows she's screwed up, and is owning it, trying to fix it. And while it's nicer if people don't screw up, making amends is the next best thing.

When we get to Brixton tube station, I'm taken by

surprise when Alison carries on walking past the entrance. She takes a right down a side street (I follow her lead) and then we work our way up through a snaking walkway created from pale blue railings. At the top, we find ourselves on the platform of Brixton station.

I had no idea Brixton had normal trains too.

The train service we get on is a regional service – the sort that missed the last vehicle upgrade because they don't stop anywhere important. The type of train you wouldn't want to get all the way to Whitstable because it might not make it. We don't pick up any great speed between frequent stops. Some stations are little more than the concrete slabs at Brixton, others with more about them – four platforms instead of two, buildings that look like they might hold waiting rooms – but none of them are places I've ever heard of.

After stopping at Shortlands, Alison stands up and walks to a particular door on the train. I join her. As we start to pull into the next station, she positions herself as if about to start the 100m sprint.

"Get ready to run," she says. "Left. Up the stairs."

The doors open and she's off, her dress hoisted up above her knees so she can take the steps two at a time. I follow her. We run across the bridge above the platforms and down the next set of steps, just as a train pulls in. I hear the end of the automated announcement "– Broadstairs, Dumpton Park and Ramsgate". It's our train.

There are plenty of seats free on the left side of the train, which means we'll get the sea views arriving into Whitstable. Even though I live there, I still get a thrill when the tracks pull close to the edge of the coast near Seasalter and you get unexpected glimpses of waves washing over pebbles.

Alison doesn't follow me into the carriage. Instead she's

standing in the train doorway. She's inside the train, but with half of her body blocking the door. From her vantage point she's able to cast an eye up the steps that we came tearing down moments ago. I realise someone else is doing the same route we did, just at a slower pace.

The doors start to beep, the signal for Alison to push against the door with all her strength. The doors give up temporarily and relax back to the open position before trying again. This time, as the doors push against Alison, the woman reaches the bottom of the steps, realises what is going on, and jumps onto the train. Alison allows the doors to close behind them.

They share polite conversation – thank you, no worries – before Alison joins me, a big grin on her face.

"Pay it forward," she says to me.

"What?"

"If you're to survive in London, you have to have a list of the little things you do – like holding the train doors – as gestures to strangers. You hope they pay it forward and do their own random acts."

Alison smiles at me but there's a sadness there too – the city has taken its toll. I wonder how I'd have survived if I'd moved there, whether it would have changed me, hardened me, or if I'd still fight back in the smallest of ways like holding the train door for a stranger.

I want to forget London, Zoe, the whole mess, want to leave it behind. I rack my brains for something to share. Some kind of gossip. Not much happens in sleepy seaside towns. Then I remember.

"Did you hear about Becky?" I ask her.

Becky's wedding was the last time we'd all seen each other, but I'm pretty sure the two of them didn't bother keeping in touch.

"No?" Her eager tone suggests she too wants to talk about anything else but the last few days.

"She's left him, Rob, for his best mate."

"What? The blonde idiot who was his best man?"

"Yep."

"God, I hated that wedding."

"Me too."

"She whinged at me because of my streaky tan. But I'd tried using a sunbed and it hadn't worked."

I look at her quizzically.

"Seriously. On my third visit, one of the staff came into the booth with me to double check I knew how to *turn* the sunbed *on!*"

We both find this funnier than it should be and dissolve into giggles. We're trying to regain our composure when the guard comes through checking tickets.

"Are you okay, you two?" he asks in mock concern.

"Yes," I say.

"It's the high of escaping London," Alison adds.

The guard nods.

"Sea air should do you both some good," he says, noting Whitstable as our destination.

I don't bother telling him it's where I live. I may not like London very much, but there's still something nice about pretending I'm the person I planned to be before I fell ill, living in London, making the occasional trips home.

ALTERNATE REALITY

Although in different halls in the first year, Alison and Ruby decide to share together in their second year. They picked Brixton. It was just a bus ride away for university for Alison and a longer but no more difficult tube journey to King's

Cross for Ruby, and a chance for her to live as part of a black community – to get a sense of the world her parents belonged to before they moved to a coastal town that was 98% white.

The first year of Ruby's course was an exploration of the various crafts involved in jewellery making, where she discovered an affinity for working with non-precious metals. True to her word to her mum, she used her second year project to trace the history of the cameo brooch, using the carving method to create a collection of pieces.

For her final year project, Ruby decided to create a fusion of cultures, a representation of her family, bringing together the hand-beaten copper techniques from Trinidad and the world of her mum, the Nigerian gold and beaded jewellery of her dad along with the Art Nouveau and Art Deco elements that defined a shift in British jewellery 80-100 years ago – and that were very much a part of the British culture she'd always known was her own and that she'd come to own while living in London.

Her mum was well enough to come to the final year show where the students displayed their work, standing proudly beside the glass cases filled with the rich gold and copper colours and stylised lines of her daughter's work, while they had their photos taken. Nobody was surprised when Ruby was awarded a First.

Except of course none of this ever happened because Ruby fell ill.

Instead, it was time off college, the pretence of accompanying her mum to the hospital when it was the other way round, of appointments to the hospital's dermatology department to be shown how to look after her skin and how to use camouflage make-up. Ruby was pleased her darker skin would make it easier to hide her inflamed cheeks. But as dark as she was, she wasn't dark enough to hide her embarrassment at having to practise with different shades of beige. (That's all the hospital had.)

RUBY

When we get off the train at Whitstable, we turn right out the station instead of following the crowd left. We walk alongside the blue railings that remind me of the walkway at Brixton station, and walk through the unassuming roads that take us up to Harbour Street.

Skipping Whitstable town centre completely, we turn right along the promenade in the direction of Herne Bay, passing in front of the small café that has changed its name *again*. We walk down by the pebbled beach. To our right, the shallow grass bank gives way to rows of beach huts, which give way again to a more dramatic grass verge known as Tankerton Slopes.

According to one of the plastic signs provided by the council's tourism team, this area is one of two homes of a rare moth – the Fisher's Estuarine Moth – that can be seen in September and October. I'm guessing it's *very* rare as I wasted many an evening down here as a teenager trying to spot one.

It's strange to me how butterflies are seen as beautiful creatures and moths are a nuisance or scary. The only real difference to the eye is the colour. I wonder if black people are like moths – that we would be seen as beautiful butterflies if only our skin was a different shade.

"I wonder how much life passes us by unawares," I say to myself.

"The moth!" Alison grins.

I smile. She's remembered. I've bored her with the stories often enough.

For the years Alison was living up in London, I was *very* aware of her life being lived without me. But I didn't come up here very often to think about it – this part of the coast carries too many heavy memories.

I look out to sea, staring out at the forlorn, isolated structure that, once upon a time, was the end of Herne Bay pier. It can be seen from Whitstable and Tankerton beaches, even though Herne Bay is five miles away, because it's so far out to sea.

"Do you remember when we were younger –" I start.

"– we used to talk about hiring a boat and rowing out to the old pier head so we could climb aboard," Alison adds.

We never did.

"We had so many plans," I say.

Most of them never amounted to anything. Many, like our pier plans, were just the puffed up talk of teenagers. But the plans to move to London had been real.

Alison is on the same train of thought. "Do you think you'd have liked London?"

"The university course, yes. The rest of it? I'm not too sure. I'm feeling battered and bruised from just a few days."

I breathe in the clean air. I'm glad to be back where I belong.

Part way between Whitstable and Herne Bay we pass a caravan park. I'm pretty sure Alison's body stiffens. It's such a tiny movement that it's almost imperceptible – it's more that I hear it and feel it than see it. I wonder if this is where she stayed?

"It's strange to think of so many people coming down to where we live for their holidays," I venture. "I wonder what it's like to stay here."

I get *nothing* from Alison. I've guessed correctly.

It takes us about two hours to reach Herne Bay pier. It would have been quicker for Alison on her own, but she notices me get out of breath easily and so stops to say "Hello" to every dog we met, giving me sideways glances to check I'm okay before we continue.

I purposefully talk very little, giving Alison the space to fill me in on her conversation with Zoe if she wants to. I'm beginning to burn with curiosity, but I can tell she's still digesting whatever they talked about, so I have to hold my tongue.

Not everything is about talking.

It's just a few miles between Whitstable and Herne Bay, but they are worlds apart. Whitstable has a moneyed feel to it, the Horsebridge Centre, the art studios and Whitstable Oyster Fishery restaurant which all live on the edge of the main beach a far cry from the rundown arcades on the front at Herne Bay, corrugated roofs obscuring the lawns in front of the beautiful Georgian terraces behind them that hint at a wealthier history.

Whitstable is in the estuary, protected by the Isle of Sheppey and the south-east coast of Essex. Herne Bay, only slightly further east has nothing between it and the Arctic Circle. So when northerly winds blow, they are particularly biting here. Alison is Whitstable – protected by those around her. Being at her side, being Herne Bay, does not give you the same protections.

Build your life on *one* friendship and you can find yourself out in the cold.

The latest pier facelift has done away with the ugly pavilion building that covered the far end. Now the pier is mostly an open wooden platform with small sheds, reminiscent of the nearby beach huts, scattered along it selling the usual seaside tat alongside a mix of food stalls that remind me of the ones I've just left behind in Brixton. There are a few kiddie rides too, including a helter skelter, but none are large enough to stop you enjoying being surrounded by the sea.

We reach the end of the shortened pier (it's an unwritten rule that you always walk its full length) and stare out at the sea. From this vantage point, the decaying structure of the isolated pier head has a foreboding air to it.

"It would have been so stupid to try and climb aboard," she says.

"Stupid and dangerous," I agree.

"We've done stupid things though," she adds.

Is she about to tell me about Zoe?

I look down at the waves lapping at the pier structure below me. My grip tightens on the railing in front of me. I know my fingers are turning white without looking at them. I should have known better than to look over the edge. From this angle, there are no long edges in my vision, not even my peripheral vision, and I need edges to stop myself from spinning.

Without edges, there is only the long drop to water. Without edges, the drop cannot be determined and this therefore infinite.

My knuckles hold on tight. My body is on the safe side of the railing but my mind is not. I'm freefalling, freediving, holding my breath underwater as I plummet the depths. And then I'm back above water, looking down, seeing my own reflection as a cold blue face looking back at me. Except it's not me. It's a face floating on the surface of the water, attached to a body that bobs between the pier scaffolding.

"Look," I say, my voice barely a whisper.

But Alison picks up on my fear and turns to me.

"What is it?"

"Look," I say again, this time a little louder, signalling with my head towards the water, my hands unable to let go of the barrier.

"Oh fuck!" I hear Alison cry.

I cannot move. But I hear her dump her bag at my feet. And I hear her take off at speed, her running footsteps stomping along the length of the pier.

"Drowning!" she cries out between breaths. "Someone's drowning!"

I hear all this but I can't see it. I can't move from my spot.

The woman in the water looks a blue-ish white. She's floating in the water face up − her eyes and mouth are closed. Her clothes balloon and billow around her. She looks strangely peaceful.

Then I hear splashing and a fully clothed Alison comes into view, lifebuoy in tow. It seems that her cries were lost on everyone because she's making a rescue attempt alone. I watch her struggle to push one side of the lifebuoy down and scoop up the woman in it. She manages to get the edge underneath the woman's head and then pulls one of her arms through as well. Alison is tiny − this woman is easily twice her size − but she has found Herculean strength from somewhere and is now towing the woman back to shore.

I then hear more splashing and people shouting "Call an ambulance" and "Call 999", but I still don't move from my spot. I watch a plastic bottle dance across the waves where the woman's body had been.

I realise I need to get to Alison. I let go of the railing with one hand, carefully crouch down and feel for her bag, my eyes not leaving the sea. When I find the strap, I pick the bag up, lift the strap onto my shoulder, and grip the railing again. I edge along, sideways like a crab, towards the shore, the smallest of steps, my eyes focused on the sea, my hands skimming over the railings, the paint crumbling as parts of it melt away in the salty air.

By the time I've reached the end of the pier, the ambulance has arrived. Two paramedics dressed in green are with the woman I saw floating in the water. Her clothes are now clinging to her, her frame shrunken. I look for Alison but cannot see her. Then I notice a flash of red sitting in the doorway of the ambulance, partly wrapped in a blanket. I recognise her slouch. I've *never* been so happy to see her.

I want to rush over to her, but I'm still unsteady on my feet. As she sees me coming she gets up and walks towards me. We embrace, the wet of her dress seeping through her blanket and into my jeans and T-shirt.

"Vertigo?" she asks me.

I nod.

And I remember *this* is why I'm friends with Alison. Because she risks her life to save a stranger and understands when I freeze and can't help. Yes she can be selfish, but I'm wondering right now if that's because the rest of us indulge her. So many of us treat her like a little sister and then we're annoyed when she seems spoilt.

We stand together by the ambulance, still half embraced, watching the paramedics strap the woman to the gurney she's on, then pick up between them and carry to the tarmac. They then raise it up on its wheels and steer it to the back of the ambulance.

The woman is still very white, but her eyes are open, moving.

Alison has saved her life.

21 lifebuoys

ALISON

"We need to have the conversation."

"The conversation?"

"Yes, *the* conversation." I stand firm – she's not just going to get away with an apology about James. "You said you couldn't leave a note. So there must have been *something* you wanted to say that you couldn't write down."

"No," Zoe says.

I don't believe her. Oh to be five years old again and allowed to shout "Liar, liar, pants on fire!"

"No? Then why all the song and dance?"

"Because it wouldn't have mattered *what* I wrote in a note, it wouldn't have been enough. It could be the simplest language and it would be overanalysed, each sentence disassembled. Goodbye is a really simple thing to say face-to-face, but impossible in a note. I *just* wanted to say goodbye and I couldn't find the right words."

Can I believe this?

"I was stupid to think it would work," she explains. "That

you'd come to my bedside upset but ready to listen. That I'd be able to explain I needed to say goodbye to you and that we'd have some kind of special moment."

I'm aghast. "You romanticised your own death."

It wasn't a cry for help. She *really* wanted to die.

"So what changed your mind?"

She hesitates.

And I realise she hasn't.

SOMETIMES YOU DON'T TELL

"I've lost it," Ruby says in a voice of syrupy innocence.

Alison watched in awe while Ruby spent a good five minutes searching her bag for her homework. The homework she *hadn't* done.

Alison had owned up at the beginning of class, blurting the words out as soon as she reached the teacher's desk. She wanted to get the confession over and done with because it was burning a hole in her brain.

But Ruby was pretending she'd done it and simply couldn't find it. Alison *knew* it wasn't true. But Alison also knew there were times when you *didn't* tell on someone.

And this was one of those times.

ALISON

I hope the woman under the pier wanted to be saved. A week ago, and this would never have occurred to me. But as the paramedics check my vitals and come back with an "all clear" I have the sense of relief that we're *supposed* to feel when we're told we're okay.

But not everyone feels relieved.

It's clear that Zoe *didn't* want saving – she didn't want to be told she was going to be okay. She's angry with the doctors for making the decision to treat her instead of giving her the palliative care she wanted. How do the rest of us (the majority, surely) who want to live, who sometimes have to fight to stay alive, how do we process the news that someone else would rather not?

And if Zoe is planning to kill herself the minute she's discharged, should I try and stop her?

What would a real friend do?

The ambulance is ready to take the woman I've saved to hospital. I get to temporarily keep my blanket: I'm asked to take it to my GP so it can be returned to the right paramedic team. I'm assuming there's a label on it somewhere but I don't have the energy to look.

We get a taxi on the seafront without any fuss even though I'm soaked through. Maybe the taxi driver witnessed what happened or he could just be used to shipping soaking wet people places, but he's happy to get a large plastic bag (a fittingly-named "bag for life" from Sainsbury's) out of the boot for me to sit on.

"What was her name?" Ruby asks me now we're securely fastened into our seatbelts and the taxi is taking us home, the throbbing engine helping soothe my nerves – the nerves that are only firing up now, once the danger has passed.

"I don't know."

It didn't occur to me to ask. I have no idea who she is or why she was in the water. But those things don't matter. All that matters is whether or not she *wanted* to be saved.

When we arrive at Ruby's I don't even realise we're here. Even though I know she's moved out of her mum's, I'm still expecting the taxi to stop there.

Ruby's flat is above a shop. It feels cramped because of

the higgledy boxes of jewellery supplies that cover most of the floor. She's also carved a studio area out of the corner of the living room by the front bay window. It's small, but not *London* small: each room has enough space to carry out its main function – a double bed fits in the bedroom, a full-sized bath in the bathroom.

I take a shower while Ruby digs out some clothes for me to wear. It feels good to have water pelting against my skin with such force – I need to get rid of the musky smell of the sea.

Afterwards, wrapped in a towel much warmer and fluffier than the blanket it has replaced, I'm feeling cleaner than I have in a long time.

Ruby has found me tracksuit bottoms with a drawstring waist that I can pull tight enough to make sure they stay up. She's also given me a vest and T-shirt, the vest to take the place of my bra and give me some semblance of modesty.

I'm beyond tired. I curse myself for buying Day Returns instead of Saver Returns – because the £20 saving means we now can't crash at Ruby's. We set off very slowly to the train station, Ruby carrying my handbag as well as the bag with my wet clothes in. My arms jangle discordantly by my sides, too tired to stay still.

Ruby has to wake me when our train pulls in at Whitstable. My normal sleep pattern has been a mess over the last few days, but I'm amazed at my ability to fall asleep on a hard wooden bench on the platform. Sleep finds me again as soon as we're on the train, with Ruby giving me a second nudge as we get close to London.

"We missed Bromley South, sorry," Ruby tells me.

I watch as we glide silently through Battersea Park station between the new high-rises that partly obscure the view of Battersea Power Station, and then over the Thames to Victoria station.

All these people living their lives, not touched by Zoe's suicide attempt, not touched by woman under the pier. There are *too many* people here to make each life matter.

I need to leave London.

This thought is a recurring one – I just hear it louder today. Living in London is like playing Jenga with your life. The population is so transient.

Nobody can afford to buy, so your whole social network is built upon renting. Then someone decides to leave, so they can buy elsewhere. And then another one leaves. And then another. And even if your social network doesn't completely collapse, you're left with some serious gaping holes.

Together, Zoe and I had formed the foundations of our social group. We'd rented together for so many years, and always in the south-east of the city so, together, we were other people's stability.

After Zoe confessed she'd been seeing James behind my back, I saw my foundations shift for the first time. How long would it be before Zoe and James moved in together? I didn't have a backup to fill the gap she'd leave. In a panic, I knew I had to get away myself, even if just for a few days.

London hadn't felt like *my* city since I got back.

The day after I arrived at the caravan park, I'd walked to Sainsbury's to get supplies and bought a box of dog biscuits on a whim. I'd then passed a few lazy hours sitting on a bench staring out to sea and feeding the biscuits to each passing dog, chatting about nothing to their owners. And I'd watched a couple of boys take impromptu lessons on how to skim stones from their dad – one of those completely useless but extremely satisfying hobbies, like being able to do tricks on a yoyo.

The slower pace was welcoming and I'd mused over the possibility of leaving London. But the slopes at Tankerton seemed so small when compared with the size they were in my memory, and it made me nervous. After London, would anywhere else be big enough? But that evening the weather answered my question: there was a storm and under the flashes of lightning, the slopes grew to be the size of mountains.

Near the caravan park I'd noticed signs for the Oyster Bay Trail and Saxon Shore Way. I wasn't sure if they'd always been there, but it made me realise there were parts of the coast I didn't know −that there was still some living to be done.

As we get off the train at Victoria, the noise hits me as a wave of heat. I'm lightheaded and unsteady on my feet. Ruby puts out an arm to hold me up.

"I need to leave London."

Not only because I'm ready to move on. But because if I'm not going to tell anyone that Zoe is going to kill herself (and I don't think I can), then I don't want to still be here when she does.

All the miles

Each Victoria line platform is 435 feet long. The Victoria line itself is 13 miles long. The total length of the London Underground network is 250 miles.

London to Whitstable is around 60 miles. It's just 1 hour and 13 minutes on the high-speed trains from St Pancras station and around 1 hour 26 minutes on the stopping train from Victoria.

But for Alison, 60 miles is another world away. And it's the world she's decided she'd like to be a part of again.

22 armbands

ZOE

Yesterday, I got acquainted with my ceiling. I was waiting for Mr Big Guns to show up, but he never made it. I expected Alison to visit. Even though I'd shared the *new* version of my goodbye story with her I thought she'd come back – especially as I'm currently still alive. It's not actually goodbye yet.

James was right; Alison did deserve better than having to hear my real reasons for not leaving a note. I hope my explanation worked. If she didn't believe me, she didn't let on.

So I spent yesterday staring upwards, finding patterns in the ceiling tiles, and formulating the next part of my plan – and deciding who should find my dead body.

There were two people up for the job. James and Tori

"Doubt that the stars are fire, doubt that the sun doth move, doubt truth to be a liar..." I didn't need to finish Hamlet's poem to Ophelia because the whole point is to *keep* doubting the things that you can't prove are true. Urghh. I'd believed James and Tori far too easily.

I'd already unceremoniously dumped James for lying about Alison. (I enjoyed pointing out to him that, yes, she *did* deserve better.)

Was his behaviour deserving enough? I didn't think so.

And what about Tori?

She was the person who tricked Alison and James into getting coffees *after* telling me Alison would want to speak to him, and after *promising* to make sure to send James straight to the ward if she saw him first. All complete and utter lies.

Why though? Why did Tori want me to think Alison was after James? What was she trying to achieve? She thought I was dying, so my opinion would only matter in the short term. What was it that she was trying to get me to do?

Aah! It's the magicians trick, the misdirection technique – *The Comedy of Errors*. She wanted me watching Alison so I *wasn't* watching her.

Tori claimed her strange behaviour at The Happenstance was because she recognised James, but he didn't recognise her and she felt awkward about it. Well the awkwardness I bought because Tori was permanently trapped in pre-teen ineptitude. But if she still fancied him, if the one-night stand wasn't enough – well, that would fit better.

And it would also explain why she'd been texting James constantly ever since I'd given her his number. (Poor James. I *almost* feel guilty about it.)

But I wasn't sure her lies were enough either, even though I'd starting seeing cracks in her awkwardness that were exposing a manipulative side to her that's more sophisticated than I'd expected.

So yesterday, I came up with a big fat nothing.

But today, as I wait for Mr Big Guns – whom I'm assured is *definitely* visiting me today – I notice a pattern in one particular ceiling tile slightly to my right, above the point where Tori sat on my bed on her first visit. It looks like cliffs.

Did Tori go up to Beachy Head to kill herself? Or was it another lie?

Her story felt a little off, but I *want* to believe her. Because if I don't, that means she's willing to lie about it. And what sort of person is that?

I want to be dead. But a person who *pretends* they want to be? That's really fucked up.

So that's decided then. Whether she's lying or not, she's the one to find me.

If she *did* think about taking her own life, she can cope with finding me. And if she *didn't*, and her story is all lies, then finding my dead body will be karma.

NOT THE WHOLE TRUTH

Couples don't always know when the rot starts to set in, so nobody should expect the kids to know. But that didn't stop Zoe from obsessively trying to work out why her parents' marriage failed.

She had the distinct advantage over her siblings of being aware that something at home wasn't quite right months before the announcement. It meant she focused on watching the culprits while her sisters mostly cried.

Old enough to notice: not old enough to understand. Zoe had no comprehension that the two adults on either side of a failing marriage might not know when the rot started to set in. So when her parents explained their separation in vague terms, wrapped in the cotton wool terms people often use to try and protect their kids, Zoe felt like she was being lied to.

Zoe and her siblings were not given a choice about who they lived with – her parents had already made the decision it was best for them to live with their mother in their current home. Their father moving out was meant to offer the minimum of disruption.

But with no concrete explanation to process, Zoe decides that their father moving out is *proof* of his crime: the divorce must be his fault. Which made sense to Zoe. He was the one going out to work every day, which gave him more opportunity to behave badly away from home.

This explanation fitted well with the anger that she carried for her father deep down inside her belly that she didn't really understand. She had nightmares about him and a pale woman dressed in blue. Had her father been cheating on their mother? It seemed likely.

Zoe now had a very clear idea of how lies could lead to the worst injustices. And when she discovered someone had lied to her, she liked to punish them the way she would have liked to punish her own father but wasn't allowed.

ZOE

I'm still waiting for a visit from Mr Big Guns when Alison turns up.

I know she's going to tell me something big before she opens her mouth to speak. Her body language gives her away: all disjointed limbs and jumbled nerves. Ruby stands guard near the Nurses Station to give Alison courage.

I know what she's going to say before I hear the words.

"I'm leaving London."

She says it so simply, yet the words hold so many complicated and conflicting messages. In leaving London, she's walking away from me. But *I'm* the one who betrayed our friendship; she has every right to walk away. And if my suicide attempt had been successful, it would have been *me* leaving her.

"How soon?" I ask. I err on the side of being practical when I start overheating emotionally. (I'm glad I'm sitting on top of the bed covers.)

She half-shrugs. I see embarrassment ripple across her face. She's already started packing.

"What about your room?" Again, nice and practical.

"I don't know," she admits. "Do you want to keep the flat?"

We've lived there just over a year, keeping our heads down around the 11-month period in the hope that we wouldn't get any new paperwork from our landlord. Without a notice period served or a new tenancy to sign, we'd automatically move onto a rolling tenancy, giving us better rights to stay and more flexibility to leave. Our stealth had been rewarded.

We could theoretically hand in our one-month notice and be free of the flat within weeks – which I'm guessing is what Alison wants.

"You could always get someone to take my room? Maybe James…?"

In the last 48 hours I've discovered I'm not dying, admitted to my best friend that I'd betrayed her (as well as admitting it to myself), and tricked the person who is now no longer my boyfriend into admitting he'd lied to me from the very beginning of our relationship.

"He lied so…"

Alison seems pleased. I'm pleased that she's pleased. It's the least I could do.

"He's free if you're interested…" I joke.

"I'll leave him to Tori," Alison replies with a pointed look. So she's has worked that out too.

And my plan falls into place in front of my eyes.

"I suppose Tori could take your old room."

Alison looks as though I've punched her in the stomach. She grips the bedframe for balance.

"Tori?" she says. There's more than just a question in her voice, there's disbelief too. I've made it no secret that I'm not a fan.

"Well, if you're moving out straight away, I need someone to take the room while I decide what to do next," I explain. "And it's not like people are queuing up to take the keys out of your hand."

I try to sound flippant, but there's an edge to my voice – an edge that's *always* there if you listen closely enough, one of the many manifestations of the anger that has consumed me.

Alison picks up on it and hardens herself against it.

"Fine, okay," she says, releasing her grip from the bedframe. She seems further away. I didn't see her take a step back, so maybe it's just because she's pulled herself up straight, but there's extra distance between us.

"I'm meant to be seeing her this evening. Getting an update about work –" there's scarcely concealed contempt in the second point: Alison hates her job "– so I can let her know if you like?"

Perfect. I don't have to give the acting performance of a lifetime when I ask her myself. And Tori will be too caught up in Alison moving back to Whitstable to question it.

"That would be great, thanks." I give Alison a warm smile. I get a watery one in return. She might not have ended our friendship as definitively as I ended my relationship with James, but there's no doubt in my mind that it's over.

I get one final nod. It's like a full stop at the end of our friendship. Then she walks towards the doors at the end of the ward without a hug or a final goodbye.

Instead of following her, Ruby walks over to the side of my bed.

"We took a trip to Whitstable yesterday," she explains.

"That's why you didn't visit. I assumed it was because I was no longer dying."

I get a strange look. Oops. That's obviously not how normal people think.

"We saw someone floating underneath the end of the pier, lifeless," she says. "Alison saved them."

"Did they want to be saved?"

"I don't know," she says slowly. I've just ruined whatever point she was making.

She tries again. "This is about Alison. Alison *needed* to save her."

Ruby squeezes my arm. A goodbye. There's more warmth in the gesture than when Tori did it – something else I add to my list of anti-Tori experiences.

I watch Ruby walk the length of the ward for what I know will be the final time. Alison is long gone. They're not just leaving the ward; they're walking out of my life.

Although my heart aches, it's better this way. I've now said my goodbyes to the two people I chose a slow death for – not in the way I planned, but the slate has been wiped clean.

Alison doesn't know about my suicide kit hidden amongst the stuff I rescued from my mother's house. Separately, they are innocent items – a helium canister, some plastic tubing, a bag fastened with twine – so I didn't bother getting rid of them.

I didn't bother sorting my belongings before my overdose because I didn't mind the thought of Alison going through my things, maybe even finding something she wanted to keep as a memory of me.

This time, I'm going to sort it all out first. There's *nothing* of mine I want Tori to have.

I suppose this is the point where Portia would ask me to show mercy.

"It is twice blest; it blesseth him that gives and him that takes."

Urghh. No, I'm sorry, Tori. No mercy for you.

Where's Elizabeth?

The Elizabeth line — the name for the new Crossrail service — is making waves by not being on the tube map yet.

Although the first section of the line is not due to open until December 2018 — with the line fully opening in 2019 — it is London Underground tradition to add the line in advance of completion as a hollow line marked only by a dotted outline.

Yet Elizabeth is still missing from the map.

And if you're wondering where Beth is. Well, she hasn't arrived yet either.

23 swimming aids

ZOE

I'm wearing one of the outfits Alison brought in for me. Navy harem pants and a light pink T-shirt. I asked her to pack clothes that would resemble loungewear and she's done a good job. I've spent 45 minutes on my make-up. I look like I'm not wearing any. I just look like a healthy version of myself – and the sort of person who would wear light pink.

I'm waiting for Mr BG to *finally* show up. He didn't come to see me yesterday and I'm hoping that's because he wanted to delay discharging me by 24 hours. Fingers crossed my meeting with him today will be my final session before they send me home. Psyches rarely talk in absolutes though, so I'll only believe it when it's written in my notes.

Your world shrinks when you're in hospital. From ward rounds and visitors to your meals, everything is delivered to your bedside – so the extra 24 hours have been especially long ones.

Trips to Costa have become the highlight of my day,

especially when Faye is working – which is most days – as I get to chat free from all the politics of my bedside.

Unfortunately, these trips mean being shadowed by my guard. I find it somewhat amusing that the person who, in my post-overdose paranoia, I suspected was watching me, was, in fact, watching me. I think it's a colossal waste of NHS funds, but I'm on 24-hour watch because I'm not on a psych ward.

My first guard – the woman who was pretending to read (but who never turned any pages) – was initially replaced by a woman who wears religion on her face, her epidermis saturated with piousness. But I now have a new shadow: a black guy that's so skinny I'm wondering if he's an imposter, escaped from the anorexia ward.

I've not asked my new guard to escort me to Costa because I don't want to miss Mr BG. They don't wait for you if you're not here, even if *they* are a day late.

It means I'm positively craving caffeine by the time Mr BG arrives, carrying a Costa coffee cup. Just seeing the maroon cup produces a Pavlovian response in me. He holds it out me to make it clear it's mine.

Thank fuck.

A few gulps confirm the coffee is bog standard strength, but it will keep me going until I can go out and get one of my own.

"Shall we?"

I follow Mr BG to the Not-Very-Quiet Room.

"You drink a lot of coffee." He says. It as a statement but looks at me in a way that tells me he wants me to confirm what he already knows.

"More than anyone else I know," I reply. I can do idle chitchat if it helps me get discharged.

"And you find it calms you?"

I haven't been so thrown by a seemingly innocent comment since the doc on the ward rounds mentioned I was in King's.

"Yes, it does."

"Caffeine is a powerful drug," he explains, but not in the voice of someone about to preach to me how bad it is for me. "It's one of a number of stimulants that can help increase your dopamine levels. It's why we use stimulant drugs to treat people with dopamine deficiencies."

He pauses. He's waiting to see how I respond.

"So you think I'm self-medicating?" I ask. "Trying to raise my dopamine levels?"

"I think it's a theory worth testing."

Gotta love a psychiatrist. Never just give a simple "Yes".

Mr BG is holding some leaflets in his hands. I'm guessing they cover whatever these dopamine deficiency disorders are.

"Low dopamine levels are linked to a number of conditions," he explains. "But the one I think you might have is Attention-Deficit Hyperactivity Disorder."

ADHD?

I miss-swallow in shock, coughing up coffee, the bitterness splurging through my nostrils.

My choking stops my comeback from being snappy, so I add extra sarcasm to compensate.

"Oh yes, I'm a seven-year-old boy running round school terrorising my classmates. Oh no, hang on. I'm not. I might not have been a model child at school, but I'm someone with GCSEs, A Levels and a degree – all passed first time. No re-sits."

I wait for an explanation. And I don't expect to be kept waiting long, seeing as I *apparently* have attention issues.

"The 'H' for hyperactivity relates to internal hyperactivity within the brain," he explains. "We used to believe that boys had ADHD and girls had ADD – Attention-Deficit Disorder. But when we took a closer look, we saw there was also a crossover area, where boys and girls had symptoms for both."

"We? As in you *personally* carried out the research?" I ask.

"So we trialled the drugs," he continues as if I haven't spoken. "We gave the drugs that worked on ADHD symptoms in boys on girls with ADD and on those with a mix of symptoms. The drugs worked for all combinations. This would suggest different variances of the same condition."

All he's getting from me at the moment is a raised eyebrow.

He continues: "So research then looked at why girls didn't typically show hyperactivity, and we discovered they did – internally. It simply manifested itself differently in external symptoms."

"Right. So I have hyperactivity... but not really? Look, I'm grateful for the coffee, but this all sounds like madness. I mean, is this some kind of plot to keep me in hospital? Give me a crazy diagnosis so I'll stay in for treatment?"

Mr BG gives me the "psych stare" – the one they use when they want to sigh or roll their eyes but they're not allowed.

"I can't just *give* you a diagnosis. But I'd like to send one of my colleagues down to go through the test with you."

I don't speak. I sip at my coffee, pretending to consider his suggestion. I want to say "No" but that's not going to help me get out of here. I know I need to say "Yes" – my stubborn streak is just holding out saying it until the last minute.

"Both suicide and suicidal thoughts are higher in those with ADHD than those without," he says. He thinks I simply need more convincing. Bless.

"The drugs we use to treat ADHD are very effective for most people," he adds. "This is a diagnosis that could significantly change your outlook on life. I think it would be worth being tested."

A minuscule flame lights up from somewhere inside me, creating a tiny glimmer of hope. The various antidepressants I've tried have made no discernable difference to my state of mind and I've never been offered anything else.

Maybe a diagnosis would be worth it.

LIKE CAGED ANIMALS

The worst time to be sitting outside the headmaster's office was at lunch, when all the teachers would walk past to go into the staffroom and every single one of them, without fail, would look each child up and down and sigh.

It was enough to make some kids shrink in fear. But not Zoe. She found it irritating that they bothered sighing. The sigh was their way of giving their opinions, which meant they thought their opinions mattered. It didn't.

Zoe found herself sitting outside the headmaster's office at least twice, if not three times, every week. She did her schoolwork and she didn't get into fights, but she was just unable to stop herself from telling people exactly what she thought. And these people included teachers. And dinner ladies.

The dinner ladies were the worst because they wouldn't bother even trying to get to the bottom of what was going on before deciding who to send inside. They could also send you in for the full lunch break, which Zoe thought was incredibly unfair. Sitting down inside for the whole of lunch would also mean she had pent up energy all afternoon, which would increase the likelihood of her finding herself sitting on the same wooden bench just a few hours later.

The worst dinner times were when it rained and Zoe and her classmates would be trapped inside their classrooms like caged animals. With the calories and sugar highs coursing through their bodies, Zoe's classmates would turn into the very creatures they were being treated like, the noise reaching deafening levels. It would make Zoe scream. The noise of her classmates would overwhelm her and the only way she knew how to combat it was by drowning it out with noise of her own.

On those days, being sent to sit outside the headmaster's office was a blessing.

It was on days when she screamed, or other days when her behaviour unnerved the teachers, that they'd call her mother in to school. But Zoe's mother never came: instead she'd tell them that it was *her* job to discipline her daughter at home and *their* job to discipline her at school.

Zoe thought it was awesome that her mother never came in because teachers used it as a massive scare tactic. In fact, Zoe had once gotten into trouble when a teacher threatened her with this very ploy and Zoe had responded, "Well, you can *try*."

Zoe knew she should keep her opinions to herself (as she was told at least once each lesson) but once the ideas had formed in her head they were bursting to get out. Holding them in made her uneasy because she couldn't swallow them down. It was easier to speak out and face the consequences.

ZOE

I'm relieved to discover the main test for ADHD is a tick-box exercise. The psych conducting the test seems impossibly young. He explains it would be best if my mother could give feedback regarding the questions about my childhood.

I wonder, if she were alive, if she'd humour him and his questions, or if she'd distance herself in the same way she did at school. At the time I thought her refusing to come in was really cool, but now I recognise it's because she didn't want to have to deal with me when it wasn't "her turn".

"My mother died last year," I explain. "And there's a very good chance, if she were alive, that she'd tell you to do your own job."

That sounds more harsh than I mean it. But it's difficult to realise negative things about a parent who's dead. You have no way of talking to them about it, getting angry at them, them explaining, maybe even apologising.

"Her death is not the reason I tried to kill myself," I add. "And I'm not in contact with my father."

So we go through the questions without any support from my parents.

I start off with no intention of being diagnosed. (My flame of hope burnt itself out about 30 seconds after Mr BG left.) But each time I'm posed with a scenario and asked if I can think of examples in my own life that would fit, my brain is flooded with them. I know before the scores are counted up at the end that I have ADHD.

My official diagnosis is an "Axis 1" diagnosis, whatever that is, and I'm "combined subtype". There's some DMS or DSM code on the end, but by the time he got to that bit of the name, there are too many words to remember and my brain had stopped listening. Which I'm sure is very ADHD of me.

The psych walks me back to my bed and picks up my notes. He carefully adds my diagnosis to the front section of my file, his handwriting neat and precise below the scrawls of various colleagues. The NHS has yet to wear him down to the point where he struggles to hold a pen.

I want to tell someone about my diagnosis and Faye is perfect. I'm also in much need of a coffee.

I dig my purse out of my bag and stand impatiently waiting for my new bodyguard to notice I want to leave. (I've worked out the best way to deal with them is to not speak to them directly.)

When I reach Costa, Faye isn't at the counter. I feel nauseous. But then she stands up: she'd been crouched down underneath the coffee machine. A wave of relief washes over me. Now I've binned my friends and boyfriend, Faye is my temporary replacement. She starts making my drink without being asked.

"I found out today I'm allowed as much coffee as I like" – I try to sound jokey and light-hearted.

"Really?" She sounds genuinely interested. But I suppose, like me, she doesn't get that much decent conversation to help the day pass.

"I've been diagnosed with ADHD."

Faye stops making my drink. The look on her face is one I'm not expecting to see: understanding.

"You're just like my friend Beth."

24 lifeguards

FAYE

Before I met her, the patient who drank rocket-fuel coffees seemed a bit like an urban myth. Once I'd met her, seen how well she looked, my curiosity as to *why* she was in hospital had piqued. Trying to work out why helped pass the time. So I chatted to her about everything and nothing each time I served her, playing detective, trying to glean what information I could.

When she openly shared her diagnosis with me, I was so thrilled that I'd blurted out Beth's name. And then one sentence led to another and then another and I found myself promising her that I'd ask my friend to visit.

Beth. My friend Beth. The person I haven't spoken to since I deserted them while they were in hospital. God, the only reason I know about her ADHD diagnosis is because Olivia messaged me to tell me. It seems strange that it's Olivia, the timid one, the one who almost *apologised* for her friendship, who is the person who is our glue, the one determined to keep us all in touch.

I'm not sure Beth is going to be thrilled that the first time she hears from me in months is to ask her a favour. So I'm going to message Olivia first, get her to soften the blow.

But I have to do this. Because there's something about this Zoe girl that reminds me of Beth – and it has underlined to me just how much I miss her.

And because if I help Zoe, however indirectly, it hopefully goes some way to negating my behaviour towards Beth.

25 lifebuoys

TORI

Now that I'm going to be sharing a flat with Zoe, I should be *more* comfortable about going in to see her. But I'm overwhelmed with nerves. Until I can see my Paul Smith and Alexander McQueen statement pieces hanging up in what is currently Alison's wardrobe, I'll be waiting for the offer to be snatched back.

Having to live with the person I told my biggest lie to is the root of my current anxieties. It's like the biggest karmatic slap across the face. I told all my lies because I wanted to live in that flat. And I'm getting what I want.

Be careful what you wish for.

I know that if you tell yourself a lie enough times, it feels like the truth. The memory of the lie leaks into the cracks and your sponge brain becomes swollen with it. It becomes part of who you are. And so that's what I need to do. I need to live and breathe my lie until it's a part of me.

And that means spending time with Zoe and *owning* my lie.

I've chosen Zoe over James. I'd not expected drinks with Alison to be so fruitful. But as soon as she arrived she blurted out they'd split up. I'd craved him for a split-second. But when she followed it with news of her own, that she was moving back down to Whitstable and offering me her room. And it made sense to have Zoe instead.

The choice was easy to make. James had gone from one-word responses to my texts to ignoring me altogether. Whereas I'd be sharing a flat with Zoe, so she'd *have* to see me every day. We'd get the chance to build up a friendship without last orders sending us on our way. I could introduce Zoe to "wine cows" and we could chat until the early hours like Alison and Ruby do.

Now I know Zoe is not going to die, I've left the sombre purples and greys in my wardrobe – my current wardrobe – and have gone for a more upbeat outfit: a Whistles off-white linen pleated top and Reiss slim-fit tailored trousers, finished off with my latest Kate Spade purchase – a pink scarf decorated with teal alligators.

I text my boss to let him know Zoe has "taken a turn for the worse" (a lie, obviously) and head to the hospital. My impeccable timing sees me arrive on the ward shortly before the morning tea round. It means I get to see Maureen too. Perfect.

Zoe and I chat about nothing while I wait for the tea trolley to make an entrance. I watch Maureen make her way up the ward, her trolley seemingly doubling up as a Zimmer frame, taking her weight as she moves from bed to bed.

Age seems to jump, not pass evenly. You go from kid to teen to adult in one fell swoop only to sit in some form of adult stasis for decades – unless you have your own kids, which ages you both instantly and considerably. And then you have retirement and people are old-ish but still strong and still with their wits about them.

And then it jumps again and you are just moments away from death, everything about you from your stooped shoulders to your shuffling feet signalling your decay. And that's where Maureen is now. And yet everything about her tells you she's not ready to die.

When Maureen reaches us, I stand up to take the brew from Maureen's shaking hands and lift it onto the table.

"I suppose you'll be wanting one too," Maureen says with a wink. She's only meant to give drinks to patients, but pours a second tea from the huge metal urn on the trolley before I get to answer.

"Oh! It's a 'tea cow'!" I exclaim, pretending the thought has popped into my head with perfect timing. I then have to explain to both Zoe and Maureen about "wine cows" – underlining to Zoe that, yes, Alison and Ruby are *that* close, and that, yes, you need a new best friend.

Maureen pats the hand on Zoe's drip-free arm.

"I've not had a chance to ask you why you're here," she says to Zoe in an unassuming way that only old ladies can do. Social rules are different for them. Instead of bristling at the question as I expect, Zoe indulges her with a smile.

"I've been diagnosed with ADHD."

Maureen looks as shocked.

"I thought that was something only young kids got. But then what do I know? At my age you stop watching the news because you've had enough of all the bad stuff you can't do anything about."

Zoe smiles again.

"I didn't know they could either until I got my diagnosis. And I thought it was a load of nonsense until they went through the different types of symptoms it causes. It was like reading through a list describing me."

"Well I never," Maureen says. "So it was as simple as that?"

"Well, the turning point for me was the drugs. They've given me new drugs to try and they seem to be helping, which would suggest the diagnosis is right. The drugs are because I've got a dopamine deficiency."

"Me too!" Maureen exclaims.

"Really?" I say, trying to inject myself into the conversation. I'm losing Maureen to Zoe.

I can't believe I'm jealous over a shared medical problem, but it *never* seems to be me. I've had to lie to Zoe about my "me too" to get her to like me. And yet Maureen breezes in and my suicide story is forgotten.

"Mine is my Parkinson's – hence these," Maureen says, holding out both hands and showing how much they shake.

"Why didn't you tell me you were poorly?" I ask, making a second attempt to join the conversation.

This time my interjection works. Maureen puts her shaking arms around my waist in a hug. She's shrunk so much it would be too difficult for her to reach my shoulders.

"It's not for you to worry about me: it's always the other way round, my little Victoria."

My heart swells with the guilt of feeling annoyed with her only moments before. Maureen is the only person in my life that has loved me unconditionally. It's good to have her back in my life again. I only hope I can hold onto her for as long as possible.

IN A BOX

Tori was adamant. Nobody was going to put her in a box and label her with a condition. All she'd been doing was sitting on a cliff top enjoying the freedom of being apart from other people. That's all. She was pretty sure that didn't warrant being labelled.

Back then, they were calling it Asperger's, not high functioning Autism, but it didn't matter to Tori – neither label would have been acceptable. And she had just enough of a stubborn streak to not to turn up to the diagnostic sessions at the local health centre, which meant she was discharged back to her GP without a diagnosis.

Her parents were angry with her – particularly her mother who felt Tori could benefit from a diagnosis and the support that went with it. But Tori's mother had never been bullied at school for being different, and so had no idea what she was talking about. Tori knew a label like Asperger's would not make her life *any* easier.

TORI

I'm shocked at how willingly Zoe has accepted being labelled. I have pushed back at every label anyone has ever tried to apply to me, especially the medical world. They are too ready to fit people into boxes: for everyone to behave a certain way or not be seen as normal.

"You're okay with the diagnosis?" I ask her.

"Nothing I can do about it," Maureen answers. She then chuckles to herself. "I know you don't mean me – I'm being silly."

"The list of symptoms is really vague," Zoe admits. "So if the drugs weren't helping, then I'd be calling them on it. But I can only get these drugs if I accept the diagnosis. So…"

"It must be a relief to know what's wrong," Maureen says to her.

"And for you too," she says to me. "It's tough having to visit a close friend in hospital, not knowing what's wrong with them."

I notice Zoe wince when Maureen refers to her as my

"close friend" but she doesn't correct her, which I'm grateful for. Maureen thinks I have friends that I'm close enough to that I visit them in hospital and that makes me proud. And I want to enjoy feeling proud even though it's a lie. It doesn't feel like a lie though because Maureen has made it the truth.

And that's why I know I can't be Autistic: I'm far too good at lying.

What I'm not good at is the ends of conversations: what to say to leave, how to tie things up. There's an unwritten rule about when to stop talking about a particular topic, when you lighten the mood. But I haven't quite worked when those points are. Sometimes I try to lighten the tone too early, other times too late.

I've yet to decide which is worse: people inching away from me because I've been too flippant too soon in a serious situation; or experiencing the same response from people because I've said something too serious, too dark, beyond the point where anyone else wanted to discuss it.

External stimuli can be perfect for solving this conundrum, which is why I suggest to Maureen that I join her on the rest of her tea round. She's thrilled. She orders me about, getting me to collect empty mugs from the first half of the ward, while filling me in on the gossip about people I don't know. But I find her company so easy to be in that I don't mind at all.

Why can't it always be like this?

26 armbands

RUBY

Alison is going through the kitchen cupboards sorting out which items are hers. The ones she wants to take with her are being added to a haphazard pile on the table.

I'm wrapping these items in sheets of the Evening Standard – which we picked up free from the station – and packing them into a cardboard box hastily bought at an extortionate price from the local storage centre.

We don't talk as we work. We're both mulling over everything we've gone through in the last week and our thoughts are making the air too thick for words to cut through. I'm going over the argument we had in the corridor outside Zoe's ward – the one where she accused me of deserting her. The one where she claimed she was never first.

I honestly thought it was *me* who let *her* go. That I let Alison leave my life to go on an adventure of her own. Back then, I didn't realise how much we'd change simply by being in different places mentally as well as physically, that we wouldn't necessarily just slot back into each other's lives when she returned from university in the summer months. And then the summer arrived and she didn't return.

To my knowledge, she didn't come back to Whitstable during her three years at university. At first we exchanged letters and phone calls, but they petered out before Christmas – my letters weren't replied to, my calls not answered or returned. I had been ghosted.

It was *she* who'd let *me* go.

By the summer after her first year, I heard how she was doing only by talking to her mum – and even then it was snippets of life in London pared down to a version palatable for parents.

Her mum called me when she was getting ready to go up to London for Alison's graduation. She wanted help choosing an outfit. Alison had phoned her to tell her the details of the event, but didn't help her mum with the planning – what to wear, which train to catch.

So I stepped into the dutiful daughter role, as I had done many times in the three years since Alison had left, and helped her organise her trip from Whitstable to the Royal Festival Hall on the South Bank – the building we'd sat in front of on her Open Day, back when we were still planning a joint future.

After her visit to London for the graduation, Alison's mum didn't make the trip up to London to see Alison again. I understood why Alison was angry with me, but I had no idea why she was punishing her mum.

Alison didn't hold onto our friendship because I was no longer palatable to her. As we get older, tomatoes become sweet to our taste. This happens to us without us choosing a particular diet. As children we'd scoffed at the idea that tomato was a fruit – as adults it makes sense. And as we grow, our palates change not just towards foods but also towards lifestyle ideas and a way of living.

Those who go to university change in ways those of us who stay at home do not. Those of us left behind are trapped in our childhood homes and we cannot fathom the changes that university brings any more than a child can taste the sweetness of a tomato as they bite into its ripened red flesh.

Through her exchanges with Zoe this past week, it's clear that London has become unpalatable to Alison. I'm not sure whether Alison truly wants to return to Whitstable or if she simply wants "not London" and just has no other place to go. I have no idea how important my friendship is in all of this either. Until she contacted me in tears, incoherently babbling about Zoe's overdose, I'd seen her twice since she left for university – at Becky's wedding and the time I spotted her on the beach.

At the wedding, our awkwardness was hidden by the general awkwardness of 12 of us who didn't know each other well enough to be thrust together in order to play our roles. Alison and I had shared superficial chat while we were milling around waiting for photos to be taken, but inside any conversation ended abruptly when we found ourselves at different tables.

It was only after a fair amount of wine had been consumed that we'd swapped mobile numbers, and even then I knew it was just a polite gesture. I sent one text saying it had been lovely to see her again and was promptly ghosted again. Us swapping numbers is the only reason she knew how to get hold of me.

I know that things won't go back to how they were before – and it's partly because I won't let them.

I told people I'd been dumped – if Alison were a boy – and the boy who dumped me came back to me because their new relationship didn't work out, I'd be told to be wary, to be careful, to make sure that I wasn't being used. Some would tell me not to take the boy back. For some reason, when it's a friend, the rules are different. I'm not meant to be as hurt by Alison's behaviour as I would be some boy. But was hurt. Am still hurting.

Also, while it's lovely to be friends again, and I'm so proud of her for rescuing that woman, I've had year upon year of a life without Alison and I've adjusted. I have the girls I know from choir, the local artists I've haphazardly collected as friends, the couple who live in the flat next door who got shopping in for me when I sprained my ankle and couldn't manage all the stairs.

None of these friendships has the same intensity, but none of them expect me to give more than I take either. I needed to be in the role of protector while sitting by Zoe's bedside, but that's not who I am any more. I'm not sure how much she realises this. I guess we'll both be figuring it out as we go along. And that figuring out starts now.

Even though I could be back in Whitstable now, and back living my life, I've somehow allowed myself to be cajoled into helping with the packing – allowed Alison to be first again.

I like working in a companionable silence. The only time Alison speaks is to query whether or not she'll need something. For some reason, she thinks my opinion on what she packs is important.

Oh God.

I can't believe I've only just twigged why. I take a deep breath and compose myself: I want my voice to come out sounding normal, calm, nonchalant.

"So have you decided how long you're going to stay at your mum's before you try and get a job?"

Alison does the pause I expect – the one where she's

recalibrating the situation in her head. Up until I mentioned her mum's she had just assumed she could stay at mine.

Five fucking years, for fuck's sake, and she's just *assumed*.

"I've not ironed out the details with her yet," Alison replies, her voice trembling.

I can tell from her tone that *something* has happened between her and her mum, but whatever it is, she's not ready to talk about it. And I'm not going to ask – because it would give her the perfect excuse to push to stay at mine.

"Are you going to hire a van to get all your stuff moved?" – it's obvious that she's going to say "Yes", but I want to carry on the conversation, as if the pause and the shaking voice didn't happen.

"I haven't thought about that yet," Alison admits. "I just want to get my stuff packed to make the mental shift – to prepare myself for leaving."

I nod.

"I have no idea how to go about hiring a van though!" she exclaims.

Alison's lifesaving behaviour seems less real and more of an aberration with each passing minute. But I need to keep it at the front of my mind because it showed that, if necessary, Alison was perfectly capable of making decisions and taking action.

Away from any emergency, she's slipped back into her role of damsel in distress, expecting other people to do things for her. I know the only way I'm going to get her to change this behaviour is if it stops working. So I keep quiet. I'm not going to start suggesting solutions. I'm not going to babysit her. Not any more.

"Zoe sorted it out each time we moved," she adds quietly.

I focus on wrapping a colourful assortment of glasses and mugs.

"Any ideas?" she ventures.

"My move was only 200 yards so I borrowed a sack trolley from the Ship Centurion."

It's the pub where we used to do karaoke. And ended up with cuts and bruises after trying to pull each other round on the sack trolley when we were drunk. I see a flicker of recognition on Alison's face, followed by a smirk.

We pack in silence for another few minutes.

"I guess I could ask about vans at the storage place?"

"Sounds like a plan."

I give her a massive grin – her reward for coming up with a way forward all by herself.

MOTHER NATURE

Ruby spotted Alison when she ventured out to watch one of Whitstable's rare but beautiful thunderstorms. Realising the person watching the storm play out just 40 or so yards down the coast was Alison made her pleased and saddened all at once. It's something they'd done together as teenagers.

As storms were carried out to sea, the thunder gets too far away to hear, but without any buildings in the way, anyone who stands on the coastline can watch the lightning dance between the clouds for miles upon miles.

Ruby had always loved the chaos of a storm – Mother Nature's way of saying it didn't matter how much you plan for, the world can still shake things up. Or maybe it wasn't Mother Nature this time; maybe somewhere else in the world a butterfly had caused the storm by flapping its wings.

Storms made the world bigger. They reminded Ruby of how tiny a role humans play: that we're just a speck of dust on the life of the earth. They made her less anxious about her illness because she knew the world would carry on just fine after both she and her mum had passed.

Instead of watching the storm, Ruby found herself staring at Alison. She thought about going over, but decided against it. She told herself she would only approach her if Alison looked over, knowing already that she wouldn't. Alison was watching the storm, totally engrossed as usual, which meant that she would be oblivious to anything going on around her.

RUBY

I've downed tools. Alison said she was going out to get us some lunch but she's been gone over an hour. And I'm not packing her stuff while she's taking a break. I've been tricked like this before. Like when we did our homework "together" except I'd work out all the answers and Alison would just copy them.

We've finished the kitchen and have moved onto the bedroom. Some of the packing we're doing is repacking – taking items out of plastic boxes underneath her bed and putting them in cardboard boxes, so the plastic ones can be used for books. I doubt if any of the stuff under her bed has seen the light of day since she moved in.

She has collected some of the same "life junk" I have – the stuff you rarely or never use but can't throw away in case it could be useful. An assortment of basic DIY tools that you use when you first move in. A mishmash of stationery, safety pins and rubber bands. A random assortment of supermarket plastic bags – although this has been shrinking since they became 5p each. If you rent, it's the kind of stuff you store under the bed; if you own, it's usually tucked away in the loft.

I leaf through the books Alison has rescued from the shelves in the lounge and piled up on top of the pillows, ready to be boxed up. There are very few textbooks: it's mostly trashy romance novels and books from her childhood. I pick up an Enid Blyton and start flicking through the pages, determined to find something to do that means I don't need to pack while I wait for Alison. I'm part way into chapter three when I hear the key in the lock, then the door open and slam shut. A flustered but excited Alison comes rushing into her bedroom.

"I've got removals details," she exclaims, waving leaflets at me, ridiculously happy with herself. "They were from the storage place."

"So that's where you've been? I thought you were getting lunch."

My stomach decides to growl in solidarity.

"Oh fuck…"

I realise that except for the leaflets, she's come back empty handed.

I head into Zoe's room (somewhere I'm far more comfortable now I know she's not dying) and grab my jacket and bag. I spotted a pizza and kebab takeaway when we were walking towards the storage place – I'm going to head there.

"I'm going for pizza. Good for you?"

I don't wait for her reply. I pick up her keys, knowing I'll need the fob to work the metal gates on the way in to the complex. I don't want to have to rely on Alison to buzz me in.

When I return with two pizzas (one veggie deluxe, one margarita) and two bottles of Sprite, I set them down on the lounge table and start to tuck in. She joins me, hesitant as if she's not sure what to expect. This must be a hangover from her friendship with Zoe because, with food in my belly, it's already forgotten.

"Sorry," she ventures.

My mouth full of pizza, I wave to say it's fine. She picks up a piece of pizza and starts on it while heading back out of the lounge. I hear rummaging and she returns with a box of star-shaped fairy lights. I instantly recognise them. The box looks unopened. She passes the box to me before sitting down in the chair.

"I bought them for you as a housewarming present when I found out we couldn't be in the same halls in first year. I thought if you put them up in your room it would stop you forgetting about me."

"You've never used them?" I ask between mouthfuls.

She shakes her head.

"They were meant to be a present for you, so I felt weird about opening them. But I was so angry when you said you weren't coming to London I didn't want you to have them."

She shrugs. I'm able to fill in the next bit myself. She kept them unopened because she always meant to give them to me, but there was never the right time – because we didn't see each other again.

"I didn't tell you I was ill because I knew there was a chance you'd pull out of university too. And I'm glad I didn't because moving to London worked out for you. I mean you never even made it back for Christmas…"

I see a look of thunder as fierce as the storms we'd watched from the beach pass across her face.

"I didn't come back for Christmas because I was scared that if I did, I wouldn't go back for the second term."

Her voice is shaking again, but this time it's with anger. She stands up abruptly and leaves the room. I let her go. We both need a few minutes to ourselves.

I eat until I'm stuffed, comforting myself with the feeling of being full.

I put the last few pieces of each pizza into just one of the pizza boxes and close it. I carry both into the kitchen, putting the empty one on top of the bin. The other goes on the kitchen worktop – only a novice puts leftover pizza in the fridge.

I clear up the rest of the debris from our lunch – the napkins, the plastic bottles – and then head back into Alison's room, carrying the fairy lights.

"Humans are fascinated with light," she says.

She nods at the fairy lights. "I was thinking about them the last time I watched a storm from Tankerton."

"When did you last watch a storm?" I ask, composing myself, ready to tell her I spotted her.

There's a brief pause. A recalibration.

"When was the last time we watched one together?" she asks.

"The summer after our A Levels."

"That'll be it then."

I nod. My throat is heavy, as if the pizza's doughy crust is swelling up inside me and up through my oesophagus. I shove the fairy lights in the half-packed box in front of me, burrowing them down into the middle of the box. I don't want to hold them for one second longer.

All the lies between her, Zoe and Tori, and yet another trips off her tongue.

And this one I have to carry now too.

27 swimming aids

BETH

I haven't been down to London since university. And I haven't seen Faye since she upped sticks and left Manchester. I suspect they are both the same but different. London has lots of new buildings, but it's so big that they just shift views rather than completely changing the landscape, like the way the regeneration work in Manchester did after the IRA bomb.

London has been hit by IRA bombs too, but a visitor wouldn't be able to pinpoint exactly where.

In Manchester, the shiny new part of the centre has somehow managed to retain its shine for 20 years – it stands out as the bit that changed the city. (It could be because no real money has been spent since, except on nondescript blocks of flats and budget hotels.)

Euston station might not have been hit by a bomb, but it *needed* the facelift it has been given. They've made it easier on the eye, but it is no less chaotic to navigate. Faye said she would meet me here but we didn't get as far as agreeing where. I can remember from the years of using this station that the arrivals screen is small and often updated late, so I'm not surprised when she's not waiting on my platform. Although spruced up, the concourse still has undertones of a dystopian nightmare.

The middle tracks are reserved for London Midland and the Overground services up to Watford, with Virgin trains being randomly allocated to platforms at either end, so there's no sensible place to stand to wait for someone getting off the train from Manchester.

But with just two places to monitor, Faye spots me before I see her.

She has to call out before I see her and I recognise her voice before I do her, partly because I'm looking for a mass of red curls. Instead, she's wearing her hair in a messy plait. I'd only ever seen her with her hair tied back – and in a bun – when she was working in the deli, and I'm surprised how different it makes her look. She has put on a little bit of weight too. But the main change is something I can't put my finger on. It's like she's mixed up all her emotions like she would her acrylic paints and sloshed it around to see what comes up.

As she spotted me first, she's half a minute ahead of me mentally. My mind is still trying to decide how to greet her when she pulls me into a fierce hug – the type you reserve for old friends.

It's a hug that says, "Let's talk about what happened and sort this out."

So I say: "We need to catch up properly."

The IRA bomb

One of the many IRA bombs to hit London went off at Victoria station in 1991, five years before the one that devastated the centre of Manchester.

Although the bomb at Victoria didn't impact the city visually in the way the bomb in Manchester did, it took one life and injured 38 others. There were no lives lost in the Manchester IRA attack.

And no matter the size of the bomb or the damage it causes to buildings or to flesh, it also causes psychological and emotional damage to those supposedly unhurt. This damage is much harder to measure and can be infinitely harder to treat.

28 lifeguards

ALISON

I'm so embarrassed my insides are on fire, blistering from the heat. My face is still hot from shame hours later. I'd just assumed I could stay with Ruby.

Assumed it.

Even though I deserted her for five years, an awkward conversation at a wedding aside, where we swapped numbers more out of politeness than anything else. Even though I only got in touch with her because I needed her support. Even though I've seen her flat and, although it's not "London" tiny, there's no way my stuff would fit even if she were willing to put me up.

I'm just so glad she asked me about staying at my mum's before I had the chance to say something stupid and put my foot in it. I'm just thankful she'll never know.

I'm meant to be picking up something for dinner at the Tesco Express. I need to concentrate on the shelves, find something to eat – I can't go back empty-handed like I did at lunch!

I'm cursing myself about the bloody fairy lights too. Ruby seemed touched that I'd kept them – and I was so pleased about it I nearly messed up. Why did I have to mention the storm? I can never let Ruby know about my visit. That way she doesn't know I *could* have gone to see her and didn't.

Although her *not* knowing about that trip is making this whole move harder. Ruby is a tad concerned that I'm moving after just a day trip: worried I've been too much affected by saving a stranger's life. But I can't explain that Whitstable was the place I turned to when things first started getting shaky in London.

When I first left, I felt as if I was attached to a strong piece of elastic, that if I stopped pulling away at any point that I'd ping back home. My mum had wanted me to go to university in Canterbury, but I'd insisted on going away and I desperately wanted to show everyone – including myself – that I'd made the right decision. I was still naïve enough at that point to believe that changing your mind automatically meant failure.

Over the years the elastic loosened. But it never went away. And when I stayed in the caravan last year, I headed back up to London a day earlier than planned because I could feel it tightening, taking hold of me again. Back then I still believed I wanted a life in London.

Moving back down should be a positive thing. Except now Ruby and I have this stupid, stupid lie between us. I wonder if this is what it's like to be Tori, falling into lies and then finding it's too late to get up.

29 lifebuoys

ZOE

Being trapped in a hospital bed is the worst form of torture. This morning I had to put up with Tori and this afternoon I have a stranger visiting me. Urghh. And this one has ADHD.

At visiting time, I know which one Beth is straight away. Not from how she looks or how she's dressed, but her mannerisms. She has the same nervous energy I do. When she walks over, she catches my look of uncertainty and rolls her eyes. It's the perfect response.

"I cannot believe how much of a *pain* it is to get here," she announced. "London runs on the tube, yet this place – a hospital, you know, something really important – is *miles* away from the closest station. And I know ambulances don't need the tube, but still."

She pauses briefly to take a breath before launching into: "I don't know this part of London at all. I went to Goldsmiths, so my bit is around New Cross, Deptford, Lewisham."

There's something about Beth that makes me want to join in.

"I think the only people who know all of it are black cab drivers."

She nods emphatically.

"They should teach 'the knowledge' in school – far more useful than a lot of the stuff we learn," she says.

"Don't get me started!"

"Finding a flat, signing a tenancy."

"And then setting up gas and electricity."

"It's like the basic practicalities of life have been missed completely, but we get to learn how to calculate the area of a triangle."

We grin at each other. It's like slipping into an old friendship, but it's just about meeting someone who I'm aligned to. It's not the banter itself; it's the lack of eggshell walking she's doing.

Beth is looking at me and it's the first time *anyone* has looked at me and seen themselves staring back at them. It's the weirdest feeling ever: meeting someone who *knows* the difference inside me that nobody else gets. She looks me in the eye and I don't see any pity, confusion or irritation.

"You're talking," she says, flumping herself down in the chair next to my bed. "That's impressive."

"Faye said that when you were in hospital you didn't?"

"It's like I was out cold," she explains. "But without being completely unconscious. I withdrew inside myself to protect myself. I hadn't taken an overdose, but a friend – not Faye, Abbie – thought I had, so she called an ambulance."

Beth shrugs – she's explaining something that happened to her that she doesn't understand. She looks around.

"I got a bed on the psych ward. But you actually took an overdose and I didn't?"

"I got assessed as not being a risk to others."

"So how you get psych support on this ward?"

"I don't."

Beth looks pissed off on my behalf.

"What the fuck? I mean a lot of the time it felt like all they did was bring me cups of tea. But I strangely felt safe and secure – like other people were taking on all my responsibilities so I just had to focus on me."

"I get cups of tea here," I say with a smile.

I feel anything but secure in this hospital, but I'm a lot calmer about being here right now than I was yesterday. I have a wave of anger each time I think about getting a diagnosis by chance. If I hadn't complained, I wouldn't have seen Mr Big Guns. And if I hadn't seen him, well…

The psychiatrist Mr BG sent to do my assessment said my diagnosis could change my outlook on life: make me feel better about being alive.

"So when should I start feeling better about wanting to be alive?" I ask.

"Ah, so you've not had the mental euphoria yet then?"

I shake my head. "I've just tried to kill myself. I'm not expecting euphoric."

"I had this high after my diagnosis," she explains. "Apparently, it's quite common. You think that for the first time in your life you get who you are and how you're gong to get better."

She sighs. "All total bollocks, of course. I just wasn't sure if you'd already been there and were on a comedown.

"No euphoric highs here," I tell her.

"Good. Hopefully, I can stop you from having one.

Seriously, I told my psychiatrist I felt as if the shadow of depression had lifted. It didn't occur to him to point out that I might be on a post-diagnostic high. The warning would have been good – the comedown would have been less of a crash if I'd been expecting it."

"My psych hasn't mentioned a high," I tell her. "But I'm wondering if that's because he doesn't know it exists."

Beth throws me a quizzical look.

"He told me my outlook would change. And it sounds like yours did, but it was short lived. If hospital psyches only ever see the initial high – and not the crash the patient suffers once they're back in the real world – maybe that's what he's seeing?"

"Fuck knows."

I like her honesty.

"So what's it like being back in the real world?" I ask her.

"I'm still trying to get used to being a 'burden' on society."

It dawns on me that if I'm going to stay alive (and it's something I'm considering) I'm not going to go back to my old job. My life has changed irrevocably.

I'm suddenly less sure about wanting to leave hospital. Here, I'm treading water. Out there, the real world is full of hidden currents that can wrap themselves around you and pull you down within seconds with no time to take a breath.

Beth flips back into random chat mode.

"Pulling into Victoria station was weird as we've got one of those in Manchester. Yours doesn't have the roof collapsing after being attacked by militant seagulls though!"

Something about what Beth is saying – Victoria station, the roof collapsing – has me reaching into the depths of my memories searching for something long forgotten. I can't find whatever memory it is, but I can't shake it off either. I try to dismiss it from my mind, hoping I'll remember the significance when I'm *not* thinking about it.

"At first they blamed the rain because when the panel broke it poured gallons of water on the people standing on the platform. But I thought that sounded a bit suspect. It rains in Manchester *a lot* and you'd think they'd design it to withstand a few showers."

I nod. "When they first built the Millennium Bridge over the Thames you couldn't use it because it swayed too much."

"Oh God, what idiots. Can you remember how much they spent on that bridge? Because the new roof at Manchester Victoria cost £20 million so you'd think it'd be built to last. Then a seagull comes along intent on destroying it and *Bam* – pieces are falling on people."

Again I'm uneasy as my brain searches itself for a memory I don't remember having. Usually when this happens it's something from a TV show I've watched or I'm recalling something that happened to a character in a book. I need to mull over everything I've watched or read that's got a train station scene in it. Great.

I have no idea how much they spent on the Millennium Bridge.

"Seagulls in Manchester?"

"Loads of them. I don't think we're close enough to the sea for them, so I don't get it. It's like they've become urbanised – like foxes."

Am I struggling to remember whatever roof story is in the recesses of my brain because I'm not used to using it? Even when I've had company, I've not been engaging my brain to the same extent I'm doing now. I have no idea what, if any, damage to my brain my overdose has caused. And my ADHD diagnosis tells me it was never firing on all cylinders anyway.

I normally have a snooze in the afternoon, but Beth keeps me company and we stay chatting. She pops out twice for coffees without me having to ask. Both times she explains Faye is unofficially giving her a 2-for-1 deal.

I know Beth is on the same drug as me, Lisdexamfetamine. I know she's settled on a dose now too, but it doesn't seem to help with her short-term memory issues. Although I don't mind being told twice about the coffee deal, as I don't remember knowing until I hear it for a second time.

I'm on the lowest dose and need to have it "titrated" – carefully increased so I can work out how many milligrams is right for me. I'm going to have to keep an eye on how many times people point out I'm repeating myself and see if it goes down as the drugs increase. Maybe Beth's memory is better than it was; maybe it was just *really* shit before.

Supping at her second coffee, Beth jumps topic again.

"You know how impulsive we are?" Beth says, a question in her voice. "Well it's a bit like an ADHD superpower. We don't get bogged down with things the same way other people do."

"I hadn't really thought about it like that."

I wonder if I get a cape.

"So why not move up to Manchester? My housemate is moving out so it's perfect timing."

I'm shocked. Yes, I'm impulsive, but this is not the sort of decision to be taken lightly.

"Unless you're planning on going back to your old job, your old life –" Beth pauses while I shake my head "– then you're going to need a new way of living. I haven't had much support from friends, except for Livvy."

"What about Faye?" I ask.

"When she texted me about you being in hospital, it's the

first time I'd heard from her in over a year. I didn't know who the text was from at first because I'd deleted her number from my phone. Livvy has to tell me. Faye texted her first to let her know she was getting in touch."

I have to massively reassess Faye in my head. It's a seismic shift. She goes from someone who cares enough about strangers to get a close friend to travel down from Manchester on the train to a flaky friend in one swoop.

"And Livvy?"

"Olivia. My flatmate. She's moving in with her fella, which is awesome news. But it means I have to find a new housemate or I move too."

"How come you moved back to Manchester?"

It's a genuine question as well as a stalling mechanism.

"It's home," she says simply.

She frowns. She's doing that thing I do – analysing why she thinks something *after* she's said it. I guess it's another ADHD thing.

"It doesn't have anything to do with family," she explains. "I don't have anything to do with them at all. I was too different and my differences weren't accepted. I was the grey sheep of the family, always on the fringes."

"Grey?"

"Black sheep equals rebel, someone who drops out of society, take drugs, gets into trouble with the police," she explains.

"They don't go to university and don't get a job," I add, realising that I too am a grey sheep. It's the reason my mum didn't come in to school whenever I got into trouble.

"But Manchester means more to me than that. When the IRA bombed Manchester in the 90s, they destroyed the heart of the city, but they didn't destroy its soul. We all pulled together as a city. It made many of us, including me, proud to be Mancunian."

"What about the new bomb?" I ask. "The one that went off at the Ariana Grande concert?"

"I don't know how I feel about the Arena bombing," Beth admits. "The IRA bomb didn't kill anyone. The Arena bomb took 22 lives. It's different when people die −" she hesitates.

"Go on."

"That bomb took the lives of people who wanted to live. Yet I've had quite enough of life − I'm ready to die. But I can't take their places. It seems unfair on both counts."

She shrugs.

"My diagnosis has helped me understand myself, but it hasn't answered all my questions and it certainly hasn't provided solutions. So I get it if you decide you don't want to move up to Manchester to share with a weirdo you've only just met who reminisces about dying!"

But it's this speech that makes me realise it's the right thing to do − and as Lucio said to Isabella: *"Our doubts are traitors, and make us lose the good we oft might win, by fearing to attempt."*

"Yes," I say, "why the fuck not."

Chatting to Beth is easy; chatting to Tori is not.

I'm not looking forward to telling Tori that we're not going to be flatmates after all. I know she's been holding onto the idea far too tightly than is healthy to the point where I started to feel guilty about setting her up.

I'm contemplating getting in touch with Alison to help me tell Tori just because I'm so bad at this stuff. I'm not sure she'll be willing to help − even though she's the reason Tori visited me in hospital in the first place − but it might still be worth asking. Maybe. Or not.

And it can't be Beth – it needs to be someone Tori already knows, so she doesn't feel like she's being ambushed. And it absolutely cannot be James.

So that leaves Faye. The half-friend of Beth's who, for whatever reason, made the effort on my behalf when I needed it. I could orchestrate it so that my conversation with Tori happens in Costa where Faye can be *accidental* backup.

I know Tori will be angry and upset – that she'll have no idea how grateful she should be. And she can never know. No matter how much she twists the truth for her own gains, it's not fair for me to tell her I wanted her to be my flatmate so she could be the person to find my dead body.

My tablets are making me less angry. Less cruel.

Flooding the network

The London Underground's engineering team has highlighted 57 different stations on the tube network it considers as at "high risk" of flooding — 11 of which are on the Victoria line.

Zoe's brain has a high risk of flooding too, but hers is the emotional flooding that's a symptom of ADHD. It happens when the executive function part of her brain misfires, when dopamine, a neurotransmitter, doesn't send signals across the brain's network correctly. The failure in the process allows what should be a fleeting emotion to flood the brain.

It's not something the psychiatrist shared with her — either in conversation or in the literature he'd given her, which was patronising and assumed the reader had a lower-than-average intelligence, even though it claimed ADHD wasn't linked to said lower-than-average intelligence.

Zoe only knows about emotional flooding because Beth explained it as the reasoning behind why someone with ADHD can experience intense thoughts of suicide 2-3 times a day brought on by the most ephemeral of experiences.

30 armbands

SIX INCHES

As children, Zoe and her sisters used to fight over who would sit next to their mother – who in turn used to joke she needed to be a triangle so she could have three sides, not just two. Charlie, being the youngest, always got one side. Zoe, who was expected to take it in turns with Clare, attempted to keep a mental tally of when it was her turn so she didn't lose out.

When it came to their mother's funeral, there was no fight over who got to stand next to their father: Clare was on one side, Charlie the other. Zoe stood a good six inches away – the sort of gap that suggested she was a stepdaughter or close cousin. She didn't want to take comfort from the man who'd deserted them.

"Mother couldn't help dying: father *could* help leaving" – that's what Zoe had said to Clare when she'd questioned the six inches afterwards, when they were all at the pub. Disjointed sections of family were milling round with old and new friends, nobody really knowing each other – and Zoe used it as an excuse to play host, to check everyone was okay. Everyone but her father. Playing host gave her the perfect excuse to be too busy to speak to him.

"Have you considered you're making things worse?" Clare had hissed at her in response.

"Our mother is dead. What could be worse than that?"

Except there could be something worse: because Zoe didn't just lose her mother, she lost her sisters too. Clare and Charlie both clung to their father for support more than they clung to each other. And their actions made it clear they were putting their father's needs before Zoe's.

ZOE

If anyone commits murder at London St Pancras station they will be able to plead diminished responsibility based on the grounds of stress caused by trying to find out which part of the station their trains go from.

I say "which part", but it's actually four stations in one, and nobody has bothered to name the different sections. So unless you want the Eurostar, which is the bit in the centre, good luck finding where your train is going from. I gave myself plenty of time to get the train to Rochester and ended up having to run up the escalator two steps at a time in order to make my train.

Hearing Beth has no contact with her family came as a shock. She's not spoken to her parents and two sisters in eight years.

I haven't spoken to any of my family since I cleared the last of my belongings out of my mother's house before it went up for sale. And I'd been quite happy to let the silence expand into being the norm, cutting them out of my life by default. But hearing that this reaction might be my ADHD talking is making me rethink.

I'd been surprised by the speed at which the house in Crystal Palace had been put on the market. Clare and I had moved out years ago, but Charlie had still been living at home at the time, taking on the role of our mother's impromptu carer.

My father seems happy in his place out in Rochester, even though he has to commute into London every day, so I get why he wouldn't want to move back in. And I'm sure any property in Crystal Palace is worth a pretty penny by now, no matter how little care and attention it's been given over the years. But it seems a bit much to expect Charlie to move in with him.

She did though. And she didn't seem angry that she'd had to move out of her home just weeks after the funeral. But I was. It felt like the decisions being made were the right ones for our father before anyone else. He just seemed too used to putting himself first.

And maybe it was time for me to sit down with my father and have the awkward, angry conversation I'd been avoiding for years, give him a few home truths. I'm in the habit of saying what I think – another ADHD trait – so people believe I'm good at coping with confrontation. I'm not. I hate awkward conversations as much as the next person.

I'm annoyed that I'm the one doing the travelling – me going down there, rather than Michael coming up here. (He's Michael to me now: defined as who he is as person in his own right, not who he is in relation to me.) But as Charlie lives there and Clare is visiting this weekend, he said he didn't want to leave them for longer than he needed to.

The train seems to be travelling through an alternate reality where places like Stratford and stations in the middle of nowhere called Ebbsfleet get called "International", as if you can get anywhere from a dump on the edge of London or some random slabs of concrete surrounded by fields.

It's as we're pulling out of Ebbsfleet *International* that I notice the list of station names parroted by the pre-recorded voice includes "Whitstable". It's strange to be travelling towards Alison even though I'm not visiting her.

When we arrive into Strood I get agitated: I know Rochester station is just three minutes away. As we pull out of Strood, the tracks take us left and over water. I was not expecting a river. I wonder if it's the Thames. I know the Thames eventually heads out to the sea, I just don't know the route it takes.

It feels strange that Rochester could be somehow connected to both London and Whitstable. And not for the first time I wonder if this feeling is normal or if it's ADHD. Where does *my* brain stop and the damage begin?

The bridge that takes us over the river is made of a metal mesh-like structure. It carves the view into a hundred different picture postcards, making the river seem prettier than it is. Michael said I should be able to see the castle ruins from the train, but I can't, so I'm assuming the road bridge to the right distorts what is the better view. I know Michael though, so there's a chance you *can't* see the castle from the train at all and he just wants to drop into conversation that there's a castle, that Rochester is nice. A hint that Charlie won't miss Crystal Palace because Rochester has an old, crumbling building.

"She's 19!" Clare had said in a way that told me she was repeating Michael – the intonation as well as the words. As if someone passes 18 and comes out of their childhood cocoon fully formed as an adult the same way a butterfly does.

Rochester station is a modern creation of angular glass. The choice of building says they've spent *money* on the city, but that it wasn't important enough to warrant any *creativity*.

I'm meeting Michael in the café at the Huguenot Museum, the back entrance of which is opposite the station. I said if he was expecting me to come all the way to Rochester, the least he could do was the rest of the journey.

The museum feels very un-museum-like, and its café an afterthought, squeezed into an unsuitable space that's more *corridor* than room. I realise I'm being unkind. I'm too used to London's grand buildings where the café would have the same size footprint as this whole building.

Michael is sitting at a table, facing towards the back entrance so that I'd be easy to spot coming in. He's lost in thought though, so I stop and wait for him to glance round the room and spot me before I walk over. The more prepared he is for me arriving, the easier the "Hellos" will be for both of us.

"So who or what are the Huguenots?" I ask after we've shared an awkward hug, knowing that Michael will know.

"They are Britain's first refugees who came over from France," he says, not being able to keep the pride of knowing out of his voice − even though anyone who bothers reading the sign on the way in can tell me that much.

I'm people-pleasing again. I know from my research that it's an ADHD thing, although I haven't yet found a good explanation as to why. Alison said empathy came more easily to me than other people and that would sit with the emotional flooding Beth told me about. I guess that theory will have to do for now.

We then get to waste a good 10 minutes while Michael insists on going up to the counter on my behalf and then having to pop back to ask me for my answer each time the lady behind the counter asks a question. It would have been easier for me to get my own coffee and cake. I can't tell if Michael believes he should pay − if he's still trying to play parent — or whether he's using it as a stalling mechanism. I guess he doesn't want to have this conversation any more than I do.

We then manage to lose another five minutes on the pleasantries of whether or not the coffee is strong enough, the cake moist enough and not too sweet.

I'm just about ready to scream "I didn't come down here to talk about cake!" when Michael puts down his coffee cup and places his hands on the top of his stomach, lacing his fingers together.

At the funeral, I hadn't noticed how much weight he'd put on. Admittedly, he'd been in a smart suit and I'd been avoiding paying any of him any attention, never mind his stomach, but I'm shocked that he has enough of a bulge to rest his hands on top of.

I fight to stop my brain going through every image of Michael to reassess them for stomach bulges — I will not let my ADHD take me wandering away at such an important time.

Michael is staring at me as if he doesn't know what to say or where to start.

So I say: "I have no idea where to start either."

He smiles. It's a real smile — a conspiratorial one; we're on the same side. And then the smile is replaced with a look that says he knows what to say: like he's known all along, he's just been waiting for it to be the right time to speak.

"I want to go back to the point when you started hating," Michael says to me as if he can pluck a date out of the air.

And then he does.

"I want to go back to Victoria station and the 18th February 1991."

31 memories

VICTORIA STATION, 18 FEBRUARY 1991

It was just after 7.30am and those using Victoria station for their daily commute had no idea of the horrors that faced them less than 10 minutes away. One of the people at the station that day is Michael Vickers, who was there with his daughter Zoe. They are taking part in a very early form of "take you child to work day".

Normally, Michael would fly through the station, from his Crystal Palace commuter service, which pulled into platforms 7 or 8, across the concourse and down the steps into the underbelly of the tube service, before jumping onto the Circle line two stops to South Kensington and his office.

But that morning he was taking time to show Zoe the different parts of the station, explaining how the trains used to be powered by steam and had once served passengers heading to France and Belgium via ferry services from Dover and Folkestone.

It all sounded very grand to the small blonde girl stood

next to him, her face shining in awe at the expanse of glass and metal that stretches above her head. She points up at the roof.

Zoe had been fascinated by glass structures since her daddy bought her a book about Crystal Palace that contained pictures of a real glass palace. The palace used to be in the park that now had dinosaurs instead.

Michael explained to her that the roof above them is a Grade II listed structure dating back to 1862.

"Is that older than you, daddy?" Zoe asked.

Michael laughed. But he didn't get to answer: because at that moment there was a huge explosion in a bin on the other side of the concourse.

Glass. Shrapnel. Dust. Chaos.

Out of instinct, Michael had thrown himself down on top of his daughter to protect her from the blast. When he lifted himself up, he was relieved and overjoyed to see his daughter in one piece underneath him, coughing from the grey dust they were both coated in.

At first, Michael was dazed and distracted by the debris and the ringing in his ears, but one look of fear from Zoe, the whites of her eyes the only thing not coated in grey, and his adrenaline kicked in. He scooped her up in both arms and ran, following the crowds of people who were still alive and uninjured enough to try and get out of the station.

Swept up in the swarms, Michael found himself on a path down into the tube and not onto the streets. With the force of bodies pushing him along, he had no choice but to keep going, fully aware there was no way of knowing whether he was carrying Zoe to safety or into the path of another bomb.

Quick-thinking tube station staff opened all the barriers

to allow people down the escalators and onto the platforms. The closest escalators took them down onto the platform for southbound Victoria line trains.

Zoe didn't understand what was going on. She knew something had gone wrong. The roof of the station sounded really old, so she wondered if it had fallen on them. She was glad her daddy had finally stopped running because the jiggling had made her feel sick.

She looked around and saw a blue and white picture of a lady on the wall that was sideways, like on stamps. The lady looked sad and it made Zoe sad too. Zoe remembered staring at the lady for a long time until they were allowed to go home. She didn't go into daddy's work after all.

Afterwards, Zoe was referred to a therapist to talk through what she witnessed, but she couldn't remember anything except for the sad lady. Her parents were told her memories of the incident may or may not return – and to seek help if they did.

Later, Zoe's unruly behaviour and acting out at school would be put down to the trauma of that fateful day, even though she still couldn't remember anything. (And back in 1991, girls didn't get diagnosed with ADHD anyway.)

The memory of the sad lady settled itself into the back of Zoe's mind, fading until it was just an uneasiness she had about her daddy. And she would spend time wondering who the pale lady was that daddy knew.

32 endings

JAMES

To me, Zoe had always been independent, spontaneous, fun. When I turned up at the hospital I'd been ready to be confronted with machines and tubes, with a girlfriend fighting for her life after a mugging or a car accident.

When Tori had suggested coffees, I'd humoured her, expecting Zoe's cup to sit unnoticed on a side table, its contents going cold as we watched round the clock, willing Zoe to wake up. I humoured Tori because I knew she was the kind of person that needing humouring.

You see, I've never slept with Tori.

Yes, I've had a fair few one-night stands, but I can remember every single one of them – their names, what drinks they drank, what lines I chatted them up with, which ones laughed at my corny jokes and which ones gave as good as they got.

When Tori claimed she'd slept with me I was pissed off – not my type at all. But there was something so desperate about her, about her story, that told me I couldn't destroy her lie. At the time I didn't understand why Zoe would be friends with someone like Tori – someone even more needy than Alison. But I get it now.

So quizzing her about it in the pub? Cruel, yes – but justified. Kissing her? Okay, I don't understand why I did that. Maybe I was just enjoying what I thought was no-strings female attention. But after that I had to change my mobile number because Tori wouldn't leave me alone. It was a kiss, for fuck's sake.

Changing my number is not just about stopping Tori's incessant texting: if Zoe ever tries to kill herself again, I don't want *anyone* to be able to get in touch to let me know.

33 lies

TORI

I still hate the way the fridge opens the wrong way, with the door into the room. But now it's *my* fridge to hate, and that in itself is awesome.

I'm no longer living in a bedsit that I pretend to myself is a studio flat.

Having your own sink and microwave in the corner of your bedroom does not mean you have your own kitchen – you still have to use one of the two washing machines in the shared kitchen to wash your clothes. And having your own "wet room" doesn't count if you have to sit on the toilet seat in order to use the shower. I was a regular at my gym simply because I wanted to be able to shower standing up.

On the top shelf of what is now *my* fridge sit two boxes of wine. And on the day she moves in, I call Faye through to the kitchen to tell her about them.

"If anyone mentions 'wine cows' this is what they are referring to," I tell her with a laugh.

"Wine cows?"

I point to the tap.

"Because of the udder," I explain. "I can't remember how the name came about, but it was a drunken conversation between me and Alison."

A lie. I realise I'm starting this new friendship off on a lie, but it says to Faye that I have friends.

When Zoe asked me to meet her at Costa, not on the ward, I didn't think anything of it. I was surprised to see her with her bags all packed, ready to leave. She explained she wanted one last chance to see me before she did. A chance to explain.

We weren't going to be housemates after all.

I cried. I *never* cry. And Faye came over to find out why.

MUSICAL CHAIRS

"It's all my fault," Faye said. "I'm the one who got Beth to visit."

"There's nobody else I know who can move in right now," Tori mumbled as she tried to stem her tears. There was nobody else. Her body ached for that flat.

"So you need a new housemate?" Faye asked, her voice full of hope.

Tori looked up at her. The spotlights in Costa shone through Faye's copper hair, creating a halo around her head.

"Your place not great?" Zoe asked her to fill the gap – Tori had been struck dumb.

"You could say that," Faye laughed, a little uneasy, still waiting for Tori to respond. "I think me and Tori sharing could be good. You know, seeing as you and Beth will be."

"Yes, it could be good," Tori replied, finally finding her voice.

TORI

I've taken Zoe's old room, not Alison's. I tell myself it's because it has the larger window, but deep down I know the truth. When Alison first told me that Zoe had taken an overdose, it was Zoe's room I ached after. So claiming it as my room feels like I've achieved what I set out to achieve.

The flat lies along the front of the building, each room looking out onto Brixton Hill's busy dual carriageway – a main route for the emergency services at all hours of the day and night. A narrow corridor runs the length of the flat so the rooms at either end were wider, although the bedroom at one end is shorter, so both bedrooms are very close in size.

It's an old council block where at least some of the flats have council tenants and the strong stench of cannabis wafts through the stairwell and helps hide the weird damp smell that seems to pervade every molecule of air in the block. I need to get to the bottom of this at some point.

I couldn't let anyone who didn't live in London visit me in this flat because they would have no understanding of what I'd achieved. But when Faye first looks round the flat, I know she sees the same thing I do – enough space to call somewhere a real home.

Really, the rent on a place this size should be crippling for both of us. But we're paying just £750 a month each – only £50 more a month than my bedsit out in Blackhorse Road. I'd always told people I lived near Finsbury Park, but choosing the most well known tube stop along from where you live is seen as an *acceptable* London lie.

Everyone in London lies. It's part of the culture.

We tell ourselves that £750 a month for a bedroom in a flat on a massive dual carriageway with some of the worst pollution levels in the UK is amazing. We collectively agree that anything under an hour is an excellent commute when the average person outside the capital is looking at less than 20 minutes.

We happily pay over the odds for a pint or a glass of wine in a complete dump that's no longer a dump because it's "hipster". We openly talk about our next career move because London is about opportunity, so it has to be the reason we're still here – and anyone who's been in the same job more than two years admit so with a shamed face.

And *all* of this is why I'm here.

I'm here because I fit in.

Because everyone in London lies.

It's how they survive.

The Victoria Lie

If you had to pick out "Victoria's lie", which would it be?

The lie that is her being in the right place at the right time in order to manipulate people when they're at their lowest, as she did with Alison when she was having presentation wobbles?

Or claiming that she had a one-night stand with James to explain away why she spent the evening staring at him, when she couldn't help herself even though she knew she needed to look away?

Or setting up Zoe to believe Alison and James were colluding behind her back in order to get Zoe to drive a wedge between them, so that she could support the two of them separately, to claim them as best friend and boyfriend for herself?

Or telling Zoe she planned to jump off Beachy Head so they could bond over their suicidal thoughts?

But Victoria's lie is none of these lies.

Instead it's the one she tells herself: *that you can shape who you are to fit the mould of what other people want you to be in order to make them like you. But Tori has forgotten this is a lie: because if you tell yourself a lie often enough, you start to believe it's true.*

So Tori believes the lie that lies are her lifeline.

Interview with Zoe

So how has life been treating you?

I've been trying to understand myself within my diagnosis, but it's an uphill battle. The diagnosis isn't the answer but the start of a whole new set of questions. And the medical profession don't understand ADHD – and can't agree on what they do know – so I feel like I'm picking and choosing what it all means.

Picking and choosing?

There's quite a lot out there about how ADHD can be seen on a CT scan and how misfiring neurotransmitters don't give the same patterns on the scan as in a normal, sorry, "neurotypical", brain. But that doesn't mean that each person with ADHD gets to have a CT scan. So I don't know if *my* scan would show the patterns they are talking about, and that's so frustrating.

And the name is all wrong: I don't have an attention deficit and my nervous energy is hardly me being hyperactive. It means people make the same assumptions about my diagnosis as I did when Mr BG first suggested it. So that's frustrating too.

Thankfully, having Beth on hand is a bit like having a guide. She was able to keep me grounded when the fake euphoria of the diagnosis hit – something I thought I'd escaped. It hit after I moved to Manchester.

The drugs help, but they also create this feeling of being well-balanced which isn't real. So you have this sense that you're going to be better, but the same problems arise again and again. The drugs just take the edge off, that's all.

What's it like sharing with Beth?

It's completely nuts. She's like a depressed version of me and I'm the angry version of her. We struggle with the same things but react in different ways.

We argue a lot, but it's healthy arguing. I've been walking round on eggshells my whole life, but any pieces of calcium carbonate stop at the door to our flat. Inside there are no platitudes and none of the social niceties bullshit.

I wouldn't recommend our flat as somewhere for NTs (neurotypicals) to stay. But for us, it's just what we need.

And how are things with your family?

We're all linked on Facebook and we do our chatting on there. I talk to Charlie a lot because she's the one who just wants everything to be okay – and she thinks the more we chat the more okay it will be. I message Clare and Michael a little, but not much.

I'm still processing the stuff about Victoria station and trying to work out how much of my anger is about that and how much of it was that Michael had an affair – something he recently admitted to.

He seems to believe that because he kept her out of our lives she hasn't affected them whereas I don't think I'm ever going to have a good relationship with him if he's not willing to take responsibility for his own actions. I guessed she existed. I didn't need to meet her in the flesh.

My diagnosis means I'm analysing my own behaviour, but I'm analysing everyone else's too. I felt, I don't know, out of sorts I guess, when I twigged that Michael is no more a grown-up than I am.

And what about Alison?

Alison and I have been chatting via WhatsApp. Mostly superficial chat, but it's been good. I get the feeling she still wants to be friends, even after everything that's happened, and I miss her company, so I'm making the effort.

Beth is doing the same with Faye, which is good too. I like to think that Beth is gaining something from her trip down to see me other than getting me as a nightmare housemate!

Faye and Tori sharing is just weird, but I guess no weirder than me and Beth. There are two types of people: those who keep all the friends they've ever made, and those who go through life losing old ones as they make new ones.

If you fall into the latter category – like me, Beth, Faye and Tori do – then you don't have older friends to fall back on. So when new ones come along, you have to rely on them, and they on you, even if the friendship isn't really cut out for that.

And James?

We've had no contact at all. There's nothing to salvage, so no point.

What's next for you?

I'm still trying to decide whether or not to stay alive. On top of the diagnosis, I'm also processing the fact that I tried to kill myself. My suicide kit travelled up to Manchester with me – it's still under my bed. I'm not ready to get rid of it just yet. In many ways, my life is better now. But I'm just not sure if it's *enough* better. I know Beth feels the same way, so I guess I should check under her bed…

Interview with Alison

So how has life been treating you?

Things are good. I'm living in Canterbury, working at the university and sharing a gorgeous house with two people who work there. And, yes, the shower works!

I'm a Marketing Officer, which is a step down from Brand Manager, but my life is less stressful and I'm not in daily competition with all my colleagues, which is lovely.

I've started dating someone. It's very casual and I'm just enjoying it for what it is. He's a single dad and doesn't have a lot of free time, but that suits me because I'm not ready for something bigger. We both have baggage, but that's allowed.

The way of life down here is so different from London it genuinely feels like I've moved countries.

How are things with Ruby?

After I moved down, Ruby got very angry with me. She'd been holding it all back while Zoe was in hospital. But once we were both down here, it all came flooding out.

She admitted seeing me the night of the storm – and me

lying about that visit made her angrier than the five years beforehand that she hadn't seen me because we were starting afresh and I fucked it up.

She told me she needed time away from me because she'd built a life without me and didn't want me taking it over. I told her to take all the time she needed – that I owed that to her. I said I'd leave her alone until she was ready to get back in touch. She didn't contact me for three months. It was really scary. But it gave me some insight into what I'd done to her – and for *years*, not months.

Now we see each other socially a couple of times a month. When we're together, we have a good time, but I'm conscious that I'm being kept at arm's length with regard to the rest of her life. I don't know if that will ever change, so I'm building my own life here – hence the house-share and the dating.

And what about your mum?

I thought this was meant to be questions about the others. Sorry, but I don't feel comfortable talking about that.

Fair enough. So how about with Zoe?

Better than I expected. In some ways, things are easier with her than with Ruby.

With me and Ruby, I was the one who was the shit friend. With me and Zoe, it was Zoe. I know what it's like to want to be forgiven, so I think that's why it's so easy to forgive Zoe. I don't know. Everything we've been through is recent – so there are no years of resentment to break down either.

How much we'll see of each other I'm not sure – Manchester is a fair way from Whitstable – but it's nice to stay in touch.

And Tori?

We ended up friends because she decided we would be, not because there was some kind of mutual agreement. It's like I was tricked into being friends with her. But then could Ruby and Zoe say the same thing about me?

What I like best about Tori is that she *wants* to be friends with me – and it's nice to be wanted. She was so supportive when Ruby took that three-month break too, so I don't know why I feel like I'm being manipulated. I just have this uneasiness. I don't know how else to explain it.

Life is certainly easier *without* Zoe and Tori at the centre of it, that's for sure!

What's next for you?

I'm hoping that *nothing* is next for me, or anyone around me, for a really, really long time! I'd like a nice easy life, thanks.

Interview with Ruby

So how has life been treating you?

Well, I'm only just settling back into my life again, even though London was months ago. It stirred up a lot of feelings and I found the whole thing difficult to process: finally dealing with the fact that I didn't go to university, working out how Alison fitted back into my life.

It was lovely to be friends again, but I was also angry that she seemed to believe she could just slot back into our friendship like nothing had happed. I was also wary that she only wanted back into my life because of the hole left by Zoe. So I felt I needed to take a step back to protect myself.

She gave me space when I asked for it, which I'm grateful for, because I was able to settle back into my routine and then start seeing her again as an added extra, rather than an integral part of my life.

She says she's moved to Canterbury?

Yes. I'm very happy about it. It means that Whitstable is still *mine* and she has a different place that's hers. We're far enough away from each other that we have to plan seeing each other, so I can keep her separate from other parts of my life while I work out what our friendship means.

Have you had any contact with Zoe or Tori?

No! Thank God. Alison gives me updates as to how they're both doing, although I'm trying to wean her off doing so, as I want to leave them both in the past. I didn't realise how much London affected me until I got back here, but it ended up being a turbulent time for me.

When we came down here for the day, as soon as we stepped off the train, I knew I couldn't face going back. My plan was to wait until the train back and just refuse to get on, to ask Alison to post my stuff to me or bring it down when she visited.

But then she rescued the woman at the pier and suddenly it wasn't okay for me to do that. I had to fight back tears on that train journey. And then Alison said she wanted to move back down here and it was all just too much for me.

What's next for you?

I want to track down the woman from the pier. I find myself thinking about her a lot – I dream about her floating in the water. In my dreams she's calling out to me, but I can't understand what she's saying.

There was *nothing* in the local paper – I checked on their website. It surprised me because I thought something like that would make the news. We don't have news down here – the murders, the muggings – the same way you get in London. I thought saving a life would make the front page.

But then if it went down simply as a 999 call-out with a woman being taken to hospital, then there's nothing to report.

I worry that she was trying to kill herself. Why else was she in the water fully clothed? I want to find her so she can tell me otherwise. I want Zoe to be a one-off. I don't want my life to be full of people trying to die.

Interview with Tori

Tori declined to be interviewed.

~ The End ~

About the Author

Sarah Marie Graye was born in Manchester, United Kingdom, in 1975, to English Catholic parents. The second eldest of five daughters, to the outside world Sarah Marie's childhood followed a relatively typical Manchester upbringing... until aged nine, when she was diagnosed with depression.

It's a diagnosis that has stayed with Graye over three decades, and something she believes has coloured every life decision, including the one to write a novel. Graye wrote *The Second Cup* as part of an MA Creative Writing practice as research degree at London South Bank University – where she was the vice-chancellor's scholarship holder.

First published in July 2017, *The Second Cup* was: longlisted for the Book Viral 2017 Millennium Book Award; a finalist in Read Freely's Best Indie Book 2017; a finalist in the 12th Annual National Indie Excellence Awards; a semi-finalist in the Online Book Club 2017 Book of the Year Award; and a "distinguished favorite" in the 2017 NYC Big Book Awards.

Graye has just released her second novel, *The Victoria Lie*, and hopes it achieves the same successes as *The Second Cup*.

A NOTE FROM THE AUTHOR

I added character interviews to my first novel, *The Second Cup*, after receiving a diagnosis of ADHD – a condition I realised I'd unwittingly given to Beth.

The interviews allowed her to be diagnosed too.

They were so popular with people who read the book that I decided to include them in *The Victoria Lie* too.

I want to **thank you** for taking time to read *The Victoria Lie*. If you enjoyed it, please consider telling your friends or posting a short review on Amazon. A recommendation is the best present you can give to an indie author.

FIND THE AUTHOR ONLINE

Website: sarahmariegraye.com
Twitter: twitter.com/SarahMarieGraye
Facebook: facebook.com/sarahmariegraye
Instagram: instagram.com/sarahmariegraye

The Second Cup

The Butterfly Effect book 1
This is how it starts…

Today's the day

Today's the day. I'm going to do this.

That's what I say to myself over and over in my head as I pull on my leathers, fasten the straps on my boots, and pull on my crash helmet and adjust the chin strap.

Actually, I'm mumbling to myself, saying it out loud: "Today's the day. Today's the day." I take a quick look round to make sure there's nobody around to hear me. Not that it would make much difference. I'm so focused on today I have no space in my thoughts for other people.

I walk up to my bike. She's a beauty. I think bikes are female, as ships are. There's something enslaving about her curves, the way she calls me. I'm addicted to the buzz I get when I ride her. I don't even need to be going quickly. I like to think she responds to my every move, but I'm also conscious of the sliver of fear I get whenever I twitch the throttle and her engine growls.

I put the key in the ignition, climb over her, then put my gloves on, taking time to pull my jacket sleeves over the edges. There's nothing quite like the pain you feel deep in your bones from riding a bike in the cold when you've got a draught between your layers. I've got a patch of skin on my lower back that I believe has been damaged from my early days of riding when my trousers and jacket didn't zip together. The nerve endings on a 10in-by-2in stretch of skin have never fully recovered, not even after hour upon hour of hot baths.

Kicking up the stand, turning the key, pulling in the clutch, putting her in first, I'm a conductor in front of an orchestra playing their favourite piece of music, I know every move. I pull down my visor, my final move before I pull off from the kerb and join the living.

"Today's the day."